Yeshua
The Young Jesus of Nazareth

The Early Years: 3 — 28 C.E.
A Historical Novel

Peter Jaksa, Ph.D.

Humanity Press

CHICAGO, IL

Peter Jaksa, Ph.D./Humanity Press
30 North Michigan Avenue, Suite 908
Chicago, Illinois 60602

Publisher's Note: This is a work of fiction. Names, characters, places, and incidents are a product of the author's imagination. Locales and public names are sometimes used for atmospheric purposes.

Book Cover Design by 100 Covers

Yeshua: The Young Jesus of Nazareth/ Peter Jaksa, Ph.D. — 1st ed.
ISBN 979-8-9901920-4-1

For humanity

Blessed are the peacemakers,
for they shall be called children of God.

—JESUS OF NAZARETH
Matthew 5:9

Contents

Preface

Yeshua: The Young Jesus of Nazareth is a novel of historical fiction. It is not a history book or a book of religion; readers wishing for pure history or pure theology are encouraged to look at the wide variety of books available in both disciplines. The aim of historical fiction is to depict the events, culture, and people of a certain historical period in a way that informs and enlightens a modern reading audience.

Religious faith is a personal matter best left to the beliefs of each individual. Therefore, no claims of any kind are made in this novel to either support or dispute any religious beliefs. This novel is neutral on issues of faith or religious orientation. Both freedom of thought and of religion are equally respected.

Some of the historical information used to shape the narrative of the novel is drawn from sparse but still helpful ancient sources, such as the historian Flavius Josephus. Much more information is available from modern-day historical studies such as the works of Jose Pagola, Paula Fredriksen, and Reza Aslan.

Some information is drawn from theological sources, including the canonical gospels of the Christian bible but also several of the "lost" non-canonical gospels such as the Gospel of Mary (Magdalene), the Gospel of Thomas, and the Gospel of Philip. Also drawn on heavily are the oldest known writings of the early Christian church known as the "Q" source materials, which predate all the gospels. Sometimes history and theology overlap, and we are the wiser for it.

Sayings or quotes used in the novel that are attributed to Jesus of Nazareth come from a wide variety of commonly accepted literature, both academic and religious. Many of the historical quotes, be they direct or paraphrased, come from the "Q" source materials or other sources such as the non-canonical gospels. Whether these match or don't match the canonical religious literature should not be taken as agreeing or disagreeing with any religious beliefs or orientations.

Whatever their religious beliefs, most people agree that Jesus of Nazareth was a profoundly important historical figure. In the Christian religion, he is recognized as the Christ, the son of God. In the Jewish and Islamic religions, he is recognized as an important prophet of God. Many who do not practice any kind of formal religion regard him as an influential philosopher and humanitarian.

Some things are easy to agree on. It is universally acknowledged that Jesus of Nazareth was born and raised in a deeply religious Jewish family. Like other people in ancient Galilee, he almost certainly spoke Aramaic, the common everyday language of that time in both Galilee and Judea. Hebrew was only the language of the educated religious scholars and priests, and the scribes who wrote contracts and other legal documents.

In his younger years he worked as a *tekton*, a Greek word for builder or carpenter. Around the age of thirty, which was the legal age for a Jewish male to enter ministry work, he began a traveling ministry in Galilee and parts of Judea and Samaria. His ministry only lasted for two to three years (we have no clear dates or timelines), but it forever changed history for much of the world.

For the sake of historical accuracy, in this book Jesus of Nazareth is called Yeshua. In Nazareth, he would have been known as *Yeshua bar Yosef*, or Jesus son of Joseph. In the first Christian gospels, which were written in Greek in the latter part of the first century, he was called Iesous. In later Latin writings, he was known as Iesus. In the year 1524, the letter "J" was added to the alphabet, and afterwards he was known by the modern name of Jesus.

In ancient Nazareth, however, his mother Mary almost certainly called him Yeshua. With respect and affection, we do the same.

Chapter 1

A Very Kind Boy

Village of Nazareth, Galilee, September 70 C.E.

J erusalem has been destroyed.

It grieves me terribly to write these words. The Roman legions of Emperor Vespasian marched into Judea to quell yet another stubborn Jewish rebellion. His son, Titus, led the army. They sieged the city for five months and starved the people into submission. Then they slaughtered them without mercy.

As an example to future rebels, the Romans razed the city to the ground. Not even the holy Temple of God was spared. All that remains of Jerusalem are ashes and rubble.

By the grace of the Eternal God, my family and other followers of the church of Yeshua were spared from death and destruction. We left the city before the Roman siege began and took refuge in Pella, on the far side of the Jordan River. What sustains us now in the wake of this devastation is our faith in God Almighty and the teachings of Yeshua.

My name is David of Nazareth, the son of Matthias. I am an old man now, but Father God still blesses me with the gift of memory. I wish to tell my story before age takes its unrelenting toll and memories fade away. The most important story is the story of Yeshua, the boy who became a man who changed the world.

Many stories are told about the life of Yeshua. Many more will surely be told in the days to come. This is my story. Most things that I describe here I witnessed with my own eyes. Some things were told to me by others who knew Yeshua well, among them his brothers, sisters, and closest disciples.

As a child, I was one of those few and fortunate children who were taught to read and write, but I am no priest or scribe. In my youth I was a shepherd, then a carpenter who for a time worked alongside Yosef and Yeshua in Sepphoris. I will tell my story plainly and sincerely.

Yeshua was only a boy of eight the first time we had a conversation. Our families in Nazareth knew each other well, as is common in small villages. His kindly parents, Yosef and Mary, asked that I take him along on my rounds. That was the first day of Yeshua's training in tending sheep. I was his teenaged sheepherding tutor.

It happened long ago, but I remember our talk on that summer day very clearly still. Over the next twenty-five years, there were many more talks. He began as my pupil, and in time became my teacher.

As the years went by, the very bright child became a young man who took care of his family after Yosef died. The young man matured into an adult fiercely devoted to the reign of God. He saw the suffering of the poor, heard the anguish of the sick and the forsaken, and brought forth God's love and compassion to ease their plight. He was divinely inspired in his mission to teach our people the true path to God's kingdom.

I joined him for a time during his ministry in Capernaum and other villages and towns, when he touched the lives of so many people. We were there with him in Jerusalem on that last Passover, when Yeshua rebelled against the Temple authorities. That greatly troubled the High Priest, Caiaphas, and the Roman governor of Judea, Pontius Pilate, which led to the momentous events that followed.

So few of us who knew Yeshua are still living. Many of the twelve apostles died as martyrs. Peter, who was the leader of the church in Rome, was crucified by the mad Emperor Nero. Yeshua's adored mother, Mary, is with God. The beloved Mary Magdalena left Judea and her fate is unknown.

Yeshua's brother, called James the Just, who headed the Christian church from Jerusalem, was stoned to death on orders from the High Priest Ananus. I had known James well since he was a boy. His unjust death made me angry, but also made me realize that I must tell my story while I am still able.

I should start at the beginning, when Yeshua and I spoke for the first time. Afterwards, the memories stayed with me, because it was clear even then that he was no ordinary eight-year-old boy.

Nazareth, Galilee, Summer 3 C.E.

Like many small villages in Galilee, Nazareth was home to less than three hundred people. It is much the same now, a small hillside hamlet built on the brow of a gently sloping hill. A large stream runs along the western edge of the village.

Nazareth is small enough so that every family knows every other family. Most people spend their entire lives there, from infant cradle to burial tomb. Over the years, our neighbors become like family.

I was fifteen years old when I became Yeshua's tutor. He and I had no prior reason to speak directly with one another before that day. Eight-year-old Jewish boys are children, while fifteen-year-olds are grown men.

It's strange how even now I can remember that day so clearly. The early morning sun was just peeking over the horizon when my deep and peaceful sleep was interrupted by a loving but insistent voice.

"David! Time to get up!" my mother Sarah called out across the room where our family slept.

Our small family — my mother, my younger sister Eva, and I — shared the one-room house. My father Matthias had been executed by the Romans as a rebel when I was a young boy. I don't remember him well, but I always thought of him as my hero.

I stirred groggily on the thin straw mattress covered with a blanket, wishing only for a few more precious minutes of sleep.

"Wake up, David! Go to Mary's house and fetch Yeshua, then take the sheep out. Up! Now!"

"Yes, *Emma*," I answered with a yawn. In Aramaic, the language of the common people of Galilee, *emma* is the casual name for mother.

On that morning, Yeshua would help me on my daily sheepherding rounds. There are no wealthy families in Nazareth, then or now. We are hard-working people, because survival requires it. Every child learns how to work from an early age.

Yeshua's father Yosef was a *tekton*, a craftsman who hired himself as a carpenter and stonemason. There was little building work to be done in the village or the money to pay for it, so he worked in the city of Sepphoris as a day laborer for the wealthy families there.

Yeshua was not yet old enough to learn woodworking and stone masonry skills. In the years to come, he would master those crafts as Yosef trained him. For a few years he would even work alongside his father before Yosef died. At eight, however, he was just old enough to watch and learn from a teenage shepherd.

Sarah handed me a small bundle wrapped in cloth. "Here is bread and cheese and radishes, and some fresh figs from Abana."

"Thank you, *Emma*."

Abana was a neighbor whose sheep I herded along with our sheep, because neighbors help each other. She had no money, so she paid us with food when she had food to spare. The fresh figs came from the fig trees next to her house. Figs were just beginning to ripen in the early summer.

"Off with you, now! Be home well before sunset."

She gave me a quick goodbye wave and turned her attention to my sister Eva, just waking up on the other side of the one-room house. Eva was stretched out on the small bed that she shared with Mother. She looked feverish, her face shiny with perspiration. She moaned and complained of stomach pain. Sarah tended to her with concern and loving care. In Nazareth, one of the many jobs that mothers performed was that of family doctor.

"Be well, little sister!" I called to Eva to comfort her.

She gave me a weak smile and waved goodbye.

I took the food satchel and my wooden shepherd's crook and went outside. Our small house was grouped together with three other houses, each built to face a common patio. The patio was open on the southward side to face the street.

We were the house on the west side. The two houses on the north side were occupied by Abana and by the family of Clopas, the older brother of Yosef. Across the patio, on the east side, was the house of Yosef and Mary.

Our shared patio was where we spent much of our daily life, when not working in the fields or orchards. The four families shared two wooden tables with benches. That is where we ate our meals, and gathered around in the evening to talk. The women shared a grindstone for grounding grain into flour, and a clay oven for baking bread. The patio was a favorite place for young children to play under the watchful eyes of their parents.

It was a short walk across the bare earth patio to the house of Yosef and Mary. On the side of their house was a plot of ground filled with green rows of ripening vegetables and melons, glistening with morning dew. The wages Yosef earned in Sepphoris could not provide the large family with all its needs. Each family in Nazareth also grew its own food from a vegetable garden, a melon patch, and a few fruit trees. Most families kept some chickens, a few sheep or goats, and if they could afford one, a cow for milk and cheese.

Mary always tended a large and bountiful vegetable garden for her growing family. After Yeshua, she gave birth to James, Joses, Judah, and Mary. In the next three years, she would bear another daughter, Salome, and another son, Shimon. In most Nazareth households, large families made for happy families.

Approaching their front door, I could hear the loud commotion of children coming from inside, the wail of a baby crying. Mary stepped out to greet me. She was gently rocking and cooing softly to the crying infant in her arms, her daughter Mary.

"Good morning to you, David," the lady of the house greeted me with a warm smile.

I enjoyed talking with Mary because she always had a pleasant disposition. Her kindness shone through her gentle eyes, dark brown and always full of life. A mature woman at twenty-six, she was already the mother of five children.

"Peace to you, Mary," I replied. "I'm here for Yeshua to help me tend the sheep."

"Yes, of course. We have been waiting for you." She turned her head and called out over her shoulder. "Husband! David is here!"

I asked: "Is Yeshua eager to learn sheepherding? Many children his age don't have the patience for it."

Mary nodded. "Yes, he's eager. He loves to learn new things, and we run out of things for him to do around the house." She paused and smiled. "He will be happier helping you with the sheep than sitting around here with nothing to do."

"Then he'll be fine," I said. "I'll keep him occupied herding in the strays. We'll be down by the stream, and with some luck we might catch a fish or two."

A moment later, Yosef appeared with Yeshua at his side, followed close behind by the brothers James and Joses. Yosef was a tall man, with the wiry but strong build of a carpenter and stonemason who spent many long days, from sunup to sundown, working on building projects in Sepphoris. He was about the same age as Mary, and blessed with the same honest face and pleasant disposition.

Yosef said to Yeshua: "Today David will be your tutor."

"Yes, *Abba*, I know." He looked up at me with a calm expression. "Peace to you, David."

He was a slim boy, somewhat tall for his age, with the wiry build of his father. He had the dark brown and gentle eyes of his mother. Even at that age, his eyes shined brightly with uncommon intelligence. He had the same tranquil demeanor as his parents.

I thought then, and not for the last time, that Yeshua looked and sounded mature beyond his years. He was a young boy, and I was a grown man, yet he greeted me as one adult to another.

"And to you, Yeshua," I said in reply. "Well, the sheep are ready for pasture. Are you ready to get to work?"

"Yes, I'm ready." His eyes were already looking down the street to my sheep-holding pen.

The younger brothers James and Joses, six and five years old at that time, had been watching me with curiosity. Now they shifted their gaze to their parents.

"Can we go with Yeshua too?" James asked. "Please? We can help!"

Joses remained silent but nodded in agreement. The three boys were close in age and friendly with each other. It was clear that the younger two looked up to Yeshua and tried to emulate him.

Mary shook her head patiently. "No, you boys aren't old enough to watch sheep. Maybe in three or four years? Be patient."

The boys groaned with disappointment but accepted her decision. It would be unthinkable for them to argue with a decision made by their parents.

Yosef handed Yeshua a stick, a slim branch trimmed of leaves and cut to be the same height as the boy. Next, he gave him a small cloth satchel.

"Here is a shepherd's staff fit for a boy, and your noonday meal."

Mary said: "Now, listen and do what David teaches you. And don't forget to eat!"

"No need to worry. Yeshua will be fine," I reassured her.

"I know, but I'm just reminding him," she replied with a smile. "Sometimes when my son gets busy, he forgets to eat."

I said to him: "We'll have our lunches at mid-day. And we'll watch the sheep to make sure they don't stray, and that no dogs or other animals bother them."

"Are you scared that wolves will eat them?" little Joses asked.

His childish fear made me smile. "If any wolves come along, we'll chase them off with our staff! Right, Yeshua?"

James giggled, but Joses stared at me with a worried look on his face. Like every child in the village, he'd heard the usual stories about wolves meant to teach children to be careful.

Yeshua looked skeptical, but amused by my joke. "But there are no wolves in the hills around Nazareth!"

"David was only talking in jest," Yosef said.

"I know that, *Abba*."

"There are no wolves, but many sheep that are hungry and waiting for us," I said. "Let's be on our way."

I bid farewell to Yosef and Mary with a nod. The two younger boys waved goodbye to their brother as we walked away.

We headed down the narrow street at a fast walk. In Nazareth, as in all villages in Galilee, the streets are unpaved. They are muddy in the winter and springtime during the wet season, and dry and dusty in the summer and fall months during the dry season.

The morning sun was rising fast, and the day would soon turn hot. Yeshua did not trail behind me, as many young children might do. He walked at a brisk pace and stayed at my side. He was barefoot because in the summer children ran around in their bare feet. Sometimes adults did as well. It was more comfortable, and the soles on our feet toughened over time.

The sheep pen was behind our family home, on the western edge of the village and closest to the stream. Our twenty sheep and the neighbor's fifteen made up my flock. I would watch them all day while they pastured so that none wandered off and got lost.

Nazareth is built on the side of a low hill. We drove the sheep to the pasture field below the village. The ground is flatter there near the stream, and there are scattered green patches of grass, clover, and wildflowers. In summer the grass is still thick, which makes for good pasture for the animals. The sheep were docile and content to roam around lazily, looking for the freshest patch of vegetation.

"Stay by me and do as I do," I told him. "There is no need to chase after the sheep. It's good enough to wave your stick and raise your voice when you need to, and they will do what you want."

"I see that," Yeshua replied. "The flock is easy to lead."

"This job isn't very exciting, but it's important," I explained. "And just think, Yeshua, in two or three years from now you can herd sheep all by yourself!"

"Yes, I understand," Yeshua said in a quiet and distracted tone.

He was being respectful, but completely lacking any sign of interest or enthusiasm. His lackadaisical tone made me curious.

"Or would you rather be doing something else entirely in two or three years?" I asked. "Instead of herding sheep, I mean."

"I will do as my Father wishes me to do," he replied.

"Oh, yes. Of course. Yosef is a carpenter. And sons usually follow in the footsteps of their fathers and learn their father's trade."

"No," Yeshua said, looking slightly puzzled. "I mean, yes, you are right that my *abba* is a carpenter. But I'm not speaking of him."

"Oh, you're not? Who, then?"

"I'm speaking of the Father who watches over us all."

His serious tone surprised me. These were words I might hear from a rabbi, but not from the mouth of a child so young.

I turned to look again at this young boy who was speaking with the voice of an elder. He was not simply parroting words he heard from others, from his parents, or perhaps at a synagogue service. He was speaking naturally, from his own heart.

Everyone in the village knew that Yosef and Mary were very devout believers in the faith. They followed and obeyed all the religious laws and celebrated the holidays. They made the pilgrimage to Jerusalem often for the feast of Passover. They passed on their strong faith to their children.

There was no school in Nazareth, or in other villages in Galilee, and no expensive private tutors to hire as in Sepphoris or Jerusalem. The rudimentary education of children was done by their parents and other adult relatives. Even with parents as devout as Yosef and Mary, however, it was unusual to hear such a proclamation of faith from such a young child.

"You are right to think of Him, Yeshua," I acknowledged. "We must always obey our great Father and do as He asks of us."

He met my gaze but said no more. I had spoken a simple truth, and no reply was needed. As I later learned over the years, this would be a lifetime habit for Yeshua. Once a point was understood, he did not wish to go on about it.

The sun beat down on us from a cloudless blue sky, and we were perspiring in the heat. A short distance away was a broad-leafed maple tree that offered shade and relief from the sun.

"Let's go sit over there," I said, gesturing toward the maple. "We can rest in the shade for a while."

As we walked, he turned his head to me with a quizzical expression on his face.

"David, I have a question for you?"

"Yes?"

"Would *you* rather be doing something else entirely, instead of herding sheep?"

Again, his words took me by surprise. Children don't ask such direct questions of adults.

"Yes, sometimes I wish I was doing something different. Sheep are not very interesting to watch all day long," I said with a chuckle.

"But you still come here and watch over the flock, day after day?"

We sat down on the grass beneath the leafy canopy of the tree and drank from our water skins. It was much more comfortable to sit in the shade, and we could still keep an eye on the sheep.

I asked: "And do you wonder why I do this every day, Yeshua?"

"Yes. Because there are many other things you could do that aren't too boring."

"Because it's a very important job to watch and protect the sheep. We depend on them for milk, cheese, and wool. We use some, and sell the rest. They provide wool for sale in the spring, and milk and cheese for the market all year round. This modest flock of sheep helps keep our family alive. What worth is a day job in Sepphoris compared to this?"

"So, you do what's more important for your family, and not what pleases you most."

"That's right," I said. "Now, tell me this. Which is more important, doing what is right or doing what pleases *you* most?"

He answered without pause. "Doing what is right is always more important. This is what our Father teaches us."

"That is true."

Yeshua continued: "We must follow our Father's commandments and obey His will." He spoke with the high-pitched voice of a child, but in a serious tone that was wise beyond his years. "And if we can't do that, then we dishonor the Lord."

I agreed with a silent nod. If only more of the adults in the village would understand and obey the Law of Moses so well.

"Your parents teach you well," I told him.

"Yes, they do. But I don't learn only from them."

"Oh? Not just from your parents? Do you have a rabbi, perhaps, who gives you lessons? But we have no rabbi in Nazareth."

"No, not a rabbi," Yeshua replied, his eyes drifting to watch over the sheep. "I mean that I learn from our Father, God Almighty. I always know what He wants from me."

I wasn't quite sure what he meant. "How do you *know* what the Lord wants from you?"

He looked at me silently for a moment, then shrugged. "I don't know how I know. I just know."

"Does God Almighty speak to you, as He did to Moses on Mount Sinai?" I asked him with a smile.

"No, I don't hear God's voice. I only know in my heart what He wants me to do."

I had no reply to that. Perhaps some educated and wise priest in Jerusalem could explain what Yeshua described as his communion with God. I was no priest, just a simple shepherd.

I glanced up between the leafy branches of the maple.

"The sun is at the mid-day point. Let's stop now and eat our meal."

"Yes!" he agreed with a cheerful grin, sounding like a typical young and carefree boy again. "I'm starving."

We each spread our food on a cloth napkin on the grass in front of us. The loaves of flat bread had been baked the night before and still emitted the delicious smell of fresh bread. Cheese was cut into small chunks, and its pleasant aroma made my mouth water. The radishes were a bright red, plump and juicy, plucked from the ground and washed only the day before.

This was simple but hearty fare, a feast for a shepherd and his helper. Yeshua's eyes brightened at the sight of the fresh figs I laid out before us.

"These are a treat from Abana," I told him. "First, eat the food that your mother prepared for you, then we can share the figs."

Yeshua said a prayer: "Blessed are You, Lord our God, who provides us with this food."

He paused, then gave a delighted grin.

"And many blessings on our kind neighbor, Abana!"

From time to time, we herded the sheep down to the stream so that they could drink. The water was only thigh high for an adult, but it flowed swiftly and was clear and cool. Yeshua waded in up to his chest to cool off. The stream bottom was sandy, not mud, and provided solid footing.

In the late afternoon, it was time to herd the sheep back to their pen. They had grazed enough for one day, and we both had enough of sweating under the scorching sun.

"I'll take this side and drive the flock up the hill," I told Yeshua. "You watch the other side. See those two strays drifting away? Bring them back to the flock."

"Yes, teacher," my pupil said eagerly.

He was just as tired of the heat and tedious work as I was, but ran after the sheep like a young fawn. Yeshua waved his stick around, shouted a few words, and guided the strays back into the fold. He was a fast learner and diligent in his work.

The sheep picked up their pace as we herded them back up the hill. They willingly filed into their holding pen, one at a time, through the narrow gate in the fence. This was a familiar daily routine for them.

As we closed and latched the gate of the sheep pen, my mother came out to greet us. She smiled sympathetically at our tired faces, glistening with sweat.

"Come inside and have some cool water," she beckoned us with a wave. "How did you like your first day as a shepherd, Yeshua?"

"It wasn't bad," he said politely as we moved into the cool shade inside the house. "The sheep were easy to herd, and also we discussed religion."

Sarah handed us cups of water and turned to me with an amused smile. "Discussed religion while herding sheep, did you?"

"Yes, *Emma*. We did. Yeshua has impressive knowledge for a boy his age."

"Mary tells me the same," she said. "He's a very smart boy."

"He will soon get tired of herding sheep, I think. Sheepherding is too simple a job." I turned to him. "We should find you a smart rabbi to be your teacher instead of me, eh, Yeshua?"

But the boy was no longer listening to me. He was looking intently at my sister on her bed, on the other side of the room. My sister was also eight years old, the same age as Yeshua. They often played games together along with other children their age.

He turned to my mother with a worried look on his face.

"Is Eva ill today?"

"Yes, she is sick. It is kind of you to ask, Yeshua."

"What is the illness?" I asked.

Eva rarely felt ill, and when she did, it did not last long. She had been sick that morning when I left.

We walked over to stand by her bedside. Eva was a small and thin girl then, with long curly black hair. Her face was pale, and her eyes were closed.

Sarah explained: "She woke up this morning with stomach pains. I made her some chicken broth, but that only helped a little."

Eva heard us and opened her eyes. She looked first to Mother, then noticed Yeshua. She gave him a shy smile. Although feeling unwell, she was happy to see her friend.

Yeshua greeted her and returned the smile. His face glowed with kindness and affection. He reached out with his right hand and took Eva's hand.

Yeshua told her: "The Lord is with you. You will be well."

Eva's face relaxed. She looked into his eyes and smiled again.

"I know so," Eva replied, her voice as gentle as his. "Thank you for coming to see me, Yeshua."

Mother took me by the arm and led me away.

"Come, walk with me. Let them visit with each other in peace for a while."

When we were a distance away, I turned to face her.

"Did you see that? He took her hand, and just like that, she grew stronger."

"Yes, I saw."

"But how can he be a healer? He's only Eva's age."

Many wise men travelled throughout Galilee and Judea and made a living as healers, exorcists, and workers of wondrous feats. These men were much sought after, and very well paid by those who hired their services. They were all grown men of mature years, however. Learned and wise men, not young boys.

"He has the healing touch," my mother said calmly, as if she was discussing the weather. "Yeshua is a very kind boy. Everyone knows that the healing touch works because it drives out the evil spirits that cause illness, but it begins with kindness."

"Maybe you're right," I said. "But I tell you, there are some things about Yeshua I really don't understand."

She gave me a curious look. "You sound perplexed. Does he trouble you for some reason?"

"No, not troubled. I agree with the things he says. I just" – I paused briefly to search for words – "there are some things I can't explain."

"What do you mean? You're not making any sense, David."

"Yeshua is not a typical eight-year-old boy."

"Ah," Sarah said. "Perhaps you're right. He is very bright for his age. He is very kind, like his father Yosef. And he has a healing touch."

She paused and raised her eyebrows in a manner that I recognized as her way of mocking me gently.

"But why should that vex you, my son?"

"Because I'm not sure it's so simple. There's more to it than that." I gave a small shrug. "I don't have the words to explain it."

"Then stop trying to explain it and accept it." She turned her head toward the children. "Look at your sister. She's feeling better already."

Eva was indeed looking better. She was sitting up in bed and talking with Yeshua in a lively manner. Her stomach pain had subsided or gone away completely.

I could not explain what I saw at that time, but I was only fifteen years old and so listened to the wise words of my mother. I took her advice to heart because she was much wiser than me about people and life. I accepted Yeshua's maturity, his comforting manner, and his healing touch. He was a very kind boy, and much more than that.

Over the years, as I watched the young boy mature, I learned to better understand Yeshua's many unique gifts and talents. He was perhaps the smartest man or woman I ever knew. He learned so easily, even as a child, and understood profound matters in a way that most people could not match. Later, in his adult years, he would teach what he knew to many thousands of people across Galilee, Samaria, and Judea. That work became Yeshua's holy mission in life.

Most remarkable of all, Yeshua had a way of showing uncommon kindness toward everyone he met. Others tried to follow his example, and by so doing also did many good things, but none could equal him. That was not a measure of their failure, but rather a measure of his grandeur. He had a rare gift for reaching and touching people, unlike anyone else.

One of his unique qualities, which at first I could not put into words, was this: when Yeshua looked into your eyes, you had the feeling that he could see into your soul. The feeling that brought forth was not fear, nor was it a feeling of being judged, not at all. It was rather a profound sense of the purest loving compassion and understanding. It was a feeling, as many described it over the years, of being touched by God.

Chapter 2

Lessons From God

Nazareth, Galilee, Spring 5 C.E.

T he Sabbath is our sacred day of rest, as commanded by God Almighty and taught by the Law of Moses. It is the day of the week that everyone awaits joyfully. All work stops. People do not get up at sunrise, or toil in the fields, or bake bread. On the Sabbath, our family meal is the most abundant meal of the week.

Our village life was simple and peaceful then. Upon waking up from a restful sleep, I turned to face south toward Jerusalem and said my morning prayer. After thanking the Lord for another blessed day, I took some quiet time to reflect on my life and the blessings that Father God bestowed on me. I then crossed the bare earth floor to the stone urn resting on the ledge by the door, dipped a gourd cup into the water, and drained it thirstily. The water, freshly drawn by my mother from the communal well down the street, was always cool and refreshing in the morning. In all my years, in all the places that I travelled to, I never found water that tasted as fresh and sweet as the water from our well in Nazareth.

After a light morning meal with Sarah and Eva, we walked to the grassy field where the village gathered for the synagogue. There was no large house or building designated for that purpose in Nazareth; indeed, we had no large houses or buildings in the village at all. In the cities, people built a large hall, with seating for a hundred people or more, for the special purpose of holding a synagogue meeting. For us, a convenient outdoor space with some benches was good enough for holding prayers, sermons, and discussions.

We walked down the familiar narrow streets and greeted our neighbors. Nazareth then was much like it is now. All the houses are built the same, small and sturdy. Each house is laid out as one large room, divided into two halves. The front half is for people, the back half for the animals. Each half of the house has a separate door. All the floors are bare earth. The wealthier homes in Sepphoris and Jerusalem have floors of wood and even marble, but such luxury is well beyond the means of small villages like Nazareth.

Most of the houses in the village have a flat roof. On hot summer days, we sometimes take our meals up on the roof, where there might be a cooling breeze. On hot summer nights, we often take our blankets up there and sleep under the stars. That is one of my favorite things, to sleep out in the cool night air and look up at the brilliant heavens sparkling with stars. Those are the moments when I feel the closest to God the Creator.

We reached the grassy spot where people were gathering and found a place to sit on the benches, neatly lined up in rows. All the men in the village attended synagogue every Sabbath day. Women were not required to attend, and many were busy looking after their young children. Even so, some women always joined the congregation.

In Nazareth, unlike many other places, women were allowed and even encouraged to speak at synagogue services. The men and women even sat together, side by side, along with their children. There were no Pharisee priests in our village to nag us about not following the laws of purity strictly enough. And although we respected the authority of the holy Temple of God in Jerusalem, and the Sadducees priests who governed the Temple, we also made practical decisions on how to live our daily lives.

Yosef and Mary came to synagogue every Sabbath and brought their children with them. James, the second son, was just old enough to help Yeshua keep an eye on the younger children while their parents took part in the services with the other adults. Joses, Judah, and young Mary still found it difficult to sit through a long service without getting bored and restless. Their mother, Mary, took care of the youngest, the baby Salome.

Sarah, Eva, and I sat at the very front of the congregation. We saved room on a bench for Mary and the children. Yosef gave the sermon that day, and we knew they would want to sit near the front.

Our neighbors, Clopas and Mary, were there early and greeted us from a nearby bench. They were also very devout and attended every synagogue service. Clopas was slightly older than his brother Yosef, and the two had always enjoyed a strong fraternal bond. Their wives, the two Marys, were as close as sisters. Clopas owned the largest and finest vineyard in Nazareth. He could always count on help from Yosef and his family, particularly at harvest time in the fall.

As we waited, we sat and talked with friends and neighbors around us, catching up on the latest news and stories. Synagogue was a time for religious service, but also a time to socialize and discuss recent events. This, as much as anything else, made our village a close-knit community. If someone was ill, or engaged to be married, or traveling, soon most people would be familiar with the news.

The weekly Sabbath meetings were familiar to all, and that made them very comforting. The older men of the village took turns giving the sermon. They recited stories from the holy Scriptures, which they had heard many times and memorized over the years. Stories were repeated often about the word of God as taught to us by the ancient prophets. Very often we were taught wisdom and law from the Torah, the sacred Law of Moses that provides us with clear and strict rules for how to live our lives.

The men always spoke in Aramaic, our common language in Galilee, and always from memory. We had no books or other written religious works in the village. Even if we had written materials, which were very expensive to buy, very few people would be able to understand the Hebrew of the ancient Scriptures.

Only a handful of people in Nazareth knew how to read or write in Aramaic, and none in Hebrew. There were no schools in Nazareth, and no highly educated people. People like us, who lived in farming and fishing villages, were the simple and uneducated peasants of Galilee. The Greek-speaking Jewish aristocracy of Herod Antipas, who lived in Sepphoris, arrogantly called us *agrammatoi*—the unlettered people.

Late spring through early fall is the dry season in Galilee, when there are few overcast or cloudy days. On that particular day, another bright and sunny day blessed us as we waited for the service to begin.

Yosef and Mary arrived shortly afterward and settled the children on the benches. Yeshua sat next to Eva, and they immediately started a lively conversation. She was always delighted to see him.

Mary sat down next to Sarah, greeting each other warmly.

"Are the children well today?" Sarah asked. "Eva told me that Judah was ill yesterday."

All mothers worried about their children's health, and often it was the first topic of conversation between them. Sadly, many children died young from illnesses that could not be easily cured.

"Yes, he had a cough. But he is recovered and feeling much better today," Mary answered.

Yosef said: "Yeshua was very good with him. He's very helpful with the younger children while Mary is looking after the baby."

I said to Mary: "Yeshua is helpful, and he has the healing touch."

"Yes, he does," Mary said in her calm voice. "We noticed that since he was very young."

Sarah gave her a big smile. "He is truly a blessing from the Lord. We are so grateful for it."

"Of course," Mary said. "Actually, healing is something that Yeshua enjoys doing for others. It comes naturally from his kind heart."

"Ah, I should begin the service," Yosef said. "It is time."

He walked to the front and turned to face the congregation. He stood patiently while everyone else settled in. The many conversations quieted and drifted away, and we were ready to begin.

Yeshua held little three-year-old Mary on his lap. She became calm and attentive, following his gaze to look at their father. Their mother Mary cradled the baby Salome to her bosom and rocked her gently to keep her feeling soothed.

As always, we began the service with a prayer. "Hear, O Israel: The Lord is our God, the Lord alone. You shall love the Lord your God with all your heart, and with all your soul, and with all your might."

Yosef began speaking in a relaxed but very clear voice. He told the story of Jonah and the fish. This was a familiar story that came from the Scriptures, but Yosef did not talk as if he was reading Scripture. He told the story from memory, and from the heart, in the simple Aramaic language that we all spoke every day of our lives.

"And the Lord told Jonah to go to the city of Nineveh, to preach the word of God to the people there because the people were very wicked. But Jonah was a stubborn man. He decided to disobey God, and even tried to run away on a ship! Oh, foolish man!"

Mindful of the religious conversations we had from time to time, I looked at Yeshua to see how well he attended to the sermon. He was completely attentive, more than the other children and more than many of the surrounding adults.

Yosef continued: "The Lord God sent a mighty storm of wind and rain, and during the storm Jonah fell overboard. Some say that he was thrown overboard because the men on the ship blamed him for God sending the storm. Now, Jonah surely would have drowned in the rough seas then, but God sent a big fish that swallowed Jonah."

Little Mary turned away, mildly frightened by the story, and buried her face in Yeshua's chest. He whispered soothingly in her ear until she relaxed again.

"Jonah was trapped in the belly of the fish, but he spent the next three days praising God and praying to God for forgiveness. After those three days of prayer, the Lord commanded the fish to spit him out onto dry land near the city of Nineveh. Jonah then obeyed the Lord, and preached to Nineveh, and the people there repented and turned away from their wickedness. From that day onward, Jonah preached the word of God Almighty and never again disobeyed the Lord. He became a prophet of God, so that we may also learn from the lessons that God taught him."

Although Yeshua knew the story of Jonah very well, having heard it many times before, he was hanging on to every word being uttered by Yosef in the sermon. Other than soothing his little sister, nothing else around him seemed to matter. Only Yosef, and what was being taught, and his own thoughts about what he was hearing.

Mary noticed my look of curiosity and smiled. "Yes, Yeshua pays attention to every word," she said. "And he never forgets a word of what is taught in synagogue."

"I can see that's true," I said. "I never noticed, but I wasn't paying attention to him before now."

"He learns quickly," Mary said with a mother's pride. "Ask him later, and he will repeat Yosef's sermon word for word."

After more discussion with people in the congregation, Yosef ended the service with some parting words. Some people would stay longer to speak with their friends, and some stirred and prepared to leave.

Yosef came back to re-join our group. Little Mary ran to her father, then laughed with delight when he picked her up and lifted her high in the air.

"Did you like the story of Jonah?" he asked her.

"The big fish was scary!" the little girl replied.

"Yes, very scary," Yosef said with a laugh. "But you see, in the end, God showed His mercy and made the big fish spit Jonah out."

That made the girl smile. "Good! I'm glad Jonah didn't die."

Yosef turned to his youngest son. "And what did you think about it, Judah? How did you like the story?"

Judah was watching some people leave. He was four years old and had no interest in sermons. "I don't know," he said, and made a small shrug. "I don't understand it."

Yeshua put an arm around his shoulder. "We can talk about it later, Jude. I will explain it to you."

James said thoughtfully: "I liked the story, *Abba*. It's a good lesson to teach us we should never disobey God."

Joses added: "Yes! And if we try to run away, then God will find us and punish us."

"That's very good! You are both right," Yosef said. "And Yeshua, what did you learn?"

Yeshua paused for a moment, collecting his thoughts. To him, it was an important question that deserved a thoughtful answer.

"I learned that God is good to us, and that He is forgiving. When Jonah acted in a very bad way, Father God did not kill him. Instead, He taught him a lesson."

"That's a very good answer," Yosef said. "And after God taught him the lesson, what happened?"

"After Jonah learned his lesson, he repented, and praised God, and became a good man. Then he did good things by obeying God's wishes, and doing God's work by preaching to the people of Nineveh."

That made Yosef smile. "That's an excellent lesson to remember. God loves all His children, and He treats us with patience and kindness if we ask forgiveness for our mistakes and then love the Lord."

"I will remember, *Abba*," Yeshua said.

Clopas and his wife Mary bid farewell to some friends and walked over to join us. She was a big-hearted woman who doted on her nieces and nephews, the children of Yosef and Mary. Within three years, she would become the mother of James and Simeon. Much later, when Yeshua was full grown and ready to start his ministry, his aunt Mary, the wife of Clopas, would become one of his most important followers.

"A very fine sermon, Brother," Clopas told Yosef. "We shall see if I can do as well next week."

"Oh, are we in competition now?" Yosef chuckled. "Let me tell you this: no matter if your sermon is better or worse than my sermon, the Lord will love you just the same."

"You're probably right about that," Clopas said. He put an arm around his wife, and said with a smile: "The Lord will love me just as much if I give a bad sermon, but I wonder, will my wife?"

Mary groaned, shaking her head at his joke. "Oh, you men and your pride. Do you want to know how to give a sermon better than Yosef?"

"Oh?" Clopas raised an eyebrow. "Tell us!"

Mary had a mischievous smile on her lips. "Give a sermon about what *you* know best. Grapes and wine and tending God's vineyard. Who doesn't love a good talk about wine?"

Everyone laughed, including Clopas.

He said: "Did not King Solomon himself wisely tell us, 'Go, eat your food with gladness, and drink your wine with a joyful heart, for God has already approved what you do!'"

"Ah, and there you have your sermon," Yosef joked.

"Shall we go back to the house?" Sarah asked. "It's almost time for the noonday meal."

Mary, the mother of Yeshua, happily agreed. "Yes, let's go. My little ones will be crying for food very shortly."

"Race you home!" Joses challenged his brothers, James and Judah. The three boys took off at a run down the street.

We followed, walking together. Yeshua did not join his younger brothers, but held back to walk with the adults. He held his sister Mary by the hand and talked to her. Eva walked on the other side of the little girl. She looked pleased to be in the company of the adults, and always seemed happier when Yeshua was around.

Chapter 3

Be Joyful at Your Feast

Nazareth, Galilee, Autumn 7 C.E.

We did not make the holiday pilgrimage to Jerusalem for the fall festivals that year. Only Clopas and his family made the journey. Yosef and Mary's three youngest children were too young for the weeklong walk—their daughter Mary was five, Salome three, and Shimon not quite two years old. Iacob and Abana were nearing old age, each approaching their fiftieth year. Like most older people, they limited their holiday pilgrimages to one holiday per year if they were healthy enough to make the trip.

We celebrated the New Year's *rashana* in Nazareth with our closest neighbors. Yom Kippur, the Day of Atonement, came ten days later. We fasted, prayed, and asked for forgiveness from God Almighty and from our fellow men and women. Yeshua was twelve years old then, just one year away from the age of majority, and was allowed to fast for a full day. Clopas would offer a sacrifice at the Temple in Jerusalem for our sins and the sins of our people.

After that came the seven days of Sukkot, the Feast of Booths. For many of us, it was the most joyous holiday of the year, a time to relax and celebrate. The young children, in particular, became very excited before the holiday. They took delight in building booths, small shelters like tents or tiny sheds, and sleeping outside under the stars.

In part, Sukkot celebrated the end of the harvest season. Much more importantly, at Sukkot we commemorated the time in our history when our ancestors, being led out of Egypt by God and Moses during the exodus, sheltered in tents and booths in the desert. They slept under the stars and joined together as one people, protected only by the loving hand of God.

Sarah, as usual, took charge of the planning for building the *sukkah*. It was part of our family tradition.

"David will build the frame, and gather the different types of wood," she instructed. "Eva, you gather the fruits and other items for decorations. Grapes are always good, so gather some nice bunches."

"I know, *Emma*. And figs and apples, too. Also many pomegranates, they smell as delicious as they taste!"

Sarah nodded her agreement. "There's a bit more sewing needed for the cloth covers, so I will finish that."

Eva asked: "Can Leila stay with us? At least for one night?"

"Of course she can," Sarah replied, placing her arm around Eva's shoulder to draw her close and plant a kiss on her cheek. "This is the time of year to enjoy and appreciate one another."

"Thank you!" Eva said. Leila was her best friend, the daughter of our neighbors, Eitan and Hila. She was three years older than Eva and an only child, and the two became fast friends from the time they were very young. They treated each other as sisters.

"Speaking of being together and appreciating one another," I said to Sarah, "are Abana and Iacob joining us? I haven't seen them around the last few days."

"No, unfortunately," she replied with sadness. "Iacob is not well. He has severe dizziness and took to his bed days ago."

That was worrisome. Any illness for an old person was something to be taken seriously. Most often, older people who were forced to become bedridden never recovered their health.

"I'm sorry to hear that," I said. "I'll stop by to see them later."

Sarah nodded. "Very kind of you. Tell Abana that we'll share our food with them, even if they can't join us."

I went outside and immediately headed toward the stream on the west side of the village. The Scriptures instruct us that a *sukkah* must be built from four different kinds of wood, which represent bringing together different types of people. Take branches from luxuriant trees, God Almighty directed—palms, willows, and other leafy trees. Bind them together and bless them every day during the holiday. In this way, we also bind our people together and rejoice in our unity before the Lord.

The previous week, I cut and shaped the wooden planks to hold up the walls and roof of the booth. Now I needed to cut some branches from a willow tree. There was a large weeping willow on the near side of the stream, with some long branches dipping down into the water.

Approaching the stream, I noticed that someone else with the same idea was already there. Yeshua saw me and gave a friendly wave.

"Peace to you, Yeshua," I said in greeting. He was almost a man, just one year shy, and it seemed more natural to greet him as a man. He had long ago outgrown the behavior of a young child.

"And to you," he replied politely, then added with a grin: "I saved some willow branches for you!"

"That's very considerate of you," I said. "Although, to be honest, I think this ancient tree will still be here for a hundred years. It will never lose all its branches to people like us, who only wish to build a booth for Sukkot."

"I think you're right. It is only one tree, but it's part of God's bounty. We should cherish and protect it so that it will be here for others to use for many more holidays to come."

I used my knife to cut down a few small branches. The light and pleasant scent of the willow leaves, like honey and citrus, was always soothing and had a calming effect on me.

"*Abba* is building our *sukkah* in Uncle Clopas' vineyard," Yeshua said. "Will you do the same? Or do you have a better spot?"

"Ah, there is no better place in Nazareth for a *sukkah* than Clopas' vineyard," I said. "Yes, we'll build our booth close to yours."

"Oh, good," he said. "Then our families can celebrate together, just as God's people did in the ancient times."

"Yes, just the same," I agreed. "Then, now, and forever."

We took our willow branches and began the walk back up the hill. Yeshua was silent, his eyes calm and gaze turned inward. I recognized it as the expression he showed when feeling contemplative.

"Are you thinking about the ancient times?"

"Yes, I was," he replied. "What do you think it was like, back then? In the time of Moses, I mean."

"Oh, not very different from how we live our lives now," I said. "We have an ancient history, much older than the Romans, but our Jewish way of life has not changed very much in over one thousand years."

Yeshua gave a small nod. "Because of the Torah."

"Yes, because of the Torah. Moses was given our Law directly from God, and the Law has not changed. It is a gift from God that tells us how to live our lives. It makes us the people we are."

"It is our sacred covenant with God," Yeshua said with a reverent tone. "It commands us to love and honor the Lord, and to love each other as He loves us."

I gave him a smile. "You understand completely. This is the spirit of Sukkot. Our religious traditions are strong, and they help us keep our covenant with God."

"Then let's celebrate this holiday with all the joy in our hearts," he said with a grin. "Our family, your family, and Iacob and Abana."

"Ah, sadly, not Iacob and Abana," I told him. "Iacob has been ill. He doesn't leave his bed. They will not join us in our booths."

The joyful smile faded, and his expression became serious. Much too serious for a twelve-year-old boy, I thought, but that was Yeshua.

"They will join us, or we will join them, one way or another," he said. "We are all one people, unified. The Lord has decreed that it must be so."

"Then it will be so," I agreed.

We built our booth very close to that of Yosef and Mary. There were only three of us and nine of them, so we had some room to spare. Sarah and Mary helped each other with preparing the meals, sharing different types of food to make each family's meal richer.

Eva and her friend Leila helped Mary watch her younger children, Mary, Salome, and Shimon. The older boys, James, Joses, and Judah, ran off to play games with children from other families camped nearby. They would be called in later for the family meal.

Yosef walked the short distance to our booth to bring us a wineskin. He and Mary only drank wine in moderation, but Clopas, his brother, was generous and made sure they always had an ample supply. Many holiday feasts, by tradition, called for sharing and enjoying some wine.

"Joyous holidays," Yosef said in greeting. "Here is some fine old wine, saved for a special occasion."

"And also to you," I replied. "Yes, this is the perfect occasion."

It was quite late in the afternoon, and we sat for a while to enjoy the sunset while sipping our wine. It was a good time to bring up a matter that had been on my mind for a while.

"You are a master craftsman, Yosef," I told him. "A *tekton* skilled in working with wood and stone."

"I like to think so," he said modestly. "But why are you telling me this?"

I saw no reason to be cryptic about my wishes, so addressed him very directly. "I would like to become your apprentice. If you will have me, of course."

"Ah, I see," he replied in a serious tone. We were close neighbors, our families friends for decades, and this was a serious manner. He would give me a thoughtful answer, and agree to my proposal only if it would be to our mutual benefit.

"You are a good and just man, David," Yosef said, looking me in the eye. "I will be pleased to work with you as my apprentice. Actually, my second apprentice."

"Thank you, Yosef," I replied gratefully. "But why do you say second apprentice?"

"Yeshua will be thirteen next year. He will reach his majority and become a man. It's time for him to learn the skills of my trade, I think. So why not two apprentices?"

Sarah overheard our conversation. "Two apprentices would keep you very busy, no? Will it be too much?"

"It can be done," said Yosef. "All three of us will work on the same projects together, so I can teach both of you side by side. It will make the work go faster on building projects, and we can earn more money by working on more projects."

"That sounds very good to me!" I said with a laugh.

Mary walked over to join the conversation and to check on the younger children. Eva and Leila had been playing with Salome and Mary to keep them entertained, and keeping an eye on little Shimon. Their patience for babysitting had reached its limits, however, and they looked pleased to return the young ones to their mother.

Mary said to us: "Yeshua is eager to start his training next year. Do you wish to start your apprenticeship sooner than that, David?"

"As soon as my teacher will have me," I said with a nod to Yosef.

He smiled amiably. "There is no reason to keep you waiting until next year. We can discuss these details later, David."

"Of course," I happily agreed.

Eva looked around, puzzled. "Speaking of Yeshua, where is he? I haven't seen him for a while."

"Neither have I," said Leila. She was a pretty girl with long brown hair and hazel eyes. Her character was relaxed and sociable, but her face always gave the impression that she took her responsibilities very seriously. She was also friends with Yeshua, as was Eva.

"Would you girls go and look for him, please?" Mary asked. "We're almost ready for our meal."

"Happy to!" Eva said. "He probably went back to the house. We'll find him."

Mary and Sarah finished preparing our meals. The booths were very near each other on a slope among the grapevines, and we wandered easily from one to the other. Mary brought a basket to our booth.

"For Abana and Iacob," she said. "Let's set aside a portion of the meal for them. The children can take it to their house."

"Good, I was thinking the same," Sarah agreed. "Iacob's illness has me worried."

Yosef turned his head to look down the hill. "Oh, here come the girls. It looks like they didn't find Yeshua."

Eva and Leila walked briskly back to our booths. For some reason, they were full of excitement.

"We healed Iacob!" Eva exclaimed happily. "He's coming here with Abana to join us in our *sukkah*!"

Sarah's eyebrows went up. "What do you mean? You and Leila healed Iacob?"

Leila laughed and shook her head. "Eva, you are being immodest! *We* only stood and watched."

"Oh, you're right, as usual," Eva said with a soft laugh. "*Yeshua* healed Iacob. We found him at Abana's house."

"And how did Yeshua do that?" I asked, curious.

"He talked to him, and touched his head," Eva said.

"He also gave Iacob a blessing, and they both said a prayer," Leila added. "And then Iacob stood up from his bed, and he walked!"

"He stopped being dizzy and sick," Eva said. "We both saw it."

I caught Sarah's eye. She gave me a patient, knowing smile.

"This is what Yeshua does," Sarah said. She looked at Mary and Yosef. "He has a gift."

"Yes," Mary said, a simple statement.

Yosef pointed to a short way down the hill. "Here they come."

Iacob and Abana approached, walking arm in arm at a slow but steady pace. Yeshua walked on the other side of Iacob, but the older man did not need his assistance.

"Joyous holidays!" Iacob said in greeting. "God be praised, I am well, so let us celebrate the holiday."

"Yes, God be praised," Abana said gratefully. "Yeshua came to us, like a blessing, but I know that he was sent by the Lord."

"Father God provides what we need," Yeshua said simply.

Yosef looked at him with great pride. "And what better time to thank Him than at Sukkot? And God Almighty commanded His people: Be joyful at your feast!"

Iacob recited the familiar Feast of Booths stories for us all to hear. He was the oldest in our group, and so we deferred to him. The children listened with rapt attention; even three-year-old Salome could sense that this was a special occasion.

"When the prophet Moses led our people out of bondage from Egypt, they wandered in the wilderness for forty years on the way to the promised land. Our people had no homes, no houses, so they set up booths, like this one, in the desert to shelter them at night."

Young James had a thoughtful question: "Were they attacked by wild beasts? Or bandits?"

"Yes, sometimes they were attacked. But each time that happened, our people banded together and fought off the attackers! We had no army then, no soldiers with swords and spears. Our people depended on God alone, and on each other, to protect them."

Abana said: "This is why we gather each year at Sukkot, so that we remember how our ancestors lived. And we come together again as one people, united very closely, just as they did."

"Did they build *sukkahs* just like this one, with leafy branches?" Eva asked. She smiled and added: "And decorate them with grapes and pomegranates, like I did?"

Iacob laughed. "They set up booths, and tents, and shelters of all kinds using whatever materials they could find. They did not have as much food as we have now, so their food was not used for decoration."

"Our *sukkah* is a symbol and a reminder of how our ancestors lived," Yosef explained. "Their lives were much harsher than our lives now."

Yeshua said: "Yes, and the fruit for decorations is a symbol of God's bounty. It reminds us to appreciate and thank God for His goodness."

"Oh, I know that," Eva replied. "And I *am* very grateful for all that we have."

Mary asked the children: "Who can tell us, why do we sit within these walls tonight? And why do we look up at the sky filled with stars through the open spaces in the roof?"

"To remind us of our ancestors in the old times!" Joses answered eagerly.

"Yes, Joses, that is true," Mary replied. "But is there another reason that you can think of?"

The children looked at each other with puzzled looks. The adults watched and waited patiently to give them time to ponder. Yeshua was the first one to smile.

"Yeshua, do you have a thought to share?"

"Yes, I think so, *Emma*. The walls of the *sukkah* embrace us, just as the hands of God embrace us," Yeshua said.

"Yes!" Eva cried. "That's just how it feels. I feel very protected by God. And when I look up at the stars, I feel more in touch with God."

"Those are very wise words, my daughter," Sarah told her. "And I feel exactly the same, sitting here with all of you."

"The loving arms of God embrace us, shelter us, and protect us," Yosef said. "In the same way, we love, embrace, and protect each other. This is the message of Sukkot."

"I love our *sukkah*!" little Mary said. "Can we sleep here tonight?"

"Yes, you children can sleep here tonight," Mary said. "If Yeshua will stay with you and watch you, that is."

The younger children turned to him, eagerly waiting for an answer.

"Of course I'll stay with you," Yeshua said with a grin. "I also love our *sukkah,* just as much as you do."

Eva said: "Leila asked me to stay with her family tonight. Will you allow me to, *Emma*?"

Sarah nodded her assent. "Yes. David and I will be at home if you should need anything."

Iacob sat up with a groan and stretched his arms. "It's time for us older folks to go home, too. Thank you for a wonderful holiday feast, my friends."

"We are blessed to share this celebration with you," Yosef said. "The Feast of Booths would not be the same without you. Thank you for sharing your joy and happiness with us."

Yeshua gave his father a quizzical look. "*Abba*, I have a question?"

"Yes?"

"I understand that Sukkot is a special time to show our love and appreciation for God, and our love and appreciation for each other. We treat each other lovingly, with great kindness and generosity. It is a time of joy and happiness."

"That is so," Yosef said. "But what is your question, Yeshua?"

He gave a small shrug. "My question is: why don't we treat each other this way *every* day of the year?"

His question made me chuckle, and all the adults around us smiled. It was such a typical Yeshua question.

"Perhaps one day we will," Yosef said. "God willing, perhaps one day we will."

Chapter 4

Lessons From Yosef

Nazareth, Galilee, Spring 9 C.E.

Sepphoris was at that time the capital city of Galilee, rebuilt by Herod Antipas after the Roman army burned it to the ground. The Roman attack was in response to the Jewish uprising led by Judas the Galilean, following the death of Herod the Great. His army of rebels plundered the homes of the wealthy and powerful who had profited from their loyalty to Rome. They then took Sepphoris and captured all the weapons in its armory. The people celebrated joyfully because it was a glorious victory over the hated foreign occupiers.

The Romans came and re-captured the city, of course. They razed it and left nothing but rubble, to set an example for other would-be rebels who would preach sedition and challenge the rule of Rome. The men in Sepphoris were slaughtered, and the women and children sold into slavery.

The Romans crucified two thousand rebels and their supporters to teach a brutal lesson that would be remembered for generations to come. Their corpses were left for weeks to rot on the crosses, which lined the roadsides for miles on end to frighten the people. For the Romans, crucifixion was a simple and inexpensive method used to punish and terrorize the local population.

My father, Matthias, was one of the men who joined the rebellion of Judas the Galilean. He died on the cross along with the other rebels.

I was just a young boy then, living with my mother and baby sister in Nazareth, and have few memories of those years.

After the death of Herod the Great, his son, Herod Antipas, called "the Fox," was appointed by Augustus Caesar to rule Galilee, Perea, and Iturea. Antipas quickly set to work to rebuild Sepphoris on a grander scale than before its destruction. This then became the major building project of its time in Galilee. It required the labor of many thousands of workers, and the work took many years to complete.

Fortunately for the men of Nazareth, Sepphoris is only a short one hour walk away. While those families who owned land still worked on their farms, men from the poorer families poured into Sepphoris six days a week to work on the building projects.

The new Sepphoris became a beautiful city, called by many "the ornament of all Galilee." Improvements were constantly being made, and so the work continued. The wealthy mansions and houses there always needed upkeep. Many of the men from our village still walked daily to Sepphoris to work on the various construction projects. They rested only on the day of the Sabbath.

Our neighbor Yosef was a man of peace. He never joined Judas the Galilean and his rebellion, and thus did not suffer the same cruel and bloody fate as my father. Yosef was a *tekton*, a skilled worker in the building trades. He worked on the rebuilding of the capital city from the beginning of its reconstruction.

By this time Yeshua was a young man of fourteen, one year past his age of majority when he became an adult. He joined his father on the trips to Sepphoris as an apprentice, to be trained in working with wood and stone.

I joined them also, as Yosef's second apprentice. Two of Yeshua's younger brothers, James and Joses, took over my sheepherding duties. I had long ago tired of watching sheep, and the two boys were happy for the work and the benefits it brought their family in extra milk and cheese.

Yosef, Yeshua, and I left Nazareth in the early hours of dawn for the hourlong walk to the city. Sepphoris is located due northwest of our village, and as we walked along the narrow dirt road the rising sun cast long shadows to our left.

There are few roads between most villages of Galilee, but there is always a road leading to Sepphoris. The big cargo wagons carrying the crops of wheat and barley, orchard fruits, olives, wool, and other goods collected for taxes travelled on those roads. The tax collectors came in person twice a year, and they needed to travel fast and work efficiently for their employer, Herod Antipas.

Yosef typically looked straight ahead and kept his eyes fixed on the road as we walked along. There were few bandits in this central part of Galilee, unlike the thinly populated mountain areas in the northern part of the province, but still one had to be alert and cautious.

Yeshua, unlike Yosef, had lively and roaming eyes. It was springtime in Galilee, which meant that everywhere the eye could see the land was covered in a rich carpet of green, dotted with a myriad of colors from various types of flowers and trees. This was a valley of fertile soil, the best farming land in all of Galilee or Judea. Sepphoris was built here to prosper in the middle of this bountiful land.

Yeshua took joyful satisfaction in looking at the signs of life all around us. These were the gifts of God's creation: the fields of wheat ripening in the sun, the neatly planted rows of vines on the hillsides laden with small unripe grapes, the fruit orchards, the groves of olive trees. He took a simple joy in the many colorful patches of wildflowers that grew by the roadside and in sections of uncultivated ground.

"Look!" Yeshua cried with delight, pointing a finger up at the sky. A hawk was diving rapidly, straight down, like a rock falling from the clear blue sky. It spotted some prey on the ground far below.

Yosef took a brief look, smiled at his son's youthful enthusiasm, and turned his eyes back to the road.

"Yes, it's a hawk," I said.

"Ah, David, is that *all* you see? Just a hawk?" Yeshua asked.

"Well, yes. What do *you* see?"

He grinned happily. "I see one of God's perfect creations. We are blessed to see it this morning." He spread his arms to indicate the land surrounding us. "We are blessed to be living in this land! Blessed to enjoy the bounty of God's goodness."

Yosef agreed with a nod. "That is very true, Yeshua. And the Lord said, I am come to deliver my people out of the hand of the Egyptians, and to bring them up out of that land unto a good land flowing with milk and honey."

"Yes!" Yeshua exclaimed. "The Lord fulfilled His promise to us. We should celebrate and enjoy His gift."

"You see the world with eyes of faith," I told him with a smile. "I'm also thankful for God's blessings, but sometimes I wish we had more freedom to enjoy the fruits of the land and of our labor."

Yeshua gave me a questioning look. "What do you mean?"

"I mean only this. Yes, the land is rich and fertile. We are good and hard-working people. But in the end, who profits most from our labors and the bounty of the land? That fox, Herod Antipas, and the Romans that he loves more than God or our own people. Every year, his taxes take almost half of what we produce."

Yosef gave a sigh. "The injustices of the world weigh heavily on your shoulders, David. You are very much like your father in that way."

My face flushed. I wanted to shout out my anger, but in respect for Yosef, I kept my voice even. "When I was a young boy, my father was crucified on this very road because he tried to fight those injustices."

Yosef said: "Matthias was a brave and righteous man. He did what he believed in his heart that God Almighty asked him to do."

"You are also a brave and righteous man. Yet you didn't join him in his fight," I said, unable to hold back a faint tone of resentment.

"No, I did not," Yosef replied. He gave me a compassionate look. "Do you wish to know my reasons why?"

"Yes. Tell me, so I may understand it better."

"I didn't take up arms because we can't win our freedom through violence. Herod has a large army. Even if we defeat his army, then Rome will come to his aid. This happens in every Jewish rebellion."

"But it *has* worked before!" I protested. "Just now you quoted to us from the Scripture of Exodus. Moses led our people from slavery in Egypt, did he not? He parted the Red Sea to let our people escape, then drowned Pharaoh's army when they tried to follow. Was that not an act of great violence?"

Yosef shook his head, staying calm and patient with me. "No, that's not right. Moses did not drown Pharaoh's army."

"What do you mean? Of course he did."

Rather than answer me directly, he turned to his son. "What do you think about that, Yeshua?"

"I understand what you're saying, *Abba*. I agree with you." He turned his head to catch my eye. "You see, David, Moses did not part the Red Sea, or drown the soldiers of Pharaoh. God Almighty parted the sea and drowned Pharaoh's army. Only the Lord has the power to create miracles."

I knew in my heart that they were right. My anger slowly subsided, only to be replaced by frustration. In my darkest moments, frustration often turned to despair. Perhaps I was similar to my father in that way, as well.

"What is the solution, then?" I asked. "How do we ever defeat these people who enslave us, then kill us if we resist?"

Yosef said: "Our people will be delivered from bondage when the Lord makes it so. Only the reign of God will sweep away the tyranny and wickedness of this world."

"Amen," Yeshua said in solemn agreement.

The city slowly came into view, rising slightly above the plain in the morning mists. We walked on the road in silence.

We entered Sepphoris through the south gate. Although we had been there for work many times before, each time it still felt like entering a new world. The capital of Galilee was a city of forty thousand people, with all the luxury and splendor that the Jewish ruling class demanded. Only the large coastal cities of Tyre and Sidon were richer, and, of course, Jerusalem.

Where Nazareth had narrow and dusty streets, Sepphoris was built with wide streets paved with stone. The larger streets were forty feet wide, which was unheard of in the villages of Galilee. The houses and mansions were large and made of wood and stone, with red-tiled roofs in the Roman fashion. Some were built two stories high, or even taller.

While the population of Sepphoris was predominantly Jewish, these were not peasants from the Galilean countryside. There were many wealthy merchantmen from Judea, members of the royal family of Herod Antipas, and government officials. Most spoke Greek, which was the language of the Herodian nobility and high-ranking officials.

This was where the legal courts were held. It was where all the tax collections were gathered and stored. The city had a large theater for more than four thousand people, built in the Roman style, to entertain its citizens with plays and athletic contests. The design of Sepphoris and its daily life was more Roman than Jewish.

Everything about Sepphoris seemed like a message to outsiders that said: this is how your masters live. Many people from Judea, and particularly those from the large cities, had a low opinion of people from Galilee. They viewed us as the "country" people, uneducated bumpkins best suited to cultivate the land and feed those in positions of authority. Much of the surrounding land was owned by the wealthy elites, who then leased it to the local Galilean farmers.

Even the Aramaic language of the common people of Galilee was spoken with a different accent than the Aramaic spoken in Judea, and our heavy accent was made fun of. A man or woman from Galilee was easily identified by their lowly "country" accent.

Yet still we trekked daily to this great city, because only the people there could afford to pay us for our labor.

The job that Yosef contracted for us was to build a stone wall that would surround a garden. It would take the three of us four days to complete, and the wages were good. When this project was finished, Yosef would find us another job. Yeshua and I were only apprentices, and our job was to help and learn as we went along.

Yosef and I did the masonry work. I was learning the art of mixing mortar, in just the right proportions and to just the right thickness and consistency. Mortar poorly made would weaken and crack when it dried, then the wall would sag and need to be repaired or rebuilt.

I learned how to lay stones following a perfect line, set by Yosef with thin wooden posts and a long string. The stones had to be set in such a way that the wall was flawlessly straight and flat along its sides. A wall with sides that were not perfectly even was a sign of poor and unacceptable workmanship. Yosef checked the sight lines often.

"Is the workmanship acceptable?" I asked as he looked to make sure that the corner I was building was perfectly squared.

"The workmanship is good," he replied. "Whether it is acceptable, well, that will be determined by the master of the house after our work is finished."

I asked: "And if the work is deemed not acceptable? What then?"

"Then we don't get paid, David, and all this work will be for nothing. But that's not the worst part."

I frowned, puzzled. "What could be worse than that?"

"It would make it more difficult for me to find work in the future," Yosef said in a serious tone. "My reputation would be damaged. And you would be back to watching sheep."

"I understand. I will never fail you in that way."

He gave a reassuring nod. "You are doing fine work. Just continue as you are. We'll make a stonemason out of you yet!"

The garden wall would have a large and ornate wooden gate, and this became Yeshua's project. This was not a rough-hewn gate of the type one might see on a country fence, but a well-designed gate that needed to be as finely crafted as a piece of furniture. Yosef first drew the design, then purchased the proper materials. He patiently guided Yeshua through each step of the work, always keeping a close eye on his progress and helping him with the more difficult parts.

Carpentry and masonry tools were very expensive, and the only tools we had were those owned by Yosef. Yeshua learned how to use the saw, chisel, plane, square edge, mallet, and hammer to shape the pieces of wood so that they fit together perfectly. He was a fast learner at this, as in most things that he put his mind to. The only times he had any difficulties was when he became impatient and rushed things. He was responsible and took pride in doing good work, but young men are often prone to impatience.

Yosef worked at a steady pace, fast enough to be efficient but never so fast that he sacrificed quality. It was pleasant and relaxing working in the warm sun. He broke into a hymn, singing softly to himself. His song was interrupted by a loud sound of wood hitting against wood.

"Ah! How careless!" Yeshua said in a low, frustrated voice that only we could hear. Yosef put down his trowel and went to him.

"How were you careless? Show me."

Yeshua held up a thin piece of wood. "This slat is cut too short. It doesn't fit properly."

"Then it can't be used," Yosef said. "How did this happen?"

Yeshua gave him an embarrassed smile. "I rushed through it."

"What is the first rule of carpentry, my son?"

"Measure twice, cut once."

"Yes. If you break that rule, it means you're no longer thinking about your work. A master craftsman can't allow such carelessness that leads to foolish mistakes."

Yeshua acknowledged with a nod. He bent down and inspected a small pile of lumber at his feet. "I am lucky. We have just enough board left to make another slat."

"Good," Yosef said. "And for your lesson, for the next week you will measure *thrice* and cut once. Will you remember that?"

Yeshua laughed. "Yes, *Abba*. I won't forget."

In the early afternoon, we found a patch of grass and sat down for our midday meal. Lunch was simple food that could be eaten quickly: bread, goat cheese, and olives. The lady of the house came out to walk around and inspect our work. She said nothing to us but appeared to be pleased. She went back inside the house, and a short time later a servant girl appeared to reward us with a pitcher of cool water.

While we ate, Yeshua watched with fascination as a wide variety of people walked by on the busy street. This was a sight that we would never see in Nazareth. Many of the people were servants running busy errands or making deliveries, but most were city residents who easily stood out by the way they were dressed.

The men wore stylish clothes made of fine linen bleached white, and sandals or shoes made of leather. The women were dressed in colorful dresses, made of thin fabrics and shiny silks that no villager could afford. Yeshua had a natural interest in watching people, and indeed, he seemed to like most people. The crowd of people on the streets of Sepphoris was a new world for him to explore.

Some distance away, at the end of this major street, we could see the tall building that was the royal palace of Herod Antipas. It was built on the highest ground in the city, massive and opulent and designed to impress. Colorful banners hung down from the walls. The flags of the Herodians flowed in the mild spring breeze. The gates were guarded by Herod's soldiers, armed with spears, swords, and shields. They wore helmets and brightly polished armor in the Roman fashion.

Yeshua said: "I wonder if Herod will walk this way? I would like to see what he looks like."

"You will see him one day if you are patient," Yosef answered. "Some days he walks on the streets and talks to the common people. He is always surrounded by his guards, of course."

"Is he afraid of his own people, *Abba*? Why is that?"

Yosef answered with mild disdain: "Every ruler is afraid of his own people. That is the way of the world."

"Even Caesar in Rome?" Yeshua wondered.

"Yes, even Caesar in Rome. The emperors of Rome are often killed by their fellow Romans."

I was not sad to hear him say that. In truth, the thought of dead Roman emperors made my heart glad. The Romans brought suffering to our people. Roman soldiers executed my father on the cross.

I looked at Yosef and said: "When there is justice in the world, *then* perhaps rulers will have less reason to be afraid?"

He gave me a sad smile. "Perhaps so, David. Perhaps so."

Yeshua said: "God Almighty will make it so."

I wanted to believe him. I did not feel as certain, however, that it would happen soon. My faith was not as strong as Yeshua's.

Yosef shot a glance up at the blue and cloudless sky. "Let's get back to work. We have another five hours of good working daylight, then I want to leave for home. Zebedee, Salome, and the children are leaving for Capernaum tomorrow, and the two Marys are preparing a special dinner for them tonight."

Yeshua sprang to his feet like a young colt. "Good! Knowing that a feast waits for us will make the work go faster now."

We arrived back in Nazareth just before sunset and were immediately met with a lively and joyful scene. The shared patio of our four houses was full of people and commotion, including the happy shouts of many young children playing their games. The air was filled with the aroma of fresh bread just out of the oven, and a spicy stew cooking in the large boiling pot.

The two Marys, meaning Mary the wife of Yosef, and Mary the wife of Clopas, were in charge of meal preparations. Cooking and serving food was women's work, so the men sat on benches around one of the tables, drinking wine and talking in loud voices. There were children happily running around everywhere.

The brothers Yosef and Clopas each married a woman named Mary. It was amusing to watch sometimes as someone called out the name

Mary, and both women looked up immediately from what they were doing and turned to the sound of the voice. Mary, mother of Yeshua, was the oldest by perhaps two years.

Salome, wife of Zebedee, was Mary's younger sister and Yeshua's other aunt. She assisted by watching the bread in the clay oven so that it did not burn. Early the next day, Zebedee and Salome, along with their two young sons and two-year-old daughter, would leave for the fishing village of Capernaum to start a new life there.

Sitting at the table with Clopas and Zebedee, well into his third or fourth cup of wine, was our neighbor Iacob. The men greeted Yosef with respect and affection. Yeshua and I were much younger than these mature men, and we were greeted politely but not with the same level of regard. That was understandable – we would grow in their esteem as we grew older and proved ourselves.

At the next table, my mother Sarah sat with Abana; their task was to watch over the younger children. Yeshua's brother Shimon was three years old, going on four. His sister Salome was five. Mary was seven.

Eight-year-old Judah was chasing after his little cousin, James, the son of Clopas. Off to one side, Yeshua's twelve-year-old brother James played a game with Joses, who was one year younger. Their game was interrupted by the sons of Zebedee, James and John. Those two boys, seven and five years old at the time, were the loudest and most active of the cousins. They would remain loud and energetic as adults.

The children ran and played games around the patio under the watchful eyes of the two older women. My sister Eva and her friend Nimura, the daughter of Clopas and Mary, played with the youngest children. These were the toddlers, Rina the daughter of Zebedee and Salome, and Simeon, the youngest of the Clopas children.

The first child who ran to welcome us was little Salome. She loved her father Yosef, of course, but she was especially fond of her oldest brother Yeshua. It was his arms that she leaped into.

"I missed you!" the girl said merrily, hugging him around the neck.

Yeshua laughed and kissed her cheek. "I'm glad to see you too, little sister," he said, then put her down. He had a rare, very gentle quality in dealing with children. Little children naturally liked and trusted him, and he cherished them.

"Come join us and have a cup of my wine!" Clopas invited us with enthusiasm. He took special pride in the quality of his black grapes and the fine red wine they produced. We gladly accepted his offer.

Iacob turned to Zebedee and resumed their conversation. "And how did you come to befriend this man from Capernaum?"

Zebedee said: "We met on the pilgrim road to Jerusalem during the last trip for Passover. Our families joined, and we walked and camped together for four days. Of course, we talked about this and that and everything else during the trip."

"Of course," Yosef said between thirsty sips of his wine. "There is no better way to make a friend than sharing the road to Jerusalem for one of the high holidays. Talking makes the long walk easier."

Zebedee continued: "He owns fishing boats, he told me, in both Bethsaida and Capernaum. He's prosperous in his business, indeed so prosperous that he was looking to hire help. He has two sons of his own, but they're too young, only a little older than my sons."

Iacob said: "So then, you're going to work for this man Jonas?"

"Yes. To start with, I will work for him. In a few years, if we prosper, with God's blessing, I might become his business partner."

Clopas raised his wine cup. "The Lord bless you with good health and good fortune, brother! The waters of Capernaum are rich fishing grounds. You will do well, I'm sure."

Yeshua lost interest in talk about the fishing business, and his eyes drifted to the women preparing food. He drained his wine cup, then walked over to greet them and talk. He never bothered to follow rules about keeping a social distance between groups of men and women.

Mary, who was stirring the stew with a long wooden spoon, looked up at him. "Did you have a good day in the city?"

"Yes, *Emma*. It was a wonderful day. But now I'm famished, and the stew smells delicious. How soon do we eat?"

"Just a little while longer. Be patient. This is your Aunt Mary's spicy partridge and lentil stew you like so much."

Mary the wife of Clopas smiled at her words. She was a buxom woman of medium height, with reddish-brown hair and lively green eyes. She asked teasingly: "Is that right, Yeshua? Do you like my stew better than all the rest?"

He smiled. "You make the best stew, Aunt Mary … *after* my mother, of course."

"Oh ho!" she exclaimed in mock protest. "Then I should be happy to be second best. Humility is a blessing, or so they tell me."

Salome the wife of Zebedee carefully took the last loaves of bread from the hot oven and placed them on a wooden tray. She was the youngest of the three women by two years, a slim woman with long brown hair. She had dark brown eyes that always seemed to have a kind expression, the same as her sister.

"Mary, don't tease our nephew," Salome said. "Right now, he looks too hungry to be in a mood for teasing."

Yeshua said: "You're right about the hungry part. Here, let me help you put the bread on the tables. The sooner we eat, the better!"

Salome gave her nephew a look of mild reproach. "Serving food is not men's work. Let us women handle it."

He raised an eyebrow. "Is it not men's work? And why is that?"

"Because that's how we are taught, Yeshua. Why question it?"

Mary sighed and gave her sister a patient look. "My son does things in his own way, as he wishes. You know that by now, Sister."

"All right!" Salome conceded with a laugh. She took two of the bread trays and handed them to Yeshua. "Here you go. And thank you for helping, my kind nephew."

My sister Eva was also listening to their conversation. She sat up abruptly from her bench and went over to them. "I'll help you carry the bread, Yeshua," she said with a shy smile.

I realized then, and with some surprise, that her smile toward him had been changing over the past few months. What had always been friendly smiles before were now becoming – adoring smiles, perhaps? Yes, they had a certain look of adoration about them. My little sister, I thought to myself, was growing up.

A short time later the stew was ready. Mary's strong and clear voice rang out across the patio: "Children! Come to table! Time to eat!"

"Ah, those are welcome words," Yeshua said happily. He poured himself a second cup of wine, then motioned toward my cup with a questioning look. I gave a nod, and he refilled my wine cup as well.

Taking joy from a good meal was another lifetime habit for Yeshua. For as long as I knew him, from boyhood to adulthood, he was happiest at a banquet or a feast. Yeshua took special delight in enjoying a good meal in the company of people he loved, and who could blame him for that? It was simply another way to celebrate God Almighty's bountiful generosity and blessings.

The women brought the food on trays and in wooden bowls that were placed at each table. Bowls of spicy stew were accompanied by salads made with sliced cucumbers, radishes, and olives. The stew was thick and savory, made with partridge, lentils, onions, and leeks, and spiced with coriander and salt. Each table had a fruit tray piled high with spring fruits: strawberries, mulberries, and melons picked fresh from the garden. Walnuts, dates, and dried figs would finish the meal.

The wives sat next to their husbands, and the children sat wherever they wished. Yosef said a prayer for all assembled. Then we feasted.

Chapter 5

Life In Galilee

Nazareth, Galilee, Spring 10 C.E.

Clopas took his turn to speak at the synagogue meeting. As always, he spoke with a clear and strong voice. He was a short but powerfully built man, with a wide chest and broad shoulders that came from many years of planting vines, working on his winepress, and tending the vineyard. When he spoke at synagogue he often did so with a twinkle in his eye, which was a sign of his zeal for teaching the word of God.

"Abraham had a son, and he named him Isaac. Isaac had a son who was named Jacob. Jacob had twelve sons. The second youngest son was called Joseph," Clopas began, speaking in relaxed and measured tones.

Stories from Scripture were recited from memory, and always told in our native Aramaic. We did not speak Hebrew in Nazareth; that was the language of the religious scholars and priests, and those educated scribes who wrote contracts and other legal documents.

The adults in the assembly knew what came next, because we heard the story of Joseph dozens of times before. It was a familiar and comforting story, and people listened patiently. Clopas would put an interesting twist on it at the end, as we would find out.

"Joseph was a hardworking and obedient boy who loved God with all his heart. He loved and honored his parents as well. Jacob loved his young son, and he rewarded Joseph with a beautiful coat that was made from fine cloth of many colors."

Clopas paused for a moment to let his listeners picture and enjoy that image in their minds. We listened to the familiar story continue.

"Joseph felt very proud, of course. He was thrilled with his beautiful coat, which was also a sign of his father's love and approval. However, that coat also caused bad feelings and misfortune. Joseph's many brothers became very jealous of him, and beat and mistreated him in many ways."

"Now, they say that Joseph was also a dreamer who was inspired by God. He told them about his dream that one day he would become a powerful man, and they would come to him to seek his help. Of course, this made his brothers even more angry and jealous, because they took it as a message that *he* was better than *them*. Finally, they got rid of him. They gave him away to a band of travelers passing by who were on their way to Egypt."

One of the older boys, sounding upset, shouted out a question: "Why didn't Jacob stop them?"

"We don't know why Jacob didn't stop them," Clopas said. "All we know is that, after many challenges and hardships, Joseph's trust in God and his hard work led him to a life of splendid success. He did many good things and was able to help many poor people. When a famine struck the land, many starving people went to him for food."

"His brothers also went to him because they, too, were hungry. Many years before, they mistreated him and abused him and gave him away to strangers. Now they humbled themselves at his feet. And how did Joseph reply to their pleas?"

We knew the answer, of course, but allowed Clopas to continue. This was the key point of the story.

"Joseph was not angry with them for the way they had mistreated him, for their evil and cruel behavior. Rather than sending his brothers away, he forgave them. He gave them food and helped them."

Clopas finished the story and gazed around at the familiar faces, his friends and neighbors sitting before him. He asked: "What lessons can we learn from the story of Joseph and his brothers?"

A man in the back spoke up: "When we face cruelty and hardship in life, we must bear it and trust in the Lord, as Joseph did. In time, through strong faith and hard work, the Lord will provide for our needs."

"Yes, that is so," Clopas agreed. "We have all seen this happen in our lives and in the lives of our neighbors. Father God guided me through many times of trouble in my life. And every time He provided what I needed to overcome my troubles."

Yeshua said: "We should treat those who hate and mistreat us with forgiveness and compassion, just as Joseph did with his brothers. This is what Father God asks of us, even when we are hurt and angry and wish for revenge or retribution."

Mary and Yosef looked at Yeshua with pride in their eyes. Clearly, however, not everyone in the assembly was as convinced as they were that Yeshua was right. Feelings of anger and the need for revenge are powerful feelings and difficult to overcome.

"Wise words, my nephew," Clopas said to him. "It is only through forgiveness and compassion that we honor and please the Lord. Acts of jealousy and anger are too common, even among brothers."

A man laughed and said: "Yes, those things are far too common — *especially* among brothers!"

Others laughed with him good-naturedly, as did Clopas. We were all very familiar with strong feelings of both love and anger in our own families.

Yosef looked at Clopas and asked: "And what moral do *you* draw from this story, Brother?"

"Ah, that's a good question," Clopas replied. "As I reflect on it now, the story of Joseph and his brothers makes me wonder about another question."

"What question is that?"

Clopas paused a moment to choose his words, then looked over the assembly with a glint in his eye. "The day will come, perhaps soon or perhaps many years from now, when God Almighty will send another Joseph to walk among us."

"How will we know him?" asked the impatient boy who interrupted Clopas earlier. "Will he wear a coat made of many colors?"

"Perhaps he will wear such a coat, and perhaps not," Clopas said. "But we will know him by his character. See it if you try – a richly blessed dreamer who loves the Lord, and who shines brightly and stands above the crowd."

Another pause, and his wife Mary smiled and sighed impatiently. "What is the question, Husband? We are all eager to hear it."

People chuckled and laughed at her gentle jibe. Clopas smiled back at her to show that he was not offended, then became serious again.

"My question, neighbors, is this: when that day comes, and God sends another Joseph to us, how will *we* treat him?"

We all looked at him in silence for a long moment. It was a serious and thought-provoking question that asked each of us to examine our own morals and values. No one offered an immediate answer, and none was expected. It was meant to be food for thought, as people stirred themselves and prepared to leave. This was a discussion surely worth having another day.

"Enjoy your Sabbath day of rest, my friends," Clopas said. "Be strong and blessed."

Sarah said: "A restful day today sounds wonderful. Tomorrow is the first day of an unpleasant week."

"Why a difficult week?" Yeshua asked.

His mother Mary answered: "The tax collector comes tomorrow. You know what that means."

"Oh, yes, the tax collector. I forgot about him," Yeshua said. His mood turned somber, matching that of the others.

"What will that robber demand from us this time, I wonder?" Mary of Clopas asked.

The tax collectors came twice a year, in the late spring after the grain harvests and in the fall after the grape and olive harvests. It was a worrisome and difficult time for all the families.

Yeshua had no farm, crops, flocks, or orchard produce to deal with, which meant that his dealing with the tax collector would involve only a simple payment. Even so, he worried about the pain and hardships of the other people in Nazareth.

Levi, the tax collector, rode into Nazareth in the early morning at the head of ten cargo wagons. Each of the large wagons was drawn by a team of oxen or mules. A fully loaded grain wagon was very heavy and required oxen to pull it.

Levi rode in the first wagon, sitting in the driver's seat next to the ox driver holding the reins. He understood clearly that his visit would not be welcomed here. Indeed, many of the villagers would treat him with scorn and loathing. He would have to put up with that grief, and more, because he had a job to do.

I knew Levi when we were boys. We attended school together for two years in Jerusalem. He was a very bright but otherwise normal and happy child then. Now he lived in Sepphoris and made a good living as a publican. Over the years, his job and his new social status changed him, and he became a different person from the boy I knew in school.

Levi's employer was Herod Antipas, the Jewish noble appointed by Rome to govern Galilee as a puppet ruler. Antipas collected all taxes. Farmers who grew wheat or barley, owners of vineyards, orchards, and olive groves, and owners of sheep and other animal herds, paid taxes with a portion of their annual production. Laborers such as Yosef paid with a money tax.

Antipas kept a good portion of tax collections for himself, however a substantial amount went to the High Priest in Jerusalem to support the Temple, and the rest was paid to the Romans. Keeping the peace and collecting taxes were by far the most important responsibilities of

Antipas. How well he did those two jobs would determine how long he remained in power, always at Rome's discretion.

The taxes imposed on the common people of Galilee were steep. Each year they paid the tax collector two-fifths or more of their crop harvests, the produce from their orchards, or the animals they bred and raised. Every adult Jewish male also paid an annual religious tax to support the Temple in Jerusalem.

The high taxes were difficult for farmers. After paying their taxes, it was difficult to feed their families and also keep enough seed to plant the next harvest. During hard times, many families went deeply into debt to the money lenders. When people could not pay their debts, their land and other possessions were taken from them.

What made things worse is that Herod Antipas paid each of his tax collectors, like Levi, with a portion of the total amount of taxes they collected. Thus, it became in the best interests of the tax collectors to collect as much as they could from each family. The most dishonest and greedy collectors made unfairly high assessments of what was owed, and used pressure and threats to squeeze all they could from the people in the countryside. While Herod and tax collectors became wealthier, the common people became more impoverished.

All those things made publicans, as tax collectors are called, a hated and reviled occupation. They were traitors to our people because they worked for Antipas, and Antipas worked for the Romans who occupied our land. Worse, they were looked upon as leeches who preyed on poor people, those less educated and powerful than them. Thus, tax collectors were viewed by the common people as the worst of sinners and unjust men.

Levi knew all these things. Yet, he still took pride in his job and the many benefits it provided. He was still young for a publican, only in his early twenties, but already financially well off and able to afford a fine house and other luxuries in Sepphoris.

As he rode on his cargo wagon past my house, Levi looked calm and composed on the outside. I knew better, however—inside, he was filled with tension and guilt. He was steeling his nerves for what would be days of questions, demands, pleading, crying, and angry arguments with the people of Nazareth. In the end, as usual, he collected what he asked for and drove the loaded wagons back to Sepphoris.

"Half the wool from my sheep was sold after the spring shearing," I told Levi, who was seated opposite me at a table on our patio. "I kept the rest bundled up in storage for the tax."

"Yes, I see. And you also go to Sepphoris to work as a builder?"

"Yes. We go to the city six days a week, but we don't find work every day, as you know."

Levi gave a grunt. The two large men who stood on either side of him looked bored, but kept a respectful silence. Their job, other than loading the tax collections into the wagons, was to discourage trouble. Levi worked for Antipas, and they worked for Levi.

"Come to my house next week. I'll have some work for you," he told me with a polite smile. There was something in his tone to hint that he was being graciously generous toward me. "There are some small repairs on my roof to be done."

I acknowledged with a nod. "I will be happy to fix your roof."

Levi quickly scanned his eyes over the waxed writing tablet in his hands. He made a small frown, then looked me in the eye. "Including the half shekel for the Temple tax, your assessment is six shekels. Plus the wool, of course."

I met his gaze but kept my voice calm, so that I sounded calmer than I felt. "Six shekels is six months' worth of income for a workman like me, *and* you also want the wool? The wool plus four shekels would be a fair assessment. Or perhaps even three shekels, if you were in a more lenient mood."

He gave a small shrug. "David, my friend, you know that Herod makes the rules. I only obey them."

"We are not friends," I said evenly. "And, yes, Herod makes the rules, but you interpret them as you see fit."

Levi's face reddened slightly. We both knew that I was right, but he would never concede that.

"This is my ruling. Six shekels and the wool."

I frowned and looked around us. Yosef, Clopas, and Yeshua already paid their taxes, and now they sat nearby and watched my negotiation with Levi. The more eyes we had on the tax collector, the less likely he would be to behave shamelessly—or so we hoped.

Iacob was sitting at the next table, looking red-faced and nervous. He was next.

Levi's two helpers and bodyguards stared at me. My next words would determine how they should act toward me. The tax collectors held all the power, and arguing with them only brought more grief. At worst, I could be arrested for disobedience to an agent of Herod and summoned to Sepphoris for punishment.

I decided not to fight a hopeless battle. "Very well, six shekels." I looked at Levi's helpers and jerked a thumb in the direction of my house. "The wool is bundled in my house. My mother, Sarah, will show you where it is."

Levi said: "Good, then we are done. Next!"

I stood up and made room for Iacob to take my place. Yeshua and Yosef looked at me with sympathy and understanding. Clopas gave me a grim smile, then poured me a cup of wine as I joined them at their table. Clopas had paid a steep price with several amphorae of his best wine and also a money payment.

"But I don't have three shekels!" Iacob cried out, his voice filled with nervous tension. Abana appeared suddenly in the doorway of their house, but stopped and came no further. Women could not take part in tax discussions.

Levi held up both hands to mollify the older man. "Be calm, Iacob! I'm not here to squeeze water from a stone!"

"Hah!" Clopas growled. "That's exactly what you're here to do!"

Yeshua looked from Levi to Iacob to Abana, and his face hardened. His expression showed anger, but also anguish. Seeing the suffering of his neighbors caused him pain. It was a look that would be familiar to us in the years to come, as he travelled and talked to people who were poor and suffering in many ways.

He opened his mouth to say something, but Yosef put a hand on his arm and shook his head. Arguing with the tax collector would not help Iacob's situation. Oftentimes, arguing only made them more stubborn and unforgiving. Yeshua sighed and looked up at the heavens.

Levi said to Iacob: "Give me two shekels and two sheep." He looked down again to check his writing tablet. "And also something more, something that is worth less than a sheep."

Iacob shrugged, looking miserable. "I have nothing else to offer you. Be done with it and leave me in peace."

Levi looked at one of his helpers. "Search this man's house and find something suitable."

The man turned and walked to where Abana stood in the doorway. She glared at him angrily, but stepped aside and allowed him to enter. Iacob lowered his head in shame. He felt humiliated, but powerless to stop the intrusion into his home.

The situation became too much for Yosef to bear. He stood up and addressed Levi in a sharp tone.

"You sinful man!" he berated the tax collector. "Must you profit so cruelly from this poor man's poverty?"

The second bodyguard instantly became tense and turned to face Yosef, ready to stop any physical confrontation. Levi knew that Yosef was not a violent man, however, and calmly waved his hand to call his bodyguard off.

Levi said: "I am bound to do my duty to our lord, Herod Antipas, who rules us in Galilee. He commands I collect his taxes in full. I have no choice in this matter, as you know, Yosef."

Yeshua sprang to his feet to stand beside Yosef, his eyes shining fiercely. "There is one Lord who rules over us, one Lord alone! He is God Almighty! Today you dishonor and shame yourself before the Lord, Levi tax collector!"

The fierce passion in Yeshua's voice surprised us because it was so unexpected, unlike his usual serene disposition. He could not accept the injustice before him calmly.

Levi looked shocked by the heated challenge to him coming from this very young man. In his heart, perhaps, he might have agreed with what Yeshua said to him. In his present position, however, he could not show weakness in front of his men and these people. He kept his face rigid and said nothing.

The man who went to search Iacob's house came back, carrying a bright and flowing piece of clothing. Abana followed closely on his heels, her face red with furious anger.

"Here is a fine man's robe that will fetch a good price," the helper said, showing the clothing to Levi. "Will this do?"

Abana turned on Levi and screamed at him: "That is the robe he wears to synagogue! It's the only robe he has! You cannot take this from him, or you are a devil!"

Levi averted his face away from her. "Yes, it will do," he said.

"God will punish you for this!" Abana yelled after the three men, who calmly walked away to their ox cart. The negotiations were over, and they were not looking back.

Iacob put his arm around Abana's shoulders and gently steered her back to their house. They were simple, honest people who worked hard to survive from one day to the next. They were powerless in the face of this kind of heartless tyranny, however, and powerless to fight back against the insult to their dignity.

We sat for a while longer, feeling sad for them and angry toward Levi and the other men who made them feel humiliated. There was nothing more to be done, however, and nothing more to be said.

Chapter 6

Summer Wedding

Nazareth, Galilee, Summer 10 C.E.

eila, the daughter of Eitan and Hila, had grown into a beautiful and virtuous woman. Her family lived several houses away on the same street in Nazareth, so we knew them well as neighbors and friends. She was a few years older than my sister Eva, but they had been good friends from a young age. After many years, Leila and I discovered that our long neighborly acquaintance turned into mutual affection. I was twenty-two and she eighteen, and most people our age were already married and raising children. We were both eager to do the same.

My own father was dead, so it was my responsibility to approach her father, Eitan, to discuss marriage terms. We agreed easily on the formal marriage contract, and I paid him the *mohar*. At the betrothal ceremony we became legally married, however Leila remained in her father's house for the time being.

The wedding celebration, now only one week away, was the second part of the marriage ceremony. This was when Leila would be brought by family and friends in a colorful procession from her father's house to my house to consummate the marriage. This was the feast that the entire village looked forward to.

With the day of the wedding celebration fast approaching, Sarah and Eva were in a buzz. They were almost as excited as Leila. The feast with family and friends would last for several days, and it seemed like there was no end to the planning and preparations that still had to get done. Some out-of-town guests were now arriving, including my uncle Abram, the Levite, who was travelling from Jerusalem.

Eitan owned some choice farmland that was well suited for growing wheat, the best cash crop to sell in Sepphoris. That also meant, happily for us, that the family had no shortage of wheat flour, which was best for baking and many other kinds of food preparation. Our neighbor Clopas would make sure that the wine never ran out.

All our neighbors pitched in to help with food preparation and other arrangements for the feast. A wedding celebration in Nazareth is a community event.

The wedding took place on a clear and bright morning. As usual, it was held outdoors, because we had no building large enough for an indoor ceremony. We were blessed with sunny skies and a gentle breeze. The food was plentiful, laid out on rows of tables. Young children ran around happily while their parents talked. Men and women, young and old, joined in the dances that never seemed to stop.

Leila was as lovely a bride as any man could wish for. She had a gentle heart but also a strong and practical mind, which I admired and cherished equally. I gazed at her happy, smiling face and once again thanked Father God for bestowing this blessing in my life.

During the wedding feast, we went around to greet and talk with our guests. Our closest neighbors were like family to me – Yosef and Mary, Clopas and Mary, and Iacob and Abana – and they all looked very happy for us. They sat around the same tables with our parents; my mother Sarah, Eitan, and Hila.

At many Jewish weddings, men and women were separated and dined at separate tables, because many men considered it beneath them to dine in public in the company of women. We would have no such stiff formality at our wedding, and our families and friends were happier for it.

The two mothers, Sarah and Hila, stopped fussing over the food and other preparations and sat together to talk and enjoy a cup of wine. They were as concerned that everything went smoothly as Leila and I were, and perhaps even more so.

Leila bent down to give her mother a kiss on the cheek. "Everything is going wonderfully. Thank you, *Emma*."

"Ah! Should my daughter deserve anything less?" Hila said. "Now don't you worry about a single thing. Your only job here is to enjoy your wedding."

"That's exactly right," Sarah said cheerfully. "Leave everything to us. Have some food and wine! Go join the dancers!"

"We will," I told them with a grateful smile. "And you two do the same."

"Come, let's talk to Mary," Leila said, pulling me away.

Yosef and Mary greeted us cheerfully. They were perhaps the most content and happy married couple that I ever knew. One can always tell happy couples from the unhappy ones by the way they look at each other, talk to each other, and express kindness and affection toward each other in a multitude of small ways. Yosef and Mary expressed their love easily, as naturally as breathing.

Yosef raised his wine cup to us and said: "To life!"

"Good life and peace to you," Mary said. Her bright and gentle eyes told us her well wishes came from the heart, and were not just a polite formality.

"And be you blessed too," I said.

"Please, enjoy the celebration," Leila said. "We are blessed to have you as our neighbors. Mary, there are so many things I wish to talk with you about. As we get to know each other better as married women, I mean!"

Mary laughed. "I would be delighted. We, too, feel blessed to have you as our new neighbor. It's good to see you both looking so happy. That's the start of a good marriage!"

"Words of wisdom, I'm sure," Leila said fondly.

"None wiser!" Yosef said.

I returned their warm smiles. "Thank you both for your kindness. Enjoy the feast!"

We walked to where my sister was seated. Leila was an only child, which was one reason why she always treated Eva as a younger sister. When we reached Eva, who was seated across from Yeshua, Leila bent down and wrapped an arm around her shoulders.

"Are you happy for me, Sister?" Leila asked.

Eva's bright eyes told us the answer. "I am joyful for you. And for you, Brother."

Leila said: "And I wish the same for you, one day. When it's your time to share the Lord's blessing, you will have a good husband and a happy marriage."

That made Eva blush. They both took a quick glance at Yeshua across the table, then looked back into each other's eyes and smiled. I pretended not to notice.

Yeshua was talking with Eitan, my new father-in-law, oblivious to this interaction between the two women. It would surprise him to know that he was the object of their attention, I thought. Yeshua and Eva grew up as friends since they were toddlers. They were now at the age when many people were getting married, so perhaps Eva's interest should not have surprised me at all.

I took Leila by the hand and we joined in the dancing. This was a slower couple's dance, not one of the lively group dances. As we danced, I looked at her with a quizzical expression.

"What?" she asked with a soft laugh.

"That look you exchanged with Eva, and the smiles. When you both looked at Yeshua, I mean."

She raised an eyebrow. "Ah, you noticed. Well, what of it?"

"Is there something I should know about?"

"No, Husband, there is not. Eva talks to me as a sister. She's at the age when girls naturally think about marriage and family. How could she not?"

We danced in silence for a while, but the thought lingered. In a quiet tone I said: "She is growing very fond of Yeshua, it seems."

"Perhaps," Leila replied, just as quietly.

"But does he feel the same about her?"

She looked at me with a glint of amusement in her eyes. "And how should I know that? He's *your* close neighbor. You talk with him all the time."

"He looks at her with great affection."

She smiled at that. "Yeshua looks at everyone with affection in his eyes. He's different from most people in that way."

"True," I admitted. "Perhaps the affection between them is only that of childhood friends?"

"Perhaps. But my heart tells me Eva wishes for more than that."

I was starting to see things that way, as well. Surprisingly, it made me feel unsettled.

Leila noticed my expression and raised an eyebrow. "Does that thought bother you?"

"I don't want my sister to pine for an impossible love."

She sighed. "Neither do I. Perhaps you can have a talk with Yeshua sometime, to get an idea about his intentions?"

"No," I said. "We don't discuss such things. Yeshua favors marriage, of course, because the Scriptures tell us to be fruitful and multiply. But he never talks about his own interest in a wife and family."

"It may be that he's simply not ready," she said. "When he *is* ready, and if he has an interest in Eva for a wife, then Yosef will come to you to talk about a marriage contract. So, *you* will still know about Yeshua's interest before me."

"Yes, you're right. I will hear about it from Yosef first."

I was the head of our family, and Eva would need my permission and blessing to marry. Yosef was the head of their family, and he would approach me with a marriage proposal for any of his sons who wished to marry Eva.

"Sometimes I worry about Eva's future," I confessed. "We have no land and little wealth. I can't offer any kind of generous dowry for her to her future husband."

"Then you should stop worrying," Leila said. "I don't know Yeshua as well as you, but there is one thing I know about him for certain."

"Oh? What do you mean?"

"Yeshua has less interest in money or wealth than any other man or woman I know."

The wedding party spent the day dancing, singing, and feasting. In the late afternoon, we took a short break from the festivities to cool off and rest inside the house. Eva brought a pitcher of cool water for us to drink. Her eyes were downcast, and her mood was curiously subdued compared to earlier in the day. We invited her to sit with us and talk.

"Are you enjoying the wedding?" Leila asked in a casual tone that could not entirely mask her concern.

"Oh, yes, very much," Eva said with a languid smile.

I said: "The musicians are very good. Have you joined in many of the dances?"

"A few," she said. "Maybe later."

Leila gave her a mild frown. "What is wrong? I know you well, and this is not your usual self. Is something making you sad?"

Eva shifted her eyes to the floor. She did not reply, but her silence answered Leila's question clearly enough.

"Eva, talk to us," I encouraged her in a gentle tone. "Or, if you would rather talk to Leila, I will go outside so that you can talk in private."

Eva lifted her head up and gazed at each of us. She was near tears.

"Am I not a good woman?" she asked. "Am I not pretty enough?"

Her questions stunned both of us for a moment. Leila reacted first and put a comforting hand on Eva's shoulder.

"Now, where do you get such silly ideas? Of course you're a good woman, and of course you're a very pretty girl."

Eva shook her head slowly. "He doesn't think so. I can just tell."

"Who doesn't think so?" I asked, although I could have guessed the answer.

Leila sighed. "Yeshua."

Eva remained silent, but a slow tear rolled down her cheek.

"Forgive me for saying these things," she said apologetically. "This is your wedding, and I don't want to spoil it."

"No, that's fine. There's no need for any apologies," I said. "But tell me, did Yeshua say anything to you to make you unhappy?"

"No! Yeshua would never do anything to hurt me," Eva said. "You know that."

I nodded. "Yes, I know that. But what makes you believe that he feels that way about you?"

Eva looked at Leila for help.

"Sometimes a girl can just tell," Leila said gloomily.

"I see how men look at the women they wish to be their wives," Eva added, speaking softly. "A few men in the village have looked at me that way. But not Yeshua. Never Yeshua."

I did not know how to reply to that. I did not know what Yeshua thought about Eva, or about marriage. Worst of all, I did not know how to comfort my sister at that moment.

"Uziel looks at you in that way," Leila said. "I noticed that he asked you to dance, at least twice. Why do you keep turning down the poor man?"

"I don't know," Eva said, frustrated.

"Ah, I think that's a conversation you two should have without me getting in the way," I said. "I'll go outside and give you some privacy."

"I'm sorry to bother you with this, and spoil your mood," Eva said.

"My dear sister, you are never a bother," I told her. "As for Yeshua, well..."

Leila raised an eyebrow. "What about Yeshua?"

"Yeshua is different," I said with a shrug.

"I know that," Eva said. Her face brightened a bit, and she gave me a smile. "Yeshua is Yeshua."

I joined some of the men at their table for a cup of wine. My uncle Abram drew a small crowd around him because he brought fresh news from Jerusalem. He was the younger brother of my father Matthias. Whereas my father picked up the sword and joined the rebellion of Judas the Galilean, and was crucified as a rebel against Rome, Abram went to Jerusalem and became a Levite assistant to the Temple priests.

My father's side of the family are descendants of the tribe of Levi, and our men claim a right of heritage to serve alongside the Sadducees priests in conducting the sacred Temple rituals. There are many more Levites than Sadducees, and the Temple could not function without men like my uncle.

"Is the Temple reconstruction truly finished?" Clopas asked him. "After thirty years of work?"

"Yes!" Abram replied enthusiastically. "Herod the Great began the work thirty years ago. Sadly for him, he didn't live long enough to see it completed, but this year we finally finished the job!"

Yeshua said: "Is it beautiful? I wish to see it."

"It is the most beautiful thing in the world," my uncle said with a tone of reverence. He said it with so much sincerity that no one doubted he meant exactly what he said. "It cost an enormous amount of money and work, as you know."

Clopas chuckled. "Yes, we know. Our religious taxes paid for it all these years. But it's good to know our money was put to good use."

"Ah, but it's worth it!" Abram exclaimed. "All the work was done by the finest craftsmen in Judea. Believe me when I tell you this, my friends – God Almighty looks down at our Temple and cannot help but smile at our gift to honor Him."

Yosef said: "Then the cost was worth it. I want to see it too. We will make the pilgrimage to Jerusalem for Passover next year."

"That would make me very happy, *Abba*," Yeshua said.

Abram said: "Good! Come with them, Nephew, and bring your new bride. You will stay as guests at my house."

"You have always been generous and kind to me, Uncle. Thank you, and one day I hope to repay your generosity."

"You and Leila will thank me next year by celebrating Passover with me. But right now," he said, holding out his cup, "you can thank me with some more wine."

"Done!" I said and re-filled the cup.

Eitan had another question about Jerusalem. "What was that nasty business with the Samaritans? We hear they are now forbidden from entering the Temple?"

Abram frowned, clearly disgusted. "A few Samaritan fools defiled the Temple by scattering human bones around it. They rebel against the Temple authority and the sacrificial rites. I am telling you, they are worse than those radical Essenes, who also oppose our authority and argue with the Temple priests. Many of those Essene fools prefer to live in the desert to maintain their purity."

"But are the Samaritans banned from the Temple, truly?" Eitan wondered.

"Some of the priests wanted the troublemakers stoned to death, but calmer heads prevailed," Abram continued. "By order of High Priest Ananus and the Roman prefect Coponius, Samaritans are now forbidden to enter the holy areas of the Temple. They must remain in the outer court, with the gentiles and the unclean."

"How terrible!" Iacob said.

Clopas laughed. "No! I say be grateful for the Samaritans! Everyone says that Galileans are rebels and troublemakers, that the only people worse than us are the Samaritans. They make us look good!"

The men chuckled and laughed at his joke. It was a popular joke, and what made it funny was that it was true.

I turned to Yeshua. "Will you walk with me for a bit, to stretch our legs? I've been sitting at tables too much."

"Of course," he replied promptly and stood up. "A groom can't be denied such a humble request on his wedding day!"

He was in a very happy mood. This was not unusual for Yeshua, but even so, I was glad to see it. Few people I ever met in my life enjoyed a wedding celebration as much as Yeshua. He took delight in the entire proceeding: the eating, drinking, dancing, singing, and simply spending time with the happy wedding couple and their guests. He was friendly and welcoming with every person there, with no sign of judgment and no regard for their social status or background.

In later years, during his ministry, Yeshua was condemned for this behavior with harsh criticism and anger from the priests. The Pharisee priests, and the even stricter Sadducees who insisted on following the Law exactly as written in the Torah, took great offense at his disregard for the purity laws. Yeshua, as always, did as he wished and didn't care what other people thought of him.

We walked leisurely along the grassy field that led down to the stream. The sun was setting in the western sky, soon evening would fall, but the wedding celebration would continue.

"Are you enjoying the feast?" I asked.

"Very much. And you look as happy as any groom could be. You are indeed blessed today, David."

"I am," I said. "Marriage is a blessing from the Lord."

Yeshua smiled. "Then God said, it is not good that the man should be alone."

We were both very familiar with that line of Scripture. We heard it repeated hundreds of times since we were children, and we strongly believed it. It is a fundamental belief ingrained in the Jewish faith.

I turned my head to catch his eye and asked: "And how about you? Are you thinking of marriage? A family with a wife at your side, and surrounded by children?"

Yeshua's reaction surprised me – he became very silent. His eyes drifted to the water gently flowing by in the stream, sparkling in the afternoon sun. Then he raised his gaze upwards toward the heavens. All this happened within a few heartbeats, but his mood changed and became more serious as he considered my question.

"Forgive me, I don't wish to pry," I said. "Perhaps you'd rather not talk about this."

"It's not prying. Yes, of course I want a happy life, a family," he said. His voice was calm and steady, as usual, but tinged with a surprising tone of sadness, and something else. Uncertainty.

"Then you shall have those things," I said. "But tell me, why do you sound so unsure?"

"Because I'm not sure it can happen," he said. "It's not as simple for me as it is for you."

"I don't understand. If you wish to marry, then marry. Many young women in Nazareth would be happy to call you husband."

He looked into the distance again. We walked in silence along the stream for a while. He wished to tell me something but did not know how. Or perhaps, I wondered, he thought that I would not understand.

Yeshua broke the silence. "Do you remember what I told you, many years ago, that somehow I know what the Lord wants from me?"

"I remember it well," I replied. "We were in the pasture field just over there, during your first lesson in being a shepherd. You told me then that you knew God's will and what He wants from you, even though you didn't understand exactly *how* you knew."

"Yes," he said softly. "I still feel that way."

"Ah. Then nothing has changed."

It took a moment to let his words settle in my mind. I believed what Yeshua told me was true, but it required more patient thought and self-reflection. With Yeshua, patience and reflection were often the keys to a better understanding of what he thought and what he meant.

"Tell me this then, if you can," I continued. "Does the Lord wish for you to have a wife and family?"

"I don't know," Yeshua replied. "I only know that in time the Lord will guide me and make it more clear to me."

"Then it will be so. You have answered my question. Thank you."

"You deserve an honest answer," Yeshua said in a very gentle tone. "And so does Eva."

I couldn't help but smile. Yeshua was very good at seeing what was in people's hearts.

"You know that Eva cherishes your friendship. She always has."

"And I cherish Eva, and always will," he said. "What plans the Lord may have for us, however, right now I cannot say."

"I understand completely."

We had walked as far as the weeping willow tree. We paused for a few moments in silence, watching the water swirl around its branches and breathing in the pleasant and soothing fragrance. My mind felt more settled, and, I hoped, so did Yeshua's.

"We should get back to the wedding feast," I said. "My uncle, the Levite, is no doubt waiting impatiently to sing a few songs for us." Like all Levites, Abram was trained in instrumental music and singing.

"Good! Some music and songs will make the occasion even more festive than it already is."

"The Eternal God has always guided you in your path, Yeshua," I said. "You are still very young, and the path is not yet clear, but trust that your faith will always guide you to the right place."

"I know that is true," he replied, "but I'm glad to hear that you also understand."

"As for me, the Lord has guided me to this day, my wedding day. Now let's go back and celebrate it with all our hearts, shall we?"

"With all our hearts," Yeshua agreed with a grin. "It would be a sin to let this blessing from God go unappreciated."

I was the groom, and this was my wedding, yet Yeshua shared my joy and happiness almost equally. I could not have asked for anything more.

Chapter 7

A Death in Galilee

Nazareth, Galilee, Fall 11 C.E.

G rapes were harvested in late summer and early fall, after the spring grain harvests and before the harvesting of the olive groves later in the fall. The harvesting of Clopas' vineyard was one of the busiest and also most festive times of the year for his family and neighbors. Because there were so many grapes to pick in a short time, all the relatives and neighbors were asked to join in the harvest for a few days. Every family that helped with the grape picking was rewarded with an abundance of fresh grapes and grape juice. Later in the season, there would be wine.

I worked in a team with Leila, Eva, and Sarah. They selected the bunches of grapes that were ripe, cut the stem with a small knife, and deposited them in a large wicker basket. It was easy work but became tedious after a while. Leila was six months pregnant then, made even more beautiful with the glow on her skin that is unique to expecting mothers. She was healthy and strong, however, and able to manage this kind of work. Sarah and Eva both kept a close eye on her and would nag her if necessary to stop and take a rest if they thought she pushed herself too hard.

My job was to be the donkey who carried the full baskets to Clopas' grape press on the side of their house, then return the empty baskets to the grape pickers. By the time I walked back up the hill with two empty baskets, they had two full ones waiting for me. The baskets of grapes were not very heavy, but walking uphill on the return trip soon made the muscles in my legs burn and ache.

The grapevines were planted in rows on small flat terraces dug into the side of the hill. On the terrace just above us, Yeshua was doing the same thing with groups of pickers from his family. Salome and Shimon were still too young to help with the harvest, but all the other children were busily engaged.

James and Joses were strong enough to carry grapes, one basket at a time, to their uncle Clopas at the house. The young boy Judah and the girl Mary worked as pickers alongside their mother. They learned quickly which bunches of grapes were ripe enough to pick, and which to leave on the vine. Yosef picked grapes for a while, then went to help his brother with the grape press.

"Who is thirsty?" a cheerful female voice called to us.

Mary of Clopas, the mistress of the vineyard, walked up with a clay jar of cool water and drinking cups. That was our signal to take a short break. The work was pleasant in the company of loved ones, and the sweet aroma of ripe grapes was delicious, but even so, people grew hot under the sun. There is no shade to be found in a vineyard.

Mary the mother of Yeshua walked over to join us. Mary Clopas greeted her with a smile and a cup of water filled to the brim.

"Thank you for being so thoughtful, Sister," Mary said. She drank the water thirstily and returned the cup. "You are blessed with another bountiful harvest this year. It looks even better than last year!"

"No, I'm the one to thank you," Mary of Clopas exclaimed, looking at us with affection. "All of you. Leila, my dear, have some water. Your face looks flushed."

"I'm feeling fine," Leila said as she took the offered cup. "This work is good for me, so don't worry."

Sarah reached out to a nearby vine, picked a plump and juicy black grape, and popped it in her mouth. She chewed it slowly and gave Mary of Clopas an appreciative smile. "Delicious! And I'm sure the wine will taste even better."

"God willing! You will have many chances to taste it and tell me about it," Mary of Clopas said to her with a grin.

The young brothers James and Joses came up the hill, each carrying an empty wicker basket. Yeshua walked right behind them, carrying his two baskets.

"My sons, you must be thirsty," Mary said to them. "Here, have some water. You've been doing a lot of walking this morning."

James said: "Yes, thank you, *Emma*. I'm very thirsty."

Twelve-year-old Joses complained: "These baskets of grapes are getting heavy!"

Yeshua laughed and ruffled his hair. "You're just getting a little tired, little brother. But remember this: hard work only makes you stronger!"

Their sister Mary gave Joses a look of sympathy. "Maybe you should put the basket down and help us pick grapes for a while? You won't get so tired doing that."

"Yes!" little Judah said, pleased with the idea. "Do the same as me. It's easy and you can keep me company."

Joses answered neither of them, but instead looked at Yeshua for guidance. His older brother gave a small shrug.

Yeshua told him: "A man must make his own decisions, and always do what he thinks is right."

"I'll carry the baskets for a while longer," Joses said with a look of stubborn determination.

"That's the spirit!" Yeshua exclaimed. "And always remember to look on the bright side."

"What's the bright side in carrying a basket of grapes?" Joses asked skeptically.

Yeshua shot me a glance. "Will you tell him, David? Or should I?"

I knew the old grape harvest joke. "Well, Joses. The bright side of carrying grapes is this: every time you carry a full basket, you're always walking downhill!"

Yeshua and James laughed, but Joses did not like being teased.

Mary looked at Joses with pride and affection. "That's fine, my son. Help with the baskets. But have some water first, and rest for a bit."

"Yes, *Emma*," the boy said gratefully.

James turned to his mother with a look of mild apprehension on his face. "I think *Abba* might not be feeling well today."

"Oh? Why do you say that?"

"He was helping Uncle Clopas with the grapes as he usually does, but then he suddenly had to stop and sit down to rest." James gave a small shrug. "He doesn't seem like himself today."

Mary shot Yeshua a glance. "Did you notice that also?"

"Yes, he looks tired," Yeshua replied. "A little more fatigued than usual, I think."

Mary of Clopas picked up the now empty water jar and glanced down the hill toward the house. She turned to Mary. "I will talk to Yosef and see if he is feeling unwell."

"Thank you, Sister," Mary said. "Let me know if he needs anything. All right then, let's get back to work. Let's pick these fine ripe grapes before the birds get them all!"

Everyone knew Mary as a woman of very strong faith and strong character. That never wavered or changed in all the years that I knew her. On that harvest morning, however, standing near her in the Clopas vineyard, I saw something in Mary's eyes that left me feeling troubled. It was glimpsed only for a brief moment, and then it was gone. It was the ephemeral, faint shadow of fear. Afterwards, it left me wondering whether there was something this gentle and gracious lady knew but was not telling us.

There are many things that make harvest time a joyous time of the year. We thank the Lord for the blessings of our crop fields, orchards, vineyards, and olive groves. We celebrate also the community spirit of helping one another in a time of need. Families, neighbors, and friends, everyone who is able joins in to help, from the very young to the very old, if they are still able to work. Then, after each day of labor in the fields or orchards, we celebrate in the evening with a feast.

We sat around the tables in the early evening relaxing, eating and talking. Everyone knew everyone else there, and there was never a shortage of things to talk about. The things that mattered all had to do with village life: the health of the elderly, the growth of children, the ongoing work on crop fields and orchards, and plans for the holidays that were such an important part of our lives. No one knew or cared much for the politics of Sepphoris, Jerusalem, or Rome. Our world was Nazareth, and we were happy with that.

Clopas was acting the gracious host and came by our table to bring wine and talk for a bit. His daughter Nimura came along to help carry the wine. She was a rather shy girl with long black hair, and tall for her age. At fourteen, she was already as tall as her father. Nimura was pleasant and friendly, but happy to let her more boisterous father do most of the talking.

"One more day of fine weather and we will finish the harvest, God be praised," Clopas said.

Yosef said: "Just look at the beautiful red sunset, Brother. It tells us that tomorrow will be a good weather day."

Clopas nodded. "You are usually right about the weather signs. Here, have more wine, you've earned it!"

Yosef placed his hand over his cup. "No more wine for me. What I need right now is a good night's sleep."

"We'll retire in a bit," Mary told him. "Have some more bread. You hardly ate anything tonight."

"Did you have enough to eat, Cousin?" Nimura asked Yeshua with a shy voice.

He gave her a bright smile. "Yes, but I can always eat more. These fresh grapes are delicious."

"Oh! Your fruit bowl is empty," Nimura said. "I'll bring you more grapes right away."

"Bless your generous heart," Yeshua told her. "Being generous to others honors the Lord."

"Yes, of course," Nimura agreed, and rushed off with the empty fruit bowl.

Clopas chuckled. "You should become a rabbi, Nephew. You think and talk like one."

"If that is the Lord's wish, then someday I will be a rabbi," Yeshua replied.

No one seated at the table that day had any doubts that being a distinguished teacher, a rabbi, was something that Yeshua would do when he was older. He showed a talent for it when he was just a boy.

We continued to feast and talk as evening fell. Oil lamps were lit on the tables. It struck me that Yosef, who was typically on the thoughtful and quiet side compared to most people, seemed even less talkative than usual that night. He did not look ill, so perhaps was just feeling tired that day. Mary did not seem concerned about him, so we were not concerned. After a short while they left and retired to their bed.

Two days later, the morning after the harvest, I left the house at first light. As usual, I stopped at the house of Yosef to join my two work companions for the walk to Sepphoris. Yeshua stepped outside, but to my surprise he was not accompanied by Yosef that morning but rather by his brother James. Yeshua carried Yosef's tool bag.

"Is Yosef not working today?" I asked him.

He shook his head. "*Abba* is feeling unwell today. And also," he looked at James with a smile, "we decided that it's time for my brother to learn the tools of our trade."

James beamed with pride. He was fourteen years old, and rapidly growing into his body as a young man. He was near the same age as Yeshua had been when he started his training as a *tekton*.

"I'm sorry that I could not tell you about this sooner," James said with an apologetic look as we started our walk. "Joses and Judah will take the sheep out to pasture this morning."

"That's fine. Joses knows what to do because he learned from you. I'm glad that you can join us, James."

"Thank you!" he said. "I hoped *Abba* could train me, but he says that both of you are also good craftsmen."

"He should know," said Yeshua. "He's the one who trained us!"

I said: "That's right. Yeshua can teach you the rules of carpentry and I can teach you how to work with stone."

"Yeshua has been teaching me already," James said. "And I watched *Abba* at work many times when he did work for people in the village."

"Here is a question for you," Yeshua said. "What is the first rule of carpentry?"

James replied without a pause: "Measure twice, cut once."

"Very good! That's an important rule, so never fail to use it. We'll make a fine carpenter out of you yet."

James' youthful enthusiasm made the hour-long walk to Sepphoris a pleasant walk. I was glad for his company, but also saddened because something important had changed. It was uncertain whether the change would be short-lived or long lasting.

In the weeks that followed, it became clear that Yosef was not his usual self. This hard-working man, full of energy and drive, cut down his trips to Sepphoris to three days a week, and then two. He became fatigued during the hour-long walk and needed to stop and rest by the roadside. Yeshua, James, and I still made the trip to the city six days a week, but it was not the same without Yosef. He was our leader, our rock, and our inspiration.

Yosef and Mary still attended synagogue every Sabbath day, the same as always. All their children came with them without fail. One Sabbath day Yosef gave the sermon. It was a beautiful sermon, but it was plain to see that his energy was diminished. There was a sadness in his eyes that had not been there before. He seemed to slowly get thinner as the weeks went by.

On the evening after Yosef gave the sermon, Leila, Eva, and I were sitting in our house talking by the light of an oil lamp before we retired to bed. Leila was eight months pregnant, and our attention was drawn to her and her health and well-being. She kept reassuring us that there was no cause for worry. We worried still because everyone knew that childbirth was risky for the life of both child and mother.

As soon as Sarah walked in the door, Eva and I knew immediately from her posture that something was wrong.

"Mother," Eva whispered quietly, then stood up and gently guided her to a chair. Sarah's eyes were downcast, and when she looked up we could see that they were moist with tears.

"You went to visit Mary," Eva said. "What's happened?"

"The worst we feared. Yosef is dying…"

Her words caught in her throat and she paused. "He gets weaker by the day. Mary is in deep sadness, but she must stay strong for the sake of the children."

Leila gave a soft cry. "Oh, that poor family! Those poor children."

"Is it the wasting disease?" I asked. "I don't know what it's called, but Yosef has been getting thinner for months now."

Sarah gave a small nod. "Mary suspects it."

"They call it *sarten*, or cancer," Leila said. "Some people live with it for many months, others less."

Eva began to sob, crying softly. Yosef and Mary were our closest neighbors and like family to us. Losing Yosef was like losing a parent or a brother. I was too young to know my father Matthias well before he was killed. Other than my uncle Abram, who lived in Jerusalem, Yosef was the closest thing I had to a father.

Sarah wiped away a tear with the sleeve of her robe. "We must trust in the mercy and goodness of God Almighty. There is nothing more to be done."

"Amen," Leila said.

"Amen," Eva said.

Be strong, I reminded myself. When life brings sorrows, when we feel the most helpless, we must stay strong.

"Amen," I said.

Yosef did not travel to Sepphoris again. Shortly afterwards he took to his sick bed, and we knew that this was his death watch. Every adult in the village knew him and was saddened by his illness. They went to visit in ones and twos to say their farewells. Yosef and Mary received each of the visitors with grace, patience, and gratitude.

Yeshua also went through a profound change at this time. He took responsibility for looking after his younger brothers and sisters. With some help from the oldest brother, James, and the older sister, Mary, he took charge of the household routines to make sure the others were cared for. With their father lying helpless in bed and their mother in a state of grief, the younger children turned to Yeshua for comfort and guidance.

One late afternoon, Leila and I went to say our farewells. Mary sat on a chair by the head of the bed. Yosef looked thin and pale, but still greeted us with a smile. His breathing was shallow, and his voice was getting hoarse.

"I pray that you have a healthy child," he said to Leila. "And many more after that."

"Thank you. I pray for the same," Leila replied. She took a glance at Mary and said: "And I also pray that the Eternal God blesses us with a marriage and a family as wonderful as yours."

Mary looked a little taken aback, but then gave her a smile. "I thank you for your kind words, Leila."

Yosef laughed softly and got a twinkle in his eye. "You are right, Leila. A wonderful marriage indeed, although sometimes I wish the good Lord would make it last a while longer."

Mary took his hand and squeezed it. "Hush now, Husband. We are grateful for the blessings that God Almighty gives us, and don't ask for more. Isn't that what you always tell me?"

"Of course you are right," Yosef said. "I am grateful for the thirty-three years of life the Lord has blessed me with. But now I must go to sleep with my fathers."

Hearing Yosef quote that ancient saying brought a lump to my throat. I told him: "And I am grateful, Yosef, to know you since the day that I was born. You have been like a father to me. I don't have the words to express my gratitude as fully as I wish to express it."

"No need to try," he said. "I understand how you feel, fully."

"I am very thankful to hear that," I said. "You have been a great teacher and guide to me, and a wonderful friend. No father could do more."

"I knew your father well. We were neighbors and friends," Yosef continued. "I told you this before: you are much like him. Matthias was a man of strength and character, and so are you."

I acknowledged with a nod. "I am humbled that you think so."

"He would be proud to see who you are now, as his only son," Yosef continued. "But I think there is one more thing he would wish to tell you if he were here."

"What is that?" I asked, deeply curious.

"He would tell you, let go of your anger. It burns inside you still, and it disquiets you like an unclean spirit."

I took a deep breath, then let it out quickly. "That might be easier said than done. Ever since the day I learned how my father died, I've felt nothing but deep hatred for the Romans."

"Everything is easier said than done," Yosef said patiently. "The only thing that matters, in the end, is that you *do* what should be done."

His voice sounded more tired, even after our brief conversation. It was time to go and let him rest.

I said: "I will remember your advice, which is as wise as always. Thank you, Yosef."

We said our farewells then. They were simple and heartfelt, which I knew was what Yosef wanted. It was the last time that we spoke.

Death came peacefully to Yosef during the night. By mid-morning, the entire village heard about it. Once again, visitors streamed to Mary's house to pay their respects. They were greeted by Yeshua, who was now the oldest adult male in the family, and the grieving Mary. The younger children stayed close by to grieve with them, joined by their friends to provide comfort. Neighbors prepared food for the family and visitors.

Yosef's funeral would be held the next day, and preparations were made quickly. Mary of Clopas already purchased the oils and spices needed for the washing and anointing of the body to prepare it for burial. She helped the widowed Mary with the sacred rite of washing the body, a task that was always performed by the loved ones of the deceased.

They anointed the body of Yosef with perfumed oil, scented with the resin of myrrh and the leaves of aloe. Aloe helped to seal the skin pores and reduce the acrid smells of death. The zesty aroma of myrrh reminded everyone of the aroma in the holy Temple in Jerusalem. The women then wrapped the body in a linen shroud.

This is how Yosef was reverently prepared for burial in the family tomb. He would be buried lying alongside the bones of his ancestors, following the strict rules described in the Torah. We did not embalm the body as the Egyptians did, or burn it as the Romans did, or bury it in the ground as some other people did. Yosef would go to sleep with his fathers and rest alongside their bones.

The following day was the day of the funeral. Villagers gathered for a memorial service and a last meal. Some people cried in their sadness, but many grieved in silence in their own way. Many people had fond memories of Yosef and shared them with each other.

Mary bore her grief with solemn dignity. She ate little and drank no wine. I noticed Yeshua did the same. The younger children looked at the shrouded figure of their father and cried. The two sisters, Mary and Salome, sobbed inconsolably.

Yeshua did not cry. It was plain to see from the look in his eyes that he carried a heavy burden on his shoulders. At the age of sixteen, as the oldest adult male, Yeshua was now the head of the family. His mother and younger brothers and sisters depended on him now, and he had to be strong for them.

At midday, Yeshua went to his mother, placed a hand gently on her arm, and said: "It is time."

On the far side of the hill of Nazareth, there is a rocky slope. Many of the families found sections of soft rock there that were suitable for carving out a space for their family tomb. The bodies of the deceased are placed on rocky shelves or on the rock floor when the shelves are filled. Yosef would be put to rest in their family tomb carved into stone.

The funeral party walked slowly in silent procession. The body of Yosef, wrapped in a linen shroud, was carried in front on a wooden pallet borne by six men. Yeshua and James were two of those men, along with their uncle, Clopas.

Mary walked close behind them, her head held high and weeping silent tears. Her younger children followed, along with Mary of Clopas, and then a long line of neighbors and friends. I walked alongside Leila and my mother and sister, near the front of the line.

Yeshua, James, and Clopas placed the body of Yosef on a stone shelf in the family tomb. That was where he would rest, alongside the bones of his ancestors.

Mary would visit the tomb each day for the next three days, along with one or more members of her family. This wise custom was also prescribed in the Torah, to make certain that the dead were truly dead and not simply unconscious. Taking care of loved ones means taking care of the body until the full transition from life to death is complete. As Yosef was loved and honored in life, he would also be loved and honored after his death.

The next morning was a cloudy and gloomy day, which matched my mood and that of most people around me. We made it a day of rest and mourning and did not travel to Sepphoris. I was concerned for Yosef's family, which was now Yeshua's family.

Sarah and Mary of Clopas prepared the noonday meal. The family and neighbors gathered around the tables on our shared patio to eat together. I noticed Yeshua was missing and asked his brother James about his whereabouts.

"He wanted to go for a walk," James said. "You will find him down by the stream, I think."

I headed down the hill toward the stream. On the near bank stood the old and familiar willow tree, ancient, tall, and broad. It had long been a favorite spot for me to sit and relax beside the calming waters, particularly when I wished to think and reflect.

I saw Yeshua sitting there, resting with his back against the trunk. He was holding something in his lap, a small gray figure. As I neared closer, I could see that it was a pigeon. He was gently stroking the bird's feathers, very slowly, to calm the creature.

Yeshua looked up when I approached. "Its wing is broken," he said. "I will tie it with a string and mend it, and it will fly again."

His words made me smile. "And how did you find a pigeon out here with a broken wing that needs your healing?"

"It flew overhead with its flock, and they were attacked by a hawk. This one was injured in the bedlam as it tried to escape. It fell just a few steps away from me."

"Ah, perhaps Father God wished for you to take care of it."

"Yes, I think so," Yeshua said.

I sat down nearby on a patch of grass. We both sat in comfortable silence for a while, watching the waters of the stream flow by.

"I grieve for Yosef," I said. "He was a good man. After my father was killed, he became more than a neighbor. Yosef was almost like a father to me."

"Yes. A very good and righteous man," Yeshua said. "He taught me to love the Lord, along with my mother."

"He taught me the same," I said. "I mourn his loss, but I know you feel the loss even more."

"My pain is deep," Yeshua said. "But it's worse for my sisters and brothers. And my mother."

I acknowledged with a small, silent nod. Sometimes there are no words to describe how we feel.

Yeshua's gaze looked inward, lost in thought. He continued to stroke the feathers of the injured bird. It did not struggle, but accepted his soothing ministrations.

"Now I am his heir," Yeshua said evenly. "Our family's well-being is my responsibility."

That was the matter that required time for his reflection. Under our laws, women cannot inherit, so a man's wealth is passed down to his sons. The oldest son receives a double share. Along with the father's wealth comes the family responsibilities.

"You are also a good and righteous man," I told him. "Yosef taught you well and prepared you for these responsibilities."

He looked up with a sad smile. "He did. And with the blessings of God Almighty, I will be a good steward of my family."

"You will," I said. I nodded toward our homes. "They are waiting for us. We should go."

"Yes, we should," Yeshua agreed. He stood up carefully, cradling the injured bird in his hands. It did not try to escape, but an accidental fall with an injured wing would cause it further harm. Yeshua's great compassion spread to all God's creatures, even one as humble as a pigeon.

Chapter 8

Head of the Family

Nazareth, Galilee, Summer 15 C.E.

Children make it easy for parents to wake up at sunrise, I discovered. Our daughter Dalia was three and a half years old, almost four, and would crawl into our bed at the first rooster's crow. Her brother Matthias, eighteen months old, was quickly learning to follow her example. Usually they shared the bed of their grandmother Sarah, but at daybreak they sought the attention of their parents. We, of course, did not mind.

Sarah was an early riser as usual and got the day started. Water had to be fetched in a large clay jar from the communal well down the street. Food for breakfast was simple and easy to prepare: bread baked the day before, cheese, olives, and fruit. Then the chickens in the coop at the back of the house needed to be fed.

Leila spent most of her time looking after the children and sewing and mending clothes. Every family in Nazareth knew how to sew and mend their own clothes, although there were two seamstresses and a cobbler who provided their services as needed. Only the wealthy bought their clothes in the cities. The very wealthy hired expert tailors and dressmakers to make clothes especially for them.

I was jarred awake as the children jumped on my sleeping body. After giving each a morning hug, I turned toward Jerusalem and said my morning prayer. Leila would see to the children while I prepared for my workday. Today was a day trip to Sepphoris to finish some work on house repairs.

"Judah and Shimon will come by to take the sheep out," I told my mother. Yeshua's youngest brothers were my most reliable shepherds. James now worked as a *tekton,* and Joses mostly helped his uncle Clopas with the vineyard.

Sarah said: "That's fine, I'll keep an eye out for them. Mary's sons are all good workers."

"Yes, they are," I agreed. "The boys can take care of the sheep on their own, but perhaps Eva wants some help with her wedding plans?"

"No need to remind me! We work on that every day," Sarah said. "Mary is coming by later to help with the menu plans and the gathering of food supplies."

I was glad to hear that. After the death of Yosef, Mary went through a year of deep grieving. Her oldest daughter, Mary, took over some of the household chores, and the younger daughter, Salome, helped in small ways. Mary relied the most on Yeshua, however, the head of their family. With Eva's wedding celebration barely a week away, it was good to see Mary so active in the preparations.

"Bring back some treats for the children if you can," Leila reminded me as I said my goodbyes before leaving. "Some candies flavored with lemon juice, if you can find them?"

"I'll find them," I said. "There is always a street peddler or two who sell trinkets and candies and such."

There were no such traders in Nazareth, but in Sepphoris one could find anything that money can buy.

The early morning walk to Sepphoris was always more energetic and talkative than the late afternoon trip back. We were better rested then and feeling excited about the day ahead. It was a time to make plans and catch up on various activities going on in our lives.

"Eva must be excited about the wedding coming up soon," Yeshua said. "I'm happy for her."

"Yes. She is anxious and excited. She was feeling impatient because the betrothal period was too long."

James laughed. The boy was growing into manhood and looking more like his father every year. He was of medium stature and had the same wiry and strong build as Yosef. His beard was trimmed short, but his long black hair flowed down to his shoulders. Yeshua and I kept our hair cut short because carpentry and masonry work gets very hot and sweaty in the summer.

Yeshua said: "We all get impatient for good things to happen."

"That includes me, Brother," James said. He took a deep breath, then caught Yeshua's eye. "This is as good a time as any to ask you, I suppose."

"To ask me what?"

James' expression became serious. "I wish to ask your permission and your blessing for me to get married."

That seemed to catch Yeshua by surprise. James never mentioned marriage before, much less that he had a plan in mind. As the head of the family, it was Yeshua's responsibility to consider any marriage plans for his younger brothers and sisters, and to grant approval or deny it. By asking for permission to marry, James made a statement that he had a bride in mind.

"Who is the woman you wish to marry?" Yeshua asked.

"Kitra," James answered proudly. There was no mistaking his strong affection for her, just from hearing him say her name.

We all knew Kitra, of course, the daughter of Alon and Ester. Her family owned some farmland. Not the most fertile kind that was best for growing wheat, but still very suitable for growing barley and olive trees. Kitra was a vibrant and healthy-looking woman with a pleasant disposition. She was about one year younger than James, who was then eighteen. It was a good age for marriage, although many people married much younger.

Yeshua put a hand on James' shoulder as we walked. "You have my permission, Brother, and my blessing."

"Thank you," James said. "You just made me a very happy man!"

"Not so fast!" Yeshua said with a chuckle. "All you have so far is my permission. I will need to speak with her father to get his agreement. Then, if he agrees, we'll have to work out the marriage contract."

"I know that. But getting your blessing was the first step."

"Have you given thought to the *mohar* payment?" Yeshua asked.

"Yes, of course! I've been saving money for over two years for a generous *mohar*."

Yeshua said: "Let's hope that her family agrees it's generous. The decision about the marriage will be made by her father, but tell me this – will Kitra be in favor?"

James hesitated for only a heartbeat, then smiled. "Yes, I think she will be pleased."

I said to him: "Then I'm also happy for you, James. Those make the best marriages, where the man and woman both desire each other. The ones designed to make a family richer … well, you never know."

Yeshua nodded agreement. "Marriage contracts are complicated things. I will ask Father God for guidance to make a good contract that will make both families happy."

"God willing, you will make it so," James said. "My faith in you is strong. You have never disappointed me."

"Then it's settled," Yeshua said. "But tell me, James. Why did you hesitate before you came to me to ask for my blessing?"

James looked mildly embarrassed. "I don't wish to cause you any offense, Brother. You're the oldest, and the head of the family, yet here I am asking to get married before you. Some people would say that's not right."

Yeshua shook his head. "Why should you care what other people think? Do what you believe is the right thing, always. Do what the Lord guides you to do. Nothing else matters besides that."

"Then you are not offended? At all?"

"Listen to me, Brother. If it's time for you to get married, then get married. It doesn't matter who is older, or who is next in line, or who might take offense for some foolish reason."

James looked relieved, and the tension drained from his face. "Well, thank you for saying that. I feel at peace now with my decision."

"Good. Kitra is a good woman," Yeshua said. He turned his head to me. "Leila is a good woman. So is Eva, a wonderful woman. Marriage is a blessing from God, so it is a good thing."

I recalled then the conversation we had at my wedding, five years earlier, about Yeshua's own plans for marriage. He would be guided by the Lord, he said. It seemed that nothing had changed since then.

We finished the work on the house repairs in the early afternoon. The owner of the house inspected the work, approved it with a pleased nod of the head, and paid Yeshua for our work. Yeshua, the foreman, would then pay us, the other workers. Many people in Sepphoris knew Yeshua as the son of Yosef of Nazareth. They trusted him to negotiate fair terms for work and ensure good quality of workmanship.

Even though I was the older of the two, I was more than happy to let him assume the role of contractor that Yosef had done before him. And also, I am not ashamed to admit, he did that job better than I ever could. More than any other person I knew, Yeshua had a gift for getting people to trust him. It required no effort, but came naturally to him.

Before we took our leave, he asked the usual question: "Sir, if I may ask, do you know of anyone else in the city who might need our work?"

The middle-aged man paused in thought for a moment, scratching his beard. Had I asked instead, I would very likely have received a polite but perfunctory answer of "no."

The man looked up and said: "Yes, I think so. My sister lives down this street, four houses past the corner. Some time ago, she talked about wanting to build a new storage room in her house."

"Thank you for this kindness," Yeshua said. "Who should I ask for?"

"Her name is Susanna. Tell her that I sent you."

Yeshua said to him: "Good health to you. Be strong and blessed."

"Be you blessed too," the man replied.

We walked as directed to the house down the street. Susanna was a woman of some thirty years of age. She welcomed us kindly once she learned that we were sent by her brother.

"Are you the son of Yosef of Nazareth?" Susanna asked.

"I am," Yeshua replied.

"I thought so," the woman said. "You have his face."

We inspected the section of the house where she wanted the room built, and Yeshua agreed on terms with her. When I mentioned the children and inquired about a place to purchase lemon candies, she generously gifted me a small bundle of candies from her own kitchen.

Susanna was a woman of substantial wealth. One week later, she paid us well for our work after we finished the addition to her house. We did not know it then, but we would see her again thirteen years later. That would be in Capernaum, when Yeshua's new ministry was in dire need of financial support.

That week we learned that in far-away Rome, the home of those who oppressed us, Emperor Augustus Caesar finally died at a very old age. He was replaced by his adopted son, Tiberius Caesar, who was an old man himself. Those events happened many months ago, but news was slow to reach Nazareth. This kind of news, about rulers in Rome and other worldly matters, did not change our lives in any way. For us, life would continue as before, no better but hopefully no worse.

The big news in Nazareth was the wedding of Uziel and Eva. Other than the High Holidays, weddings were the most festive time of the year. A wedding was a community celebration. We honored the union of the wedding couple, and we also celebrated the simple joys of life.

A large group of family and friends delivered Eva to the house of Uziel for the wedding. She was dressed colorfully in her bridal finery, which took several weeks to prepare. She wore a necklace of bright gemstones that dazzled in the bright sunshine.

Yeshua and his brothers joined the procession to escort Eva to the groom's house. So did Clopas and his sons, and other male friends.

Uziel's parents, Daniel and Mehira, set up tables in a grassy field behind their house. This is where the guests were ushered to after the wedding ceremony. Our family, which now comprised Sarah, Leila, our children, and me, held a place of honor at a table alongside the groom's family. Uncle Abram travelled north again from Jerusalem to join us, because no force could stop him from attending the wedding of his only niece.

In the evening, as the wine continued to flow, the conversation among the men turned to politics. Uncle Abram once again had the latest news from Jerusalem, which made him a center of attention.

"So, the Roman prefect Rufus only lasted three years?" Clopas asked in a loud voice. "He was a corrupt tyrant, like most of them."

Abram said: "They are all corrupt. They'll do anything they can to enrich themselves while they're in office. This happens in every place where Rome rules, not just in Judea."

"Then this new man Valerius Gratus will not be any better?"

"No, Clopas, I expect he won't be any different," Abram said. "As soon as he arrived in Jerusalem, he asked Ananus for an enormous sum of money if he wished to keep his position as High Priest." Uncle paused and chuckled. "Now you must understand, Ananus was High Priest for many years and is likely the richest man in Judea. But Ananus refused to pay!"

"Good for Ananus!" Iacob said. "Don't let the Romans rob us!"

Yeshua was listening from a distance, but now he joined our table. "Wait, let me understand this. Did you say that Ananus *was* the High Priest? Is he no longer the High Priest?"

"That's right," Abram said. "Gratus just dismissed the High Priest. He will appoint a new one unless Ananus pays him what he wants."

Yeshua's jaw went tight, which only happened when he was angry but didn't want to show it. "The Romans treat our High Priest like a monkey on a chain," he said bitterly. "They insult us and shame us, with no fear of God Almighty in their hearts."

"You are right, young man," Abram said. "They control Judea, so they control Jerusalem. Yes, they allow the High Priest to run the Holy Temple, but they sell the office of High Priest to the highest bidder from among the Jewish aristocracy."

"That is blasphemy!" Clopas bellowed angrily, slamming his wine cup down on the table with a loud bang.

Eva turned around to look at the commotion and gave him a sharp look. She wanted her guests to enjoy themselves, not argue.

Yeshua put a calming hand on his uncle's shoulder. "Blasphemy it may be, but it's not a blasphemy that we can stop ourselves."

Clopas immediately grew calm right before our eyes. Leila looked surprised to see the sudden transformation in his mood, but it did not surprise me at all. I watched Yeshua do similar things before with other people who were feeling agitated. He calmed their spirits.

Iacob frowned. "Well, if we can't stop it, then who can?"

"Not Jewish men with swords, certainly," Abram said in a gruff tone. "My brother tried that, and the Romans crucified him for it, along with two thousand other rebels."

His words stung me and made me angry. I caught Yeshua's eye and saw only calmness there. He spoke no words, but I knew what he was saying to me at that moment. Anger and violence were not the answer.

I said: "Only the Lord of Hosts can stop the Roman injustice. God Almighty is our protector, and we must look to Him for salvation."

All around us, the table became quiet. We were feeling sad, angry, and frustrated. All except one.

"The reign of God is near," Yeshua said in a strong but calm voice. "It is almost here. It will wash away the injustice and the tyranny of evil men. Only the Eternal God will rule then."

"How do you know this?" asked Abram, the Levite.

Yeshua met his gaze evenly. "I simply know."

Clopas said: "I pray with my soul that you are right, my nephew, but right now it is difficult to not feel discouraged."

A fresh voice approached from the darkness, clear and firm: "My son is not wrong in matters of the Lord."

We all turned to look at Mary.

"Clopas, you most of all should know this about him. You have known Yeshua since he was born." She walked over to Yeshua and stood by his side. Her face looked just as calm, but determined, as his.

Clopas gave Mary an indulgent look. "I know that Yeshua is smart. Smarter even than me, I'm willing to admit," he said with a laugh. "Then again, I don't believe that anyone is always right in matters of the Lord. Even the highest priests often disagree."

"Then your faith is not yet strong enough," Mary said patiently.

Yeshua caught her eye. "The time for this discussion will come later. But not now, and not here."

"Of course," she said. "I understand. Come, let's go and talk with Eva and Uziel for a bit. Let's help them celebrate this happy day."

Yeshua gave a farewell nod to the assembled men and followed Mary to where the bride and groom were chatting with guests. The political discussions at the table came to an end.

As we walked home down the familiar street, lit only by the light of the moon and the stars, I could tell that Leila was struggling with many unanswered questions. She walked on my left, deep in thought. Sarah was on my right, holding a tired and sleepy Dalia by the hand. I carried little Matthias, who was sound asleep in my arms. All around us was quiet except for the chirping of crickets in the darkness.

"Did you enjoy the wedding?" I asked Leila in a casual tone.

She came out of her reverie, mildly startled by my voice. "Yes, it's a beautiful wedding. But my mind was elsewhere just now."

"I could tell."

"I don't know," Leila said. "I feel happy, but also a little confused."

Sarah chuckled. "Happy and a little confused is not a bad way to go through life. But tell me, what makes you feel a bit confused?"

"I'm confused about some things that Yeshua said tonight."

Sarah replied: "Ah, I see. Well, Daughter, one thing I can tell you is that you're not the only one who feels that way."

"Truly, you feel the same about Yeshua?" Leila asked. "When he said that the reign of God is very near, what did he mean by that?"

"I don't know," Sarah said. "But David might have a better notion."

They both looked at me for an answer. I paused briefly to gather my thoughts because they needed to hear a serious answer.

"Let me try to explain it this way," I began. "Uncle Abram is a Levite. He works daily in the Temple. Yet, in all the years I have known him, I never had the feeling that he is as close to the Lord as Yeshua is."

"Are you saying that Yeshua is very close to God?" Leila asked.

"Yes. But it's more than that." I paused again, searching for the right words. "Yeshua knows things that I never thought about. I don't know if he fully understands them himself, at least not yet. But he tries to explain sometimes, and that helps me understand him better."

Leila looked away and sighed. "That sounds mystical. Very spiritual. But it doesn't help me understand what he said any better."

Sarah said: "We learn a little more as we go along. That is just how Yeshua is."

"But what did he mean when he told Mary that now was not the right time to discuss it?" Leila wondered. "Will he explain himself more fully, in time?"

"Yes," I said. "When he is ready, Yeshua will explain himself fully."

We walked on in silence along the moonlit street, listening to the crickets play their soothing melody.

Chapter 9

Thirst For Justice

Sepphoris, Galilee, Fall 20 C.E.

J oses did not like working with wood or stone. He did not like the city, but much preferred the open green spaces and fresh air of the countryside. However, Joses was now a married man with a wife who was expecting their first child in the spring. Like other poor men who owned no land, he needed to earn his wages as a laborer. He joined our working party of Yeshua, James, and me on our day trips to Sepphoris because that was his only means of making a living.

"Add a little more water and keep stirring vigorously," I told him as he bent over a large stirring vat. "The mortar must be perfectly even and smooth. No lumps whatsoever, or it will mar the finish."

We were building a stone patio in front of a garden at a mansion near the palace of Antipas. The garden was large and ornate, with a marble fountain and beautiful statuary in the Roman style. The owner wanted a patio, made with slabs of exquisite green marble, to connect the house and the garden. Materials for building the patio cost much more than my house in Nazareth, but that kind of expense was not a concern for a man of his wealth.

"This work is very hard on your back," Joses complained. "I would rather work on the soil, and plant vines for Uncle Clopas."

Yeshua gave him a patient look. "There will be no more vines planted until early spring, Brother. Be thankful that you have this work now and can earn a few shekels from it."

"Don't get me wrong, I am grateful for that," Joses said. "And I'm thankful to you for bringing me along, Yeshua. I know there is less work for everyone in Sepphoris now."

Yeshua said: "There will always be some work in Sepphoris, just not as much as before. We earn lower wages, but the Lord will provide as He always does."

"The Fox moving his capital to Tiberias makes our lives harder," James said. "But Antipas wanted to live on the shores of Lake Kinneret. And of course, whatever Herod wants, Herod gets."

"That is the privilege of royalty," I said with disdain. "It will never change."

For several years, Herod Antipas had been building his luxurious new capital city on the western shore of Lake Kinneret, the very large freshwater lake that the Romans called the Sea of Galilee. He named his new capital Tiberias, to honor his Roman patron Tiberius Caesar.

The construction of the new capital was just completed in the past year. Although Herod Antipas would always keep a strong presence in Sepphoris, his royal court was in the process of moving to Tiberias. Sepphoris was built in the center of the best farmland in Galilee, and would remain an important and vital city, but perhaps not as busy and prosperous as it once had been for workers like us. Tiberias, of course, was much too far away to travel for work.

"I heard that Antipas is in the city today," Joses said. "Maybe we can catch a glimpse of him?"

James scoffed. "Why would you wish to see Herod? He loves the Romans more than he loves us."

"He loves the Romans," Yeshua said with a frown, "more than he loves God. That is the much greater sin."

Joses gave a casual shrug. "I only want to see what he looks like. I didn't say that I like or revere the man."

A very thin old man dressed in torn and ragged clothes approached us, walking along the side of the house. He was a beggar wandering the streets and heard our voices as he passed by. He walked nervously onto the rich man's property without permission because sometimes hunger overcomes politeness. We paused in our work and watched him approach, shy and halting.

"Forgive me for interrupting your work, sirs, but do you have some bread to share?" the man asked James, who was standing closest to him. "Or a few coins you can spare for food? The Lord blesses those who are generous."

James turned to Yeshua, who was the leader and also carried all the money for the three brothers. The old man followed his gaze.

"We have no extra food to spare, brother," Yeshua said to him in a gentle voice. "But here, I will give you a coin to buy some food."

The man reached out eagerly with a trembling hand and took it. "Good health to you! Father God blesses you for your kind heart!"

I reached into my coin purse and took out two *sesterces*, the brass Roman coins that were worth one fourth of a penny. It would provide a few meals for him. He took them gratefully and gave me his blessings as well.

The back door of the house flew open and Nadav, the owner, rushed out. He glared at us furiously, his face red with anger. He closed the distance to us in a hurry, which frightened the old man. The owner pointed an accusing finger, not at the beggar, but at Yeshua.

"I don't allow beggars to invade my garden!" Nadav shouted. He was a big man with a hefty gut. Fatty jowls drooped down his cheeks.

He turned and pointed at the beggar. "Throw him out!"

The old man meekly backed away a few steps, almost tripping over his own feet. He started walking fearfully toward the street.

"Wait!" Nadav yelled sharply after him. He gave Yeshua a piercing look. "I insist you take back the money you gave him. You can't reward this creature for trespassing on my property! It will only encourage more like him to do the same."

I felt my temper rising at the cruelty of this man. Still, I resisted the urge to reply with anger because he was our employer in this job.

Yeshua maintained his equanimity. He said calmly: "I will not take back in anger what I gave away in kindness. That would be an offense to the Lord."

"Don't tell me what *you* think would offend God Almighty!" the man spluttered. "In my house I decide what is right and wrong, and what pleases or offends the Lord."

"We all live in God's house," Yeshua replied. "And in God's house, you are in the wrong. No other house matters."

Nadav turned his red and now sweating face to me. "You! Catch that beggar and take your money back."

I shook my head. "I will not. Yeshua is right in this, and you are in the wrong. Let that poor man go in peace."

Nadav threw his hands up, indignant. "I will dismiss you from your employment!" He looked around from me to Joses, then James, then settled on Yeshua. "Do you want to work or not? On this job I am your master, and you will follow my directions."

Yeshua spoke for all of us. We had no doubt about what he would say. "I obey a higher master than you. Do as you wish with the work on your house."

Nadav looked away and seemed to calm down for a brief moment, but then gave in to his pride. His lips curled into a sneer. "You are all dismissed! I will hire other builders to replace you." He pointed to the street. "Now get out!"

"We leave you in peace," said Yeshua. "But first, pay us the fair wages for the work done so far."

Nadav scowled and stared at him scornfully. Yeshua calmly met his gaze and waited patiently. We stood and watched the battle of wills.

Finally, the mansion owner reached for the money purse that was tied to his belt. He counted out a handful of coins, then threw them on the ground at Yeshua's feet. He turned on his heels and walked back inside his house without a further word.

Joses made the thoughtful gesture of picking up the coins from the ground, which he then handed to Yeshua. We left the unfinished green marble patio of Nadav and went in search of other employment.

There was no other employment to be found that day. That was not unusual. At times we went for two or three days in a row without work, then found a job that lasted for one or two weeks. Repeat customers were the best because they knew and trusted Yeshua. Sometimes they sought him out for special projects, beyond making repairs.

In the late afternoon, as we prepared to leave the city for the trip home, we came across a crowd of people lining up on either side of a wide street near the palace of Herod Antipas. It was a very mixed crowd of all types of people, some well-dressed and clearly wealthy, but also many from the lower classes. Some parents brought their young children, and held them by the hand or hoisted them up on their shoulders for a better view. There was a festive air all around.

"It looks like we might see a parade," James said.

"No, not a parade," said Yeshua. "A high dignitary of some kind."

I caught the eye of a man standing nearby and asked: "What are people waiting to see?"

"Herod is coming!" the man said.

Joses overheard us and grew excited. "Herod Antipas is coming?"

Yeshua laughed. "Your wish came true, Brother. You will get to see the Fox after all."

We found a spot in the front row and waited along with the rest. More people arrived and crowded in behind us. Antipas did not often venture out into the streets, and when he did, he always drew a crowd. It was important for the common people to see their ruler now and then, he thought. It helped to gain their loyalty.

A small troop of foot soldiers led the way, dressed in full armor and armed with spears. They gave bland looks to the cheering onlookers while keeping an eye out for any potential threats. Next came several of Herod's personal guards, armed with swords but dressed in fine robes befitting their status in the royal court.

Next came Herod Antipas himself, walking with the dignified but stiff gait of a nobleman or high official. He was in his middle years then, his early forties perhaps. Herod was short in stature compared to most men, as was his father, Herod the Great. He was growing thick around the middle, the product of rich foods and fine wines while living an easy life of leisure. He wore his hair long and styled in curls, dyed black and oiled so that it glistened in the sun.

Most eyes fixed on Antipas as he leisurely strolled by, and only then wandered to the other members of his court who followed in his wake. Herod scanned the lines of people as he walked by them, but did not make eye contact with anyone in the crowd. His gaze swept over the people standing near us. He took no particular notice of us, and just as quickly, he was past us and moving away.

The sight of Herod did not impress me. On the contrary, his looks and pompous manner irritated me. This was the Jewish nobleman who was a puppet ruler subservient to Rome. He shamelessly named the new capital of Galilee after his Roman patron Tiberius Caesar, because his fate depended on pleasing Emperor Tiberius.

Following close behind was an imposing man, about the same age as Antipas, but taller and strongly built. This was Chuza the Nabatean, Herod's finance minister. He was easy to identify because of the woman who walked beside him, his wife Joanna.

Even before she married Chuza at a young age, Joanna was already famed for her beauty as the daughter of one of the wealthiest and most prominent noble families in Galilee. She was ten years younger than her husband, and still a tall and regal beauty with long brown hair elaborately styled in curls.

Unlike the aloof Antipas, she smiled at people in the crowd and acknowledged their shouted greetings and friendly waves. The people of Galilee were her people, and she still felt loyal to them and not to the Herodian nobility or the Roman authorities. As I learned many years later, the Galileans who knew Joanna knew this about her and loved her for it.

As she walked by Joanna smiled brightly in our direction, and I couldn't help but smile back at her. I noticed that Yeshua, standing near me, had the same smiling reaction. For a brief moment her eyes met his, and then she was past us.

There wasn't much of interest to see after that. The lesser nobles were all finely dressed, but that did not impress us. Some looked friendlier than others, but too many copied the haughty and arrogant style of Antipas. After the rear guard passed by, people began to walk away, and the crowd quickly dispersed. We headed for the city gates and the road south to Nazareth.

"You look deep in thought, Brother," Yeshua said to Joses as we walked along the hard beaten and dusty road.

"Ah, I'm just thinking about what happened today," Joses said. "He looks like any other ordinary man."

"The Fox, you mean?"

"Yes, Antipas. He looks like a common man, just dressed in fancy clothes and done up with cosmetics."

"I disagree!" James exclaimed with a wry smile. "Common men are not so fat in the belly. Many are quite thin, if you think about it."

"That's true, but you know what I mean," Joses replied.

"What did you expect Herod to look like?" I asked.

Joses gave a small shrug. "I don't know. A bit more regal, perhaps?"

"He's not a god," Yeshua said. "He is just a man."

"A man who is the son of Herod the Great, and who is appointed by Rome to rule over us," James said. "Those are the only things that make him uncommon."

Joses frowned. "But where is the justice in that? That Rome should rule us and use a toad like Herod to lord over us?"

Yeshua's face hardened at that, and he grew very serious.

"There is no justice in it," he said. "Those things are decided by birth and military conquest. After that, justice is decided by the people who rule."

"And *that* justice is only determined by what benefits *them*," James said sourly. "We don't live in a just world."

"Only God can bring justice to the world," Yeshua said. "Blessed are they who wait for Him. And I tell you this, my brothers, the Kingdom of God is near."

James said: "I believe you, Brother. But is there nothing we can do while we wait for God Almighty to bring justice to this sinful world?"

"Of course there is!" Yeshua said. "We create justice by the things that we do every day of our lives. We bring justice into the world in the way that we treat each other."

"An act of compassion and justice was done this morning," I said with a nod to Yeshua. "You helped that poor man and stood up against the cruelty of Nadav."

"Yes, I'm happy you did that!" Joses said. He paused and smiled ruefully. "Even though it cost us the job."

James said: "That was an act of goodness and grace. A hungry man was fed, and a wicked man was stopped from committing a sinful act."

Yeshua smiled. "Ah, now you see. This is how we honor the Lord, by how we treat each other. When we are guided by compassion and love, we create justice in the world."

We walked in silence for a while. What Yeshua told us was exactly right, and we agreed with him completely. The hard part, of course, was living up to it as we went about our day-to-day lives.

Joses broke the silence. "I hate Sepphoris," he said.

We all gave him a puzzled look, but waited for him to explain.

"Sepphoris is a reminder of all the injustices in this sinful world," Joses continued. "We don't have any starving beggars in Nazareth, like that poor man we saw this morning, because his neighbors would take care of him and never let him starve. But in Sepphoris, rich men like Nadav spit on him and throw him to the roadside."

"That's very true about our village," I said. "Many good things come from Nazareth. One of them is neighborly kindness."

Joses continued to fume. "If Nadav sold that green marble for his patio, he could feed that man for five years!"

"More years than that, very likely," James said. "But for some, living in comfort and luxury is more important than righteous behavior and doing good deeds."

"I never saw that in people before, until we went to Sepphoris," Joses said. "This is why I hate Sepphoris."

Yeshua turned to him. "You are right to hate the injustices, my brother, but do not hate the people there. Teach them to do better if you can. Show them how to turn away from their sinful behavior."

"But how?" Joses wondered, exasperated. "Should I tell Nadav to change his callous heart? Or tell Herod to throw off the yoke of Rome and stop oppressing his own people?"

"No, that will not work," Yeshua said. "We can only change the world through our own acts of kindness. Yes, that means even toward people like Nadav and Herod. This is the way of the Lord."

Joses sighed. "I will try. But I wish I had your patience and your strong faith, Brother."

"You have it already. It is inside you," Yeshua told him. "Trust in the Lord to give you guidance. Use that faith to guide you in everything you do."

We reached Nazareth just before sunset. Seeing our homes and our families again was always a happy occasion, and the aromas of supper cooking over the fire made my stomach growl with hunger. Mary the mother of Yeshua and the other Mary, the wife of Clopas, were busy with preparing the meal. Joses' young wife, Rachel, was assisting them and baking the bread. At the age of sixteen, she was already an able and experienced cook.

My mother Sarah was sitting at a table with Kitra, the wife of James. The younger woman held their infant daughter, Ruth, while their three-year-old daughter Penina sat beside her playing with a doll. My sister Eva was now living in the house of her husband, Uziel, with two small children of her own, and my mother practically adopted Kitra and Rachel as her surrogate daughters.

A great deal had changed in living arrangements over the past few years. Two years past, the winter had been especially severe, and our elderly neighbors Iacob and Abana both died from bad fevers. Their house was now shared by James and Joses and their wives. Leila gave birth to our second daughter, Gila, so we had three children in our household.

Clopas was finishing up work at his wine press, assisted by his sons James and Simeon. James was then fourteen and capable of doing men's work. Clopas' daughter Nimura married a man from the nearby village of Naim, and was living there with her own family.

So many of the younger people were married, or engaged to be married. That included Yeshua's brother Judah, engaged to a woman named Chana. His sister Mary, then eighteen, was engaged to a man from the nearby farming village of Kokhaba. She would be married there the next year. His younger sister Salome, then sixteen, had no suitors but also no interest in marriage yet. She was a pretty and lively girl, and in time would not be lacking for suitors.

Leila came out of our house to join us, followed close behind by Dalia, Matthias, and four-year-old Gila. At the moment of seeing them, all the injustices of the world ceased to matter, and my heart rejoined in the great blessings that God Almighty bestowed upon me.

Chapter 10

A Holiday in Jerusalem

Nazareth, Galilee, Spring 27 C.E.

Pesach, the Passover holiday, was our favorite time of the year. The festival is also the most holy time of the year, a celebration of the time when Moses freed God's people from slavery in Egypt. With the help of God's mighty hand, Moses led our people out by parting the sea to escape the army of Pharaoh. When Pharaoh's army rushed in pursuit, the hand of God drowned them and allowed Moses to lead our people to freedom.

Our family and neighbors from Nazareth, and other nearby villages, made the Passover pilgrimage to Jerusalem as frequently as we could. We did this for religious reasons, and also for family reasons. Many families had relatives in Jerusalem, such as my Uncle Abram, and only got to see them during the holiday trips.

We travelled on the road in groups as large as a hundred or more. This was done for both safety and social reasons. We walked, talked, ate, and camped together every day during the several days it takes to walk to the city. It was a relaxed and joyous time, a welcome break away from the usual routines and hard work of our day-to-day lives.

The families of Mary's children, of Clopas and his children, along with Leila and our family, all made the pilgrimage that year. Only my mother Sarah, and Joses and his wife Rachel, stayed behind to make sure the animals were protected, fed, and watered. Rachel now had two young sons to take care of, three-year-old Yosef and six-month-old Levi, and she and Joses were not willing to make such a long trip until the children grew older.

Sarah complained she was getting too old to make the trip on foot. I promised her we would buy a horse and carriage so that she would travel in comfort on the next trip. I was no longer a *tekton* working in Sepphoris now, but a wheat farmer for the past three years after we inherited farmland from Leila's parents. We sold the extra grain from each wheat crop, which considerably improved our family's financial situation.

The day before we left, eleven-year-old Gila announced that she wished to stay behind to help her grandmother with her work, and to keep her company. We approved her decision and praised her loving compassion.

Early the next morning, Sarah gave a hearty embrace in turn to Eitan, Matthias, and Dalia, and we were on our way. It would take us a week to walk to Jerusalem.

Valley of Jezreel, Spring 27 C.E.

There were sixty of us from Nazareth in our group. We took along three donkeys to carry some supplies, but otherwise each adult carried their own satchel on their backs. The spring weather was mild and pleasant—the summer heat of the dry season was still a month away. As we walked further south, we were joined by people from nearby Naim and Kokhaba, and the size of our travelling party grew.

The flat and fertile plain of Jezreel, between the highlands of lower Galilee and the hills of northern Samaria, was a delightful place to travel through. Through the ages, it was the easy and favored path of Galileans on their way to Judea, rather than going through the rugged mountains on either side.

It was also the favored path, the Scriptures tell us, of many invading armies over the past thousand years that fought mighty battles and decided the fates of nations. The armies of Gideon fought here, and

King Saul. And also King Jehu, he who ordered the killing of Jezebel and exterminated the house of Ahab.

The soil here was black and fertile, covered as far as the eye could see with a green coat of grasses, wildflowers, shrubs, and trees. Fig and pomegranate trees grew along the roadsides, but unfortunately, their fruits were undeveloped and not yet ripe enough to eat.

As we walked along, some of us settled into groups of like-minded people, as often happens. In front were the older adults: Mary the mother of Yeshua, his uncle Clopas, and Mary of Clopas. They were the leaders of our party and decided for us all, such as when and where to stop and camp for the night. Yeshua walked with them, leading one of the three donkeys by a rope tether.

My group was the second group, who were the adults with young children to watch over. Besides Leila and myself, these also included James and Kitra, Yeshua's sister Mary and her husband Asher who joined us from Kokhaba, and my sister Eva and her husband Uziel. Ours was the noisiest and most lively group, with the older children running around and playing games with each other and with children from other families.

The children between the ages of seven and twelve soon formed a close-knit gang. These included our Matthias, James' two daughters, Penina and Ruth, and Eva's sons, Yonatan and Shimon. Dalia was now fourteen years old and not interested in childish games, so she walked with the adults. The youngest children did not venture far from the security of their mothers; six-year-old Eitan stayed close to Leila, and three-year-old Saul kept close to Mary, the sister of Yeshua.

The third group were the younger people and married couples, which included Yeshua's siblings and cousins: his brother Judah and wife Channa, his sister Salome, his brother Shimon and wife Talia, and Simeon the son of Clopas and his new bride Leah. The firstborn son of Clopas, James, was unmarried.

There was joy in travelling together for almost a week on the way to Jerusalem, and another week on the return trip. We would be in

Jerusalem for the purification rites, and then the Passover feast. This long and intimate pilgrimage, shared with family and neighbors from one generation to the next, made it truly the best time of the year.

In the early afternoon, we passed by a small group of people resting by the side of the road. Suddenly a loud voice called out: "Clopas! Brother! Wait!"

We turned to see the tall figure of Zebedee striding rapidly toward us. He reached Clopas and wrapped him in a mighty embrace.

"Peace to you, Brother," Clopas said with a laugh. "It's a blessing to meet you here!"

Close behind Zebedee came his wife, Salome. She headed straight for her sister Mary, who had seen her and was walking towards her. The two sisters embraced with tears of joy in their eyes. It had been perhaps four years since the last time Zebedee and Salome travelled from their home in Capernaum to visit their relatives in Nazareth.

Mary said: "You look healthy and happy, Sister! But I don't see your children. Did they not come with you?"

"No, they're all too busy this year," Salome said. "Rina is with her husband and their little girl. James and John are very busy with their new fishing boat."

"Oh, they have their own boat now?" Mary exclaimed. "The last time I saw them, they were barely past boyhood!"

Salome laughed. "They are both hard-working young men now. You will see them again soon, God willing."

The women gathered around Salome, including Mary of Clopas, Leila, Mary and Salome the sisters of Yeshua, and my sister Eva. I joined the brothers Yeshua, James, Judah, and Shimon, who were all greeting their uncle with affection.

"Peace to you, David," Zebedee said as he firmly shook my hand. "You are a wheat farmer now, I hear!"

"And also to you," I replied. "It's lucky that you saw us, we almost passed you by!" Zebedee had been my neighbor when I was young, and always treated me well. I was very happy to see him again.

"It is truly God's blessing to find you all here today," he said. "Now we can share the joy of the holiday with you."

Zebedee and Salome joined our group, and we continued on. It would be another five or six hours before dusk approached and we stopped to set up camp for the night.

As we walked along at a comfortable pace, Clopas began to sing in a deep and powerful voice. Yeshua, Mary, Zebedee, and Salome joined in the song. Within a few moments, everyone in our party was singing heartily. We were quickly joined by other groups walking in front of or behind us. The air filled with hundreds of voices singing the ancient pilgrim song.

I was glad when they said to me,
"Let us go to the House of the Lord!"
Our feet have been standing within your gates, O Jerusalem!
Jerusalem, built as a city which is bound firmly together,
To which the tribes go up, the tribes of the Lord,
As was decreed for Israel, to give thanks to the name of the Lord.
There thrones for judgment were set,
The thrones of the house of David.
Pray for the peace of Jerusalem!
May they prosper who love you!
Peace be within your walls, security within your towers!
For my brothers' and my companions' sake, I will pray,
"Peace be within you!"
For the sake of the house of the Lord our God,
I will seek your good.

The further one travels south in Palestine, the hotter it gets. The city of Jericho, located several miles from the western bank of the Jordan

River, is an oasis in the middle of a large desert. The surrounding land is mountainous and dry for miles around. Almost nothing grows there except scattered shrubs and desert plants. It is empty of people.

We camped in our tents outside Jericho for a night. At first light, we turned right and headed due west toward Bethany and Jerusalem. The path from Jericho to Bethany is through a deep desert valley. The ground there is extremely dry. We made good time to get through it quickly, but not so quickly that we become exhausted. Those who are foolish enough to exhaust themselves in the Judean desert become food for vultures and crows.

Jerusalem, Judea, Spring 27 C.E.

Climbing up from the Jericho desert valley toward the hill country east of Jerusalem always gave us a thrilling sight. Jerusalem was a vast city, unlike anything we have in Galilee or Judea now. Most impressive of all, rising from atop Mount Moriah, the highest point in the city, was the Temple of God. Each time I saw it again, I agreed with my Uncle Abram: it was the most beautiful sight in the world.

Outside the eastern walls of Jerusalem, we found another city, this one made of tents and flimsy temporary shelters built by the tens of thousands of pilgrims just like us. It was not possible for all the holiday visitors to find housing inside the city, so we made do. No one would even think of complaining, for we were just happy to be there. The group from Nazareth settled down on a grassy patch of land below the Mount of Olives. We pitched our tents bunched closely together.

Our family would spend Passover Day with my Uncle Abram in the city, but until then we preferred to stay with our friends. This was the busiest time of the year for the Temple priests and Levites, and my uncle would have his hands full from morning till night. The Day of Preparation on the 14th day of Nisan, when thousands of sacrifices had to be performed in the Temple before sunset, always left the priests and Levites fully exhausted.

"*Abba*, can we go see the Temple?" Matthias asked eagerly. We had just finished our morning meal, and he was eager for adventure.

"Yes!" Dalia echoed his enthusiasm. "I want to see it too."

"Me too!" said Eitan. He was only six, and this was his first trip to Jerusalem. In his mind, the Holy Temple of God was a place of stories, magic, and wonder.

"I don't see why not," I said to their smiling faces. Leila nodded her agreement.

"Dress lightly," Leila told them. "We'll be walking a *lot*. Jerusalem is a big place!"

We approached the city from the east, along a well-travelled road past the Mount of Olives. The spring weather was mild here, and a sweet breeze blew in from the west. The stream of people walking along with us created an air of anticipation and excitement. Everyone was in a holiday mood.

Just inside the tall, thick city walls, the vast expanse of the Temple walls stretched out before us. Eitan's eyes grew wide.

He said in wonder: "I didn't know the Temple was so big!"

"It's one thousand cubits long and six hundred cubits wide," Dalia said with pride in her voice. When Eitan gave her a puzzled look, she smiled and added: "That means one thousand and six hundred feet long, and one thousand feet wide!"

"Very good!" Leila said. "You remembered from our last trip."

Just inside the Temple walls was a very large and broad plaza, by far the largest open space on Temple grounds. It was teeming with a crowd of people of many races and cultures, all dressed in a variety of colorful and sometimes exotic looking clothes. Jewish people from all over the world gathered here for Passover.

Leila turned to our oldest son. "Matthias, can you tell your brother what this place is called?"

"Yes, *Emma*. This is the Court of Gentiles. Everyone is allowed here, even gentiles and people who are unclean." He turned to his sister with a teasing grin. "Even girls!"

Dalia turned to punch him in the shoulder, which made Matthias laugh. "I can go to the Court of Women, and you know it! And I'm not unclean!"

"No fighting in the Temple!" Leila admonished them.

Eitan looked around, eyes searching. "Where are all the lambs and other animals that people buy for the sacrifices?"

I pointed his attention toward the long inside wall. "Over there are the cages with pigeons and doves for sale. And the people behind those tables are the money changers. All these people from other lands must exchange their money for silver shekels, which is the only money the priests will accept."

"I don't see any lambs or big animals," he said. "Don't you buy a lamb for the *coban*?"

"Sometimes, but not always," I explained. "But the sheep, goats, and oxen are kept outside the Temple. They're not allowed for sale inside the Temple because they make too big a mess."

"Which is a very good thing!" Dalia said, laughing. "We don't want the Temple to smell like a sheep shed or a barn, do we?"

We approached the next plaza, which was separated from the Court of Gentiles by a beautifully carved stone balustrade that was about four feet high. On some of the stone pillars, placed at regular intervals, were small stone slabs engraved with warning signs in both Greek and Latin.

"This is the Court of Women," Leila explained. "This is as far as women can go. Only Jews can enter this holy place, both men and women, but no foreigners and no one who is unclean."

Eitan pointed curiously at the engraved sign on the pillar in front of him. "That's a pretty sign. What does it say?"

"It's a very serious warning," I told him. "It is written in Latin, but I know what it says because all the signs have the same message. I will translate it for you."

*"No man of another nation to enter within
the fence and enclosure round the Temple.
And whoever is caught will have himself
to blame that his death ensues."*

Eitan raised his eyebrows. "I don't understand what that means."

Matthias said: "It means, if you are not Jewish and you go inside this fence, you are dead!" He raised a finger and made a quick slicing motion across his throat. "Dead! No questions asked!"

Eitan gave me a doubtful look.

"Yes, it's true," I told him. "The Temple priests are very strict about that. The punishment for any gentile who enters beyond this point is death. They would violate the purity of the holy places in the Temple."

The Court of Women was very much smaller than the vast Court of Gentiles. The pleasant scent of incense was strong here, and in other areas of the inner courts. Wood, oils, and wines to be purchased for the sacrifices were stored here. Some people offered animals for the burnt offerings and sacrifices, while others offered grains and oils.

"This is as far as women are allowed to go," Leila told Eitan. "You go ahead with your *abba*. Dalia and I will wait for you here."

We entered the third plaza, the Court of Israelites, with a mild sense of awe. This was the farthest that men were allowed unless they were Temple priests. Just beyond the inner balustrade we could see into the Court of Priests, where the Temple's altar stood. Made from bronze and wood, five cubits long and five cubits wide, this four-horned pedestal was where the sacrifices were made.

A short distance beyond the altar were the twelve steps that led up to the sanctuary housing the Holy of Holies. This was the most sacred place in the Temple, and the most sacred place in the world.

Eitan gazed at the magnificent building with gold-plated columns with his mouth slightly ajar. Matthias noticed his look and placed a hand on his brother's shoulder.

"This is where the glory of God lives on Earth," he said in a whisper.

Eitan said: "Can we see it?"

"No," I told him. "No one is allowed inside the sanctuary except for the High Priest. And he is allowed to enter only one day a year, on Yom Kippur, the Day of Atonement."

"But what is inside, *Abba*? I want to know."

"Nothing," I explained. "It is an empty room. A very long time ago, the sacred Ark of the Covenant rested there, which contained God's commandments to our people. Nobody knows where it is now."

Eitan's face dropped. "That's sad."

"Yes," I said. "It is very sad."

In the afternoon, Yeshua stopped by our tent. His cheerful smile told us that he had some good news.

"We are invited to the town of Bethany for supper, at the house of Lazarus," he announced. "Martha and Mary will cook a wonderful meal for us. They always do! So, will you join us?"

"Yes, of course," I replied, very pleased. The parents of Martha, Mary, and Lazarus had been friends with Yosef and Mary for many years. Happily, their children wished to continue the family friendship.

"We are honored to accept," Leila said. "When do we leave?"

"Right now!" Yeshua said enthusiastically. "Let's not keep our hosts waiting."

Chapter 11

Sacrificial Lamb

Bethany, Judea, Spring 27 C.E.

The town of Bethany is a short distance east of Jerusalem, and we arrived there well before sunset. Martha's house was in the town center, near the marketplace where fresh produce and other goods were sold. It was one of the few two-story houses in town, with a spacious patio in the back designed for entertaining guests. This was a family of substantial wealth.

Although Lazarus was the man of the house, both he and Mary clearly deferred to their older sister on matters that required making decisions. Martha was a short and stout woman, with a fiery character and a strong, determined look in her eyes. She was in her early thirties then, ten years older than Lazarus and four years older than Mary.

"Welcome!" Martha greeted us amicably. She addressed herself first to the three older women: Mary, the mother of Yeshua, Salome, the wife of Zebedee, and Mary the wife of Clopas.

Lazarus greeted the men. He was a tall and thin young man, of a quiet nature and gentle disposition. He spent his time reading books, playing music, and in other intellectual pursuits. He never developed the strong physical build of the men from Nazareth, who toiled in the fields or did other types of strenuous work.

"Peace to you," Yeshua said to Lazarus and his sisters. "I am happy to see you again."

Mary gestured at the tables arranged on the patio. "Come! Sit! The servants will bring us wine. It's been four years since we last spoke. There is so much to talk about!"

After wine, dinner, and casual family talk, the after-dinner discussion turned, as it so often did, to Jerusalem. What happened in Jerusalem and the Temple of God affected the lives of all Jews.

"This new Roman governor, what do you know about him?" a very curious Zebedee asked Lazarus. "It's been less than a year since his arrival in Judea, but we hear that he's already caused major trouble?"

Lazarus frowned. "He's no different from the last one. Imperious and greedy. He cares nothing about our religion and traditions."

"As arrogant as all the rest, eh?" Clopas asked.

"Pontius Pilate is a big-nosed man," Lazarus said. "That makes him arrogant enough!"

James laughed hard and spilled some of his wine. "What does his nose have to do with being arrogant?"

"It's a well-known fact, Brother," Yeshua told him with an amused smile. "Romans believe that a big nose is a sign of strong leadership. We see it in many of their nobles who are appointed to high office."

"It's true," Lazarus chuckled. "And Pilate showed his disdain for us from the very first day he marched to Jerusalem."

"Bringing the images of Tiberius Caesar into Jerusalem, you mean?" asked Clopas.

Lazarus frowned. "Yes. They proclaim that Caesar is divine, a god. But such images are forbidden in Jerusalem by Jewish law. Pilate knew that, but he didn't care. Large crowds protested in the streets for many days until he finally removed the images."

Zebedee shook his head sadly. "But people were beaten to death during those protests. Isn't that right?"

"No, that came later," Lazarus said. "Pilate took large sums of money from the Temple treasury to build a new aqueduct. There were more large protests, and people were beaten with clubs by the Roman soldiers. Many died from their beatings."

"Pilate *stole* money from the Temple treasury, you mean," Yeshua said, his voice tense with anger. "That money belongs to God Almighty. It was not his to use."

"Stole money is right," James grumbled. "Why didn't Caiaphas and the priests stop him and protect what belongs to the Temple?"

"The High Priest answers to the Roman prefect," Clopas explained. "If Caiaphas doesn't do Pilate's bidding, then Pilate will remove him and appoint another man in his place."

Lazarus gave a sigh. "The High Priest will never oppose the Roman prefect, and certainly not this High Priest. Joseph Caiaphas and Pontius Pilate work together closer than brothers."

"That is sacrilege," Yeshua said indignantly. "It's a crime against all Jewish people. It's a crime against the Lord!"

Mary, Yeshua's mother, joined the table, accompanied by Martha of Bethany. They were drawn by the excited conversation.

"You are exactly right, Yeshua," Martha said in a firm tone. "The High Priest betrays us every single day. He rules Jerusalem, along with his council of priests, but he answers to the Roman prefect. We all know that Pilate is the true ruler."

"When will it ever change?" James asked.

Martha shook her head. "Perhaps never. Sadly, we are getting used to it. People protest and rebel, and the soldiers of Herod Antipas and Pontius Pilate beat them and kill them for it."

"Things *must* change," Yeshua said. "These injustices are profane. They are sinful, an offense against the Lord."

His mother placed a gentle hand on his shoulder. "It will change, my son. The Lord will not allow this injustice to go on."

"We wait patiently for the *mashiach* to come and free us from our Roman rulers," Lazarus said. He smiled and raised his hands upward, toward the heavens. "Must you try our patience so mightily, O Lord?"

Peter Jaksa

Martha frowned at him. "Show more reverence, Brother. Nobody knows when the messiah will come, or from where. Still, we must not question the will of God."

"Ah, but the messiah is promised," Clopas said brightly. "We don't know whether he will be a warrior messiah, in the line of King David, or a prophet messiah, in the line of Ezekiel — but he will come."

"I know that is true," Yeshua said in a solemn tone. "The reign of God is near."

Jerusalem, Judea, Spring 27 C.E.

The Day of Preparation begins on the morning of the 14th day of the month of Nisan. The day is spent in preparation for Passover, the most holy day of the year. In that year, when the Temple still stood in all its glory, this hectic and busy day was when all the offerings and sacrifices had to be made at the Temple, and all completed before sundown.

On the Jewish calendar, a new day begins at sundown. At sunset the 14th day becomes the 15th day of Nisan, Passover day. Passover is celebrated that evening with the *seder* meal, and then all the next day.

Families often joined together to purchase a lamb, goat, or other animal for the Passover sacrifice. This was done for both practical and financial reasons. We shared the expenses of purchasing all the items required, and also shared our portion of the sacrificial animal to make our Passover meal. An entire lamb is too much food for one family.

That year, our family shared the sacrifice with Yeshua's family, and also the family of Uziel and Eva. My brother-in-law asked to take the lead in purchasing the lamb and presenting it to the Temple priests. He was very eager because this was his first experience in carrying out that important task. We agreed to accommodate him.

In the afternoon, Uziel, Yeshua, and I went to the Temple. Many thousands of people were on the same mission as us. The road into Jerusalem was very crowded, even before we reached the city gates.

We purchased the lamb at a stand where sacrificial animals were sold. The one-year-old lamb was a male, without any blemish, as was required by law. The animal was very docile and allowed itself to be carried in Uziel's arms without putting up a struggle.

When we finally entered the Temple, we saw that the outer court, the Court of Gentiles, was packed with people. There was hardly any room to move.

"I've never seen so many people in one place!" Uziel exclaimed.

"This is when patience is truly a virtue," I told him with a chuckle.

Yeshua gave a nod. "It will get worse before it gets better, Uziel. The animal will get restless, so hold on to it well."

When we entered the Court of Women, we could hear the panicked bleating and cries of pain from animals in the distance. The lamb in Uziel's arms became very tense and still. Then it made a sudden surge to break free, but Uziel tightened his grip and held fast.

Yeshua caught my eye and motioned upwards, to the top of the nearest section of Temple wall. Dozens of Roman soldiers patrolled there, their highly polished armor glistering in the bright sun. One man with a stance of authority stood perfectly still and calm, watching the crowded scene below. He was a man of medium height, about forty years old. His black hair, graying at the temples, was cut very short in the Roman style. The unmistakable air of haughtiness told us he was a person of high rank.

"That must be Governor Pontius Pilate," I said. "He stands there looking as if he owns the place."

Yeshua said: "He is Pilate, no other. And, truthfully, he *does* own the place. Rome owns Jerusalem and everything in it. Rome owns even the Temple and the ground where we stand."

His words were discouraging, but irrefutable. I looked away from the Romans in anger and disgust. We continued shuffling forward, moving slowly with the crowd.

Entering the Court of Israelites, the cries of the sacrificial animals became much louder and the smell of blood was very strong. The lamb became more agitated. Uziel held a tight grip on the animal, which was making pitiful bleating noises and kicking its legs.

Several altars had been erected besides the main sacrificial altar. Hundreds of priests and Levites were working at a rapid pace, but still our progress was slow because the crowd was so large. Levites, priests' assistants, let in one small group of men only when another group left. My Uncle Abram was somewhere in that tumult, doing his job, but we did not see him.

We finally reached a gate where two priests waited for us beside one of the smaller altars. Their hands, arms, and clothes were covered with blood, like a butcher on a busy day. Uziel carefully handed the lamb, bleating with fright and kicking its legs, to one of the priests. Then we took a step back to watch the sacrificial rite.

While one priest held the animal tightly around its middle, the other priest held a bowl under its head to catch the blood. He slashed a long and sharp knife across the animal's throat, and a thick stream of blood gushed into the bowl. The lamb made one last desperate kick, which caught the edge of the bowl and splashed the blood across the front of the priest's robe.

The priest muttered an angry curse under his breath. The blood should have been sprinkled on the walls of the altar, just as the blood was painted on the door-posts of the Israelites on the night before the Exodus from Egypt.

The other priest, working hurriedly, hung the lamb's carcass on a hook, then skinned it and gutted it. The fat was cut away for the Lord's portion, to be burned on the altar along with the entrails. The meat of the lamb was divided between the altar, the priests, and us. Uziel took our share, and we left immediately to make room for those still waiting behind us.

As we walked back to the Temple gates, at times having to push our way forcefully through the crowd, Yeshua seemed very quiet. This was usually a sign that he was deep in thought. He looked troubled, and I said nothing because I did not wish to disturb his contemplation. Uziel walked with a proud and pleased expression on his face. He was just happy that the sacrifice went well and our work was behind us.

Outside the Temple gate, it was time to part ways. My family and Eva's would celebrate the Passover dinner with our Uncle Abram at his house in Jerusalem, while Yeshua and his family would spend it in Bethany with Martha, Mary, and Lazarus. Yeshua took his share of the sacrificial animal from Uziel and placed it in a small leather sack that he brought along for that purpose.

"Were you not pleased with the sacrifice?" I finally asked Yeshua.

He looked away for a moment, then in a calm but sad voice asked: "Why do we do this?"

Uziel was startled by the question. "What do you mean, why? The Passover offering thanks God for passing over and sparing our people when He killed the first-born of the Egyptians. And as the Law teaches, a blood sacrifice is an offering to please and honor the Lord."

Yeshua gave a nod. "I know what the Law teaches us about a blood sacrifice. It is a custom older than Abraham."

"Do you question it now?" I asked.

He paused again in thoughtful silence. "I don't know. I think there must be a better way to honor the Lord."

Uziel's face twisted into a frown, but he kept his tongue.

I said: "That's a discussion for another time. On our trip home to Nazareth, perhaps?"

Yeshua nodded. "Yes. We'll have plenty of time to talk on the road."

We said our farewells and went our separate ways.

Now it was Uziel's turn to look troubled. He frowned again as we walked to the house of Abram.

"Why does Yeshua have to question everything?" he asked. "We have ancient laws and honored traditions to guide us in our lives. Are they not good enough for him?"

"No, he doesn't question everything," I said. "Yeshua is guided by the search for wisdom."

"And what, exactly, is this search for wisdom?"

"The first rule of wisdom is to seek knowledge and truth," I replied. "Wisdom doesn't come from simply accepting what everyone thinks. If we do only that, then nothing changes or gets better. Wisdom comes from asking questions about how things can be different. Better."

Uziel gave a sharp snort. "That's a dangerous way of thinking. Some things should not be questioned."

"Many people agree with you."

He shook his head, frustrated. "But not Yeshua?"

"No," I said. "Not Yeshua."

Leila and Eva prepared our Passover meal. After evening fell, Uncle Abram returned to the house. He was drained to near exhaustion from his busy day at the Temple, the busiest day of the year. He was the one to give the purification blessing, however, and we each drank our first cup of wine or grape juice. Everyone except the youngest children was familiar with the rituals of the seder meal.

We all ate slices of vegetables and boiled potatoes dipped in salt water. The salt water represented the tears of our ancestors when they lived in captivity in Egypt. Later came the *matzot,* and many other foods. We ate bitter herbs to remind us of the harshness of slavery.

Eitan, the youngest child, asked the first of the four questions, as we taught him: "Why is this night different from all other nights?"

We took turns telling the stories of Moses and the Exodus, when he led our people to freedom from slavery. After the main meal, we sang songs of praise to Father God, then drank the fourth and final cup. Even the youngest children understood by then that this was a special day, the most holy day of the year.

In late evening, as people were preparing for sleep, we took a few minutes to thank Uncle Abram for his hospitality.

Our uncle looked tired, but content. "All the work and expense is nothing, compared to the joy of seeing us all together on this holiday," he said. "You are always welcomed in my home."

"It was a lovely dinner," Eva told him. "You must visit Nazareth and let us treat you with equal love and kindness."

"It will be my pleasure, my dear niece," he said, and squeezed her offered hand gently.

Uziel gave me a broad smile. "You see, David? This is what I love about our people and our traditions. Why should anyone want to change them?"

"Who wants to change them?" Abram asked with a raised eyebrow, mildly curious.

I smiled and shook my head. "Nobody, Uncle. Perhaps a discussion for another time."

"Very well," the older man said. "The day is late and we're all tired. But let me tell you one thing about changing our traditions?"

He had our attention, and we stood quietly in respectful silence.

"Any man who tries to do that will find that it's a very rocky and cursed road to travel. The pharaohs of Egypt tried it, for four hundred and thirty years, and look what happened to them."

Nazareth, Galilee, Spring 27 CE

The trip back from Jerusalem is always less energetic than the walk to Jerusalem. The anticipation and excitement of the holiday are behind us. Ahead are weeks and months of our day-to-day work and routines. Our group grew smaller by the day as different groups of people split off and headed to their own villages and towns. Zebedee and Salome took a road heading northeast, to their home in Capernaum.

Yeshua was as social as ever and talked with everyone who wished to talk, friends and strangers alike. One thing that made him different from most people is that he treated strangers no differently from friends or family. We were all children of God, and that made us all equal in his eyes.

We talked briefly, on only one occasion, about the Temple sacrifice. It was clearly something still on his mind, and he was reflecting on it.

He offered no further opinion at that time, other than to repeat his initial comment: "There must be a better way to honor the Lord." It was a troubling issue for him, and many would be offended to hear him question this ancient ritual. We put off discussion for a later time.

On a late afternoon, we approached Nazareth from the south, climbing up the gently sloping hill. People were weary but eager to be home, looking forward to a meal and then rest. As we approached our houses some of the younger children ran ahead.

"Shimon, stop! Don't run!" Eva called in a futile effort to slow down her youngest son. Our Eitan quickly ran after his cousin.

"Ah, let it go," I said. "They're just eager to see their grandmother."

Rachel stood in the doorway of our house, holding the baby, Levi. She did not greet us, but turned her head and called into the house. Her husband, Joses, came out a moment later and stood beside her, silent and still.

Our daughter, eleven-year-old Gila, came outside and immediately started running straight to Leila. Her face was anguished, and she was sobbing loudly.

"Oh, no," Eva said very softly, and dropped the small satchel she was holding in her hand. "Oh, no."

Leila gathered the crying Gila in her arms to comfort her. Joses and Rachel walked closer to meet us.

"When?" I asked Joses.

"Sarah died two days ago," he said. "We decided to wait before making funeral plans, until today at least. We hoped that you would return in time."

Yeshua joined us, his face filled with sorrow. "A very sad day for us all. I pray that Father God will ease your pain."

Eva suddenly looked unsteady on her feet, and Yeshua put an arm around her shoulders to help steady her. Uziel then took Eva by the hand to walk her toward the house.

We were shaken by the news and stunned with grief. When we left for Jerusalem, Sarah looked weary, but otherwise in good health. We even discussed plans for her to make the Passover pilgrimage next year in a carriage. Those discussions seemed like a long time ago.

"Thank you for waiting," I told Joses. "It was the right thing to do. Now let's go inside. I want to see my mother."

"We just put the sheep back in their pen," Gila told us that evening. "Then grandmother fell down on the grass, and she didn't move or open her eyes when I went to her. I was so scared! I didn't know what to do!"

"It's all right," I said, placing a comforting hand on her shoulder as she began sobbing again. "Your grandmama died quickly, and there was nothing you could do to save her."

Leila said: "You ran and told Joses and Rachel. That was the right thing to do."

Her words made Gila cry even harder. It would take some time for her to get over the shock of what happened.

Dalia took her sister by the hand. "Let's go outside and walk a bit. You can tell me about it if you want."

"All right," Gila said, using her hand to wipe away the tears from her cheeks. She followed her older sister out the door.

Leila looked to the side of the room, where Sarah was laid out on her bed, wrapped in a funeral shroud. Rachel and another female neighbor had washed her body, anointed her with oils and spices for burial, and wrapped her body in the shroud.

"Tomorrow is the funeral," Leila said. "I'm very grateful we arrived in time."

"Yes, so am I. The Lord was merciful in giving her so many years of life, and merciful in giving us time to give her a proper burial."

"She will sleep with the bones of all your ancestors in the family tomb," Leila said. She stopped suddenly, a pained look in her eyes.

"That's all right, you can say it. All except for my father," I said. "We never found his body after he was executed."

Leila sighed. "She survived on her own after him. That takes a strong woman, to take care of you and Eva by herself with no other family to help."

I nodded across the room to Mary, the mother of Yeshua, and Mary the wife of Clopas, who were quietly talking with Eva. "Those two women embraced her and became like sisters to her. Our neighbors became our family."

"Another small blessing from living in Nazareth," Leila said.

Yeshua and his sister Salome walked over to join us. She carried plates of food, and he brought a pitcher of water.

"This is for you," Yeshua said. "You've had no food since our last meal on the road. You must be famished."

"We are," Leila said with a grateful smile as she took a plate from Salome. "God bless you, Sister."

"You are very welcome," Salome said. She turned to me. "I will miss Sarah terribly. She was always good to me, from the time I was old enough to walk and talk."

I thanked her silently with my eyes. Sarah loved Mary's daughters almost as much as her own.

"The Lord blessed her with a good heart and a good life," Yeshua said. "Everyone who knew Sarah will remember her fondly. She was a virtuous woman, kind and generous. She had a gentle heart, and she made no enemies."

"That is a rare thing for any person, man or woman," I said.

"Yes, it is," he said wistfully. "Many strive for it, but few are blessed enough to achieve it."

Chapter 12

John the Baptizer

Nazareth, Galilee, Spring 28 C.E.

"He is ascetic to an extreme. He's lived in the desert like that for many years. He wears only a robe of rough-spun cloth, made from camels' hair. Never cuts his hair, so he looks like a wild man. He eats only locusts and wild honey, and drinks no wine. Some believe that he comes from a priestly family of Essenes, but he lives a simpler and more frugal life than even Essenes. He preaches about the end days."

Uncle Abram was visiting Nazareth for a week. On his trip, he rode his donkey past Jericho and saw firsthand the teacher and sage people called John the Baptizer. Some were saying that he was a prophet, sent by God Almighty to prepare our people for the coming reign of God.

All of us who were gathered around the table, enjoying a cup of after-dinner wine, were paying rapt attention. We had been hearing stories about John for many months, but Abram was the first person we talked to who saw the man and witnessed his ritual of baptism on the banks of the Jordan River.

Yeshua said: "Essenes reject the authority of the Temple priests, so many go to live in the desert to find a life of purity. They wish to escape the corruption of Jerusalem and the Temple authorities."

"That is true," Abram agreed. "They see themselves as the true tribe of Israel. A voice crying out in the wilderness against the sins and corruption of the Temple priests!"

"Including you, Uncle?" I asked with a chuckle.

He smiled. "Yes, including a poor Levite like me, because my work supports the Temple functions. But I don't mind."

"But this man John is different from other Essenes," said James. "He didn't stay in the desert, but brings his call for change and salvation to the banks of the Jordan. He brazenly challenges the Temple priests out in the open!"

Abram said: "True, and not only the priests. I saw many cavalry scouts of Herod Antipas on the outskirts of the crowd who were there watching John. The Fox is also keeping an eye on him."

Mary frowned. "Well, that can't be good for John. We know how Antipas deals with rebels."

Yeshua agreed with a small, somber nod. He turned to my uncle with a questioning look. "This full-body baptism sounds unusual. It's unusual even for Essenes, is it not?"

"Yes, it certainly is," Abram replied. "We use water in our rites of purification, of course, but only to sprinkle it on our bodies, or to wash our hands and feet. John the Baptizer immerses people fully under the river water."

"How strange!" Salome exclaimed. "Why would anyone do that?"

Abram shrugged. "I don't really know, my dear. You would have to ask John that question."

"How the water ritual is performed is not important," Yeshua said. "What *is* important is the message. People do not baptize themselves, they allow John to baptize them. It means they accept the purification of baptism as a gift from God, and accept John as a messenger from God."

Everyone became quiet, reflecting on his words. These new rituals and ideas required a new way of thinking.

Mary was the first to speak. "You are right, that John is acting as a messenger from God. This is why many people are calling him a prophet and comparing him to the prophet Ezekiel."

"He is no prophet," Abram scoffed. "He's a wild man who emerged from the desert to frighten people. And, whether the fool knows it or not, he places himself and his followers in great danger. By challenging the Temple authority so brazenly, he also challenges the authority of Herod and our Jewish rulers."

"And challenges the authority of the Romans, who rule Herod and the High Priest of the Temple," I said. "But you are too harsh, Uncle. When thousands of people flock to see this man, surely there must be something good in his message to the people?"

Yeshua said: "I think so, too. I would like to see him myself and hear what he has to say."

"So would I!" James exclaimed. "Let's make the trip together?"

"Yes, let's," Yeshua agreed. "Anyone else who wishes to come, join us. It's a long walk to Jericho, and your company is welcome."

Salome looked up eagerly. "I will come with you. But I won't be dunked in the river!"

That made some people chuckle, including Leila. She turned to me. "Do you wish to go? You've been talking about this John the Baptizer for weeks. I know you're curious to see what he's doing."

"You're right," I said. "It will be a few weeks before the wheat fields need my attention, so why not? I'll go with you, Yeshua."

Abram said: "Good! Then it's settled. When I leave, why don't you all come with me? I'll go with you as far as Jericho, and we'll use my donkey as a pack animal."

East of Jericho, Jordan River bank, Spring 28 C.E.

As we walked along the west bank of the Jordan River, we could tell, even from a distance, the crowd of people numbered in the hundreds. There were perhaps as many as one thousand people gathered on both sides of the river. All were drawn here to this desolate spot for one purpose — to see the man who was called a prophet of God.

This spot on the river, near Jericho, was chosen very strategically by John the Baptizer as the location for his sermons and baptisms. It had immense historical and symbolic meaning for Jewish people. There was a ford in the river where the water was shallow enough to allow people and animals to walk across. This was also the exact spot where Joshua, the prophet and successor to Moses, led his people across the Jordan River and into the promised land. By doing his work of baptism and purification here, on the east bank of the river, John the Baptizer also sent people across the Jordan River and into the promised land.

Over many centuries of time, this location on the river also became a trade route between Judea and the lands east of the Jordan. It brought streams of travelers at all times of the year.

"He is very clever, this John," Abram said with grudging admiration. "There is no other place in Judea where he can draw bigger crowds."

"Yes, he's clever," Yeshua agreed. "But if he challenges the Temple priests and Herod before such crowds, he will need to be very clever."

"Ah, we shall see what happens with him," Abram said dismissively. As a Levite, and thus part of the Temple establishment, my uncle had no sympathy for John the Baptizer.

He pointed me toward a group of soldiers on the edge of the crowd. "As you can see, the soldiers of Antipas are already here. Be careful not to cause any trouble, Nephew."

"Don't worry, Uncle. We're not here to cause any trouble. Thank you for your help on the trip."

Abram mounted his donkey. "I bid you farewell, Yeshua, James, and Salome. You are good travelling company."

The others said their farewells in return. Abram took one last look at the crowd on the far bank, a worried frown on his face, then turned his donkey and headed due west toward Jericho and Jerusalem.

John was in the middle of giving a sermon on the east bank of the river, where the larger crowd gathered around him. We joined the others who were streaming across the river in that direction. We walked slowly in the waist-deep water, holding our shoes and bags high over our heads so they would not get wet. The river bottom was sandy mud, but solid enough to provide firm footing.

"Evil and corruption are everywhere! I tell you this: God's chosen people have failed Him! Failed Him most shamefully! Our covenant with God is broken, and it must be renewed! Now, prepare the way of the Lord! Make his paths straight!"

John's voice was strong and clear and carried well along the riverbank. We were finally close enough to get a good look. He was a tall, very thin man of perhaps forty years. His long black hair had streaks of gray. His beard was long, shaggy, and unkempt. He was dressed in a garment of coarsely woven camel's hair that fell below his knees, and a thin leather belt around his waist. He stood very straight as he talked, his head held high, which gave him a look of authority.

"The reign of God is near!" John shouted to the surrounding crowd. "You offspring of vipers, who warned you to flee from the fury to come? So, bear fruit worthy of change! Don't start to say to yourselves, 'We have Abraham for our ancestor,' because your salvation will only come if you prove yourselves worthy!"

Listening to the sermon, and watching the crowd, it was clear that every person around us was caught up in John's spell. There were no priests here, no authorities, only common people of every variety. Many showed the unmistakable look of poverty, but that didn't matter to anyone in this crowd. Here, they all humbly joined together to form a community of spiritual bonds and hope.

"Now I offer you God's gift of baptism! Those who accept the Lord's blessing will find a path into the new tribe of Israel!"

John paused briefly to look over the multitudes, his coal-black eyes afire, then raised his voice to an even higher pitch.

"But know this! Baptism only prepares you for God's kingdom! It is not for the *remission* of sins, but for the *purification* of the body! Your salvation can only be earned through your good deeds! Go then, back to your homes, and bear good fruit, or the axe will fall on your roots and you will be cast into the fire!"

People embraced John's every word. No priest in Jerusalem could hope to earn such devotion. In my life, I only ever saw one person who was better at capturing the attention and moving the hearts of people. That was Yeshua, during his ministry.

Many in the crowd wept; not with fear, but joy. They had waited their whole lives for such a messenger from God. This was a message that touched their hearts and strengthened their love for the Lord. I had to admit, it touched my heart as well.

Salome turned to Yeshua and asked: "Do you think that he is right?"

He gave a solemn nod. "Yes. He describes what I also believe, but until today I never heard anyone put words to it so well."

"Then coming here was the right decision," James said.

I pointed to where John was walking toward the water's edge. "Look, people are gathering for the baptisms. Should we join them?"

"Yes," Yeshua said in a calm voice. "We should join them."

People waited patiently for their turn, talking quietly amongst themselves. There was a feeling of conversion and salvation in the air. For many, this would mark a new beginning in their lives.

When we reached the front of the line, Salome turned to us with a smile. "To atone for my earlier doubts, I shall go first."

James laughed. "You are forgiven. Now go, John waits for you."

Salome stepped out of her shoes, then walked to the water's edge. John took her by the hand and walked her slowly into the river. They stopped when the water level reached up to her waist. He supported her with one hand as she leaned backwards until she was immersed completely under the water's surface for a brief moment. John pulled Salome up to her feet and walked her back to shore. He then took James by the hand to walk him into the river.

Salome was soaking wet, water dripping from her robe, but smiling. "That wasn't bad," she said. "The water is cold, but nothing terrible."

When James returned, Yeshua kindly motioned for me to go next. John the Baptizer led me by the hand until we were waist deep, then pushed lightly on my chest. I was familiar with the ritual then, having seen it performed many times, and allowed myself to lean back and be submerged. My toes started to slip in the sandy mud, but John pulled me upright again. He was surprisingly strong for a man so thin and wiry. Where did he find the strength to perform this ritual with many hundreds of people every day, I wondered?

Once back on the river shore, I stood dripping wet beside Salome and James to watch Yeshua go through the ritual. His baptism took longer because, surprisingly, they stopped and exchanged some words while standing in the water. John had not spoken a word to me, nor to any other person before then. We were too far away on the shore to hear what was said between them.

"Oh, look!" a woman standing nearby cried out with delight.

I followed her gaze upward and watched a white dove flying away. It had been flying low, then rose high into the sky.

Yeshua said nothing when he returned to us, but he looked at peace. We were all feeling more at peace. Someone had built a fire some distance away, and we walked there to warm ourselves. The heat of the fire would also dry our clothes a bit faster. The dry summer season would begin in a month, but for now, the air was chilly as late afternoon turned to early evening.

Small groups of people camped for the night near the river. John had many loyal followers and disciples who stayed with him year-round. We settled down near one of the campfires for a simple meal of bread, cheese, and wine. There was much to think about and talk about.

"John preaches of the coming of the reign of God," Yeshua said. "It will happen soon, but only if we prepare the way properly. This is what I have also believed for a long time."

I tipped my head to him. "This is something you have talked about since you were a young man."

"But what does that mean, to prepare the way properly?" Salome asked.

"It means to have a spiritual renewal of our people," Yeshua said in a solemn tone. "People are suffering terribly, but the Temple rituals of atonement are not helping them at all. Nothing changes, and suffering continues."

"The offerings and sacrifices make the Temple wealthy," I said. "The money paid to the Temple makes the High Priest obscenely wealthy. But the common people still live in poverty and despair."

James said: "We are God's chosen people, but look at us now! John tells us that our covenant with God has been broken, and that it must be renewed. But *can* it be renewed?"

Two men approached our fire, shyly and almost apologetically. They had been sitting nearby and overheard our talk.

"May we join you?" the older one asked. He was a man of middle age, with a stocky build and reddish-brown curly hair. "We are both disciples of John, and your conversation is very interesting."

"Of course, please join us," Yeshua said. "We have little wine left to share with you, unfortunately."

The man dismissed the comment with a casual wave of his hand. "We drank enough wine. My name is Philip of Bethsaida. We wish to enjoy your company, not drink your wine."

"I am Matthias, also from Bethsaida," the younger man said. He was thin, and perhaps twenty years younger than his companion. "I can tell from your accent that you are all from central Galilee, yes?"

Salome chuckled. "Is our accent so strong? But you are right. We're from Nazareth."

"Ah, Nazareth," Philip said. He opened his mouth as if to say more, then smiled and remained silent.

"Have you been to Nazareth?" James asked.

Philip shook his head. "No, I have not yet had the pleasure. But to answer your earlier question, young man — yes, it is entirely possible for the people of Israel to renew our covenant with God."

"How can you be so sure?" asked Salome, doubtful. "It seems to me that it would take a miracle."

Matthias answered her. "We are certain of it because John tells us so. John is a prophet; I know it in my heart. He speaks with the voice of God."

"Is John a priest?" James asked.

"No one really knows," Philip said. "He does not tell us where he comes from, or from what family. John is, simply, John."

"It doesn't matter where he comes from," Matthias added. "We accept him as a messenger from God. When he plunges us into the living waters of the Jordan River, we accept his call to become part of the renewal of Israel."

Philip said: "Over the past year, many thousands of people have also accepted the call. We are the new Israel." He paused and glanced at James. "We are the people of Israel who will renew our covenant with God."

Salome still looked skeptical. "It takes powerful faith to believe that a stranger who was living in the desert can do such a thing. Does John the Baptizer have the power to offer purification and salvation to our people and renew our covenant with God?"

Philip and Matthias remained silent, but Yeshua answered her.

"No, John has no such power. But it's not John the Baptizer who offers purification through baptism to prepare the way for the reign of God."

"What do you mean, Brother?" Salome asked.

"God Almighty offers us purification through baptism," Yeshua said. "God is doing these works through John the Baptizer. John is only a vessel. He is God's mediator."

"Ah, I understand," Salome said.

Philip, who had been studying Yeshua, addressed him with a look of respect and admiration: "You understand perfectly."

The young Matthias, face glowing with excitement, followed his lead. "Not only that, but *you* understand immediately what, for many of us, takes weeks and months to understand."

"My brother is very wise in the ways of the Lord," James said with a proud tone.

I added: "Yes, I agree. This has been true of Yeshua ever since he was a boy."

"Then, will you join us in doing the Lord's work?" Philip asked him. "Nothing is more important!"

Although John's disciples were eager to hear his answer, Yeshua paused in thought. This was not a decision to be made lightly. He was the head of his family, and that entailed heavy responsibilities. When we left Nazareth, he had no intention of making any such life-changing decisions. He gazed first at Salome and studied her face, then at James. They returned his gaze calmly and waited for him to speak.

"I know how important it is to do the Lord's work," Yeshua said. "This is a big decision, however. It deserves thought, reflection, and prayer. I will not give you an answer tonight."

"Of course," Philip said respectfully. "Surely this is not a matter to be decided hastily. We leave you in peace now, Yeshua, but please give it proper consideration."

The two disciples of John stood up, said their farewells in a humble manner, and took their leave.

Salome gave a sigh. "Ah, Yeshua. I think I know which way your heart is leaning."

"Do you?"

"Yes, I do. *Emma* knows you best, and she always said that one day you would follow your mission to serve the Lord."

James said: "I agree with Salome, and with Mother. Your mission in life is greater than being the head of our family. I have thought so since I was a boy."

Yeshua acknowledged their show of faith with a grateful nod. Even so, it would pain him to leave his family in Nazareth, although they were now all grown adults and capable of managing their own lives.

"And what about you, David?" he asked. "You look like you have something to say."

I gave him the most honest answer I could. "I think that you already know what to do. I think you have always known."

The next morning, James, Salome, and I ate a sparse breakfast before starting our trip back to Nazareth. Yeshua had gone for a walk along the riverside. We ate in silence, enjoying the warm sun and mild breeze of a pleasant spring day.

"Here comes Yeshua now," James said. "Judging from his stride, I would say that he's made a decision."

Salome laughed. "Yes, that's his determined look. I would know that walk anywhere."

He greeted us with a resolute expression and gave us the news we all expected to hear.

"I will stay here and join in doing God's work. I will baptize people alongside John. His disciples are right — nothing is more important."

"How long will you be doing this?" Salome asked.

"For as long as needed, Sister. The reign of God is near, I am sure of it. I will do everything in my power to prepare the way."

James placed a hand on his shoulder. "I commend you, Brother. You are truly doing God's work. I will tell the people back home about what you are doing here."

Yeshua looked him in the eye. "While I am here, *you* will be the head of the family. You are wise and fair, and have good judgement."

"I'm humbled to know that you think so," James replied. "I accept this responsibility."

We gathered our things and prepared to leave. An early morning start was best. It would take us four days to walk to Nazareth, or longer if the weather turned rainy.

"You have waited a long time for this day to come," I told Yeshua as we bid farewell.

"I have, truly." He looked at me directly and added: "You asked me, more than once, why did I not take a wife?"

"Yes. And you were never quite certain of the reason why."

"This is the reason why," Yeshua said. "It's not because I disapprove of marriage, and not because I did not wish for a family. It's because I could not take a wife, or do any other such thing, that would place a burden before my service to the coming reign of God."

"I understand. You listen to the voice of Father God, and do as He wishes. This is something you have always done."

"It's what we all must do," he said.

"You are right," I replied. "However, the Lord speaks to some more powerfully than to others. And clearly, Yeshua, in this you are truly blessed. God Almighty speaks to you with a very powerful voice."

Salome said: "Let's be off. Be well, Brother. And be careful of the soldiers of Antipas. They are here for a reason, and not one that would be to your benefit."

"Have a safe and pleasant trip," Yeshua said. "And don't worry, no harm will come to me. I do not fear Herod Antipas and his soldiers. I serve a much greater power."

Chapter 13

Return to Nazareth

Nazareth, Summer 28 C.E.

G rapes were ripening quickly in the late summer. Once again, Clopas relied on the kindness of relatives and neighbors to help him harvest the fruit of his vineyard. Birds of all kinds were voracious in picking away at the ripe black grapes, round, sweet, and plump with juice. The children of the village loved them as well and were eager and excited to help with the grape harvest.

My family, six of us including the children, picked grapes for two days straight. We enjoyed the bright sunshine and light breezes, and the delicious aroma of ripe grapes on the vine. We worked beside Mary and her children, and her children's children. All except Salome were married, with children of their own. Yeshua was still away on his mission along the Jordan River, giving sermons and baptizing people alongside John the Baptizer and his followers.

At the end of the second day, the grape harvest was completed. We were all tired but happy with the fruits of our labor. Each family received enough table grapes to last for a week or longer, along with clay jars of grape juice. Gifts of wine would come later in the season. Clopas and Mary were generous to those who helped with the harvest.

"The Lord blessed me with another good harvest," Clopas said with a happy smile as he joined our table. We were in the middle of our evening meal on the shared patio in front of our houses. Mary shared our table, along with Salome, James and Kitra and their family, and our neighbors from down the street, Oren and Liva.

"You are blessed in many ways, Clopas," Mary said. "Your family are all healthy and prospering, and your vineyard grows the best grapes in Nazareth."

James said: "That is true. Have you thought about planting more vines, Uncle?"

Clopas clapped him on the shoulder. "Buy some land next to mine, and we can extend my vineyard to your land and work it together, eh?"

Kitra laughed and shook her head. "If only we could! But James has enough work on our own farm, small as it is, along with his carpentry work."

"I thank you for your kind offer, Uncle Clopas," James said. He turned to our elderly neighbor, Oren. "Is this something that Avner might be interested in, I wonder?"

"Ah, my son will never work as a farmer again," Oren replied. "He is nearly finished with his priestly studies in Jerusalem."

Liva, the wife of Oren, beamed with motherly pride. "Avner will be a wonderful Pharisee priest! I am certain of it." She shot Mary a glance. "He is blessed with a passion to serve the Lord, just like Yeshua."

Salome said: "Yes, but they show their love for God in different ways. Yeshua has no wish to become a priest."

Liva shook her head with a look of disapproval. "That is a shame. He could be doing God's work in Jerusalem, like my Avner, instead of wasting his time with that troublemaker, John the Baptizer."

Salome opened her mouth to protest, but Mary silenced her with a gentle touch of her hand.

"Yeshua is not wasting his time," Mary said calmly. "He is serving the Lord in the way that he knows best."

Liva turned to her husband for support. "We have talked about this before. Is Yeshua on the right path to serve God Almighty?"

"Some say there are different ways to serve the Lord," Oren said. "I don't know if that is true, or whether Yeshua follows the true path. But Avner knows what I believe, and he honors my wishes."

Clopas' face flushed red. "Then Avner is being a loyal and dutiful son, Oren. But don't presume to judge how another man chooses to show his devotion to the Lord."

We were interrupted by a young man's voice approaching in the darkness, laughing good-naturedly. "How did my name get involved in this discussion?"

"Avner!" Liva cried and quickly rose to embrace her son. "Welcome home. But I expected you yesterday!"

"I'm sorry to disappoint you, *Emma*," the young man said. "There was a disturbance near Jericho, and it delayed me on my trip."

His father raised an eyebrow. "What kind of disturbance?"

Avner looked around at the people sitting at the table before he answered. His eyes finally rested on Mary.

"The rebel John the Baptizer was arrested by soldiers of Herod."

Salome gave a soft gasp. James became tense. There was a flash of concern in Mary's eyes, but her face and her voice remained calm.

Mary asked: "Were other people arrested? Did you happen to see Yeshua there?"

"Only John was arrested, from what I heard," Avner said. "I have no news about Yeshua, I'm sorry to say."

This news of the arrest did not surprise me, but it was nonetheless troubling.

"What was the reason for John being arrested?" I asked.

Avner shrugged. "No one knows. Many reasons, I expect. John had been speaking out bitterly against Antipas for a long time. He often complained about Herod's sinful marriage to his brother's wife."

"He calls him an immoral and unjust ruler," James said.

Mary, the wife of Clopas, scoffed. "John only speaks the truth. Herod Antipas *is* an immoral and unjust ruler."

Oren shook his head. "But is it wise to call him that publicly in front of large crowds of people?"

"I don't care about John or Herod!" Salome cried out impatiently. She turned to Avner sharply. "I only care about my brother. What were John's followers doing when you passed through there?"

"Most are confused, discouraged," Avner said. "John was their leader, and tonight he sleeps in Herod's dungeon."

"If he's still alive," Clopas said.

Mary said: "No, I don't think that John is dead. Antipas had John arrested, not killed. There must be a reason why he wanted to make him a prisoner, rather than have him killed on the spot."

"Some priests in Jerusalem believe that Antipas is afraid of John," Avner explained, finally sitting down and pouring himself a cup of wine. "He thinks that John might be the prophet Ezekiel, come back to life. Even some of his own soldiers flocked to John to be baptized."

"He has reason to worry," I said. "John has thousands of followers, and his flock kept growing."

"That must be the reason why he was arrested," James said. "Herod is afraid that John was gaining enough followers to start a revolt."

"It always happens this way," Oren grumbled and threw up his hands. "Every generation, there is a Jew who becomes popular enough to start a revolt against the Jewish authorities and the Romans."

"And then the authorities and their armies crush them," Leila said. She glanced at me as she finished her sentence, and I felt the familiar stab of pain in my heart. Leila was not to blame for that; it was simply a reaction I could not control when I thought about my father.

"Yeshua is not someone who starts revolts," I said. "He's also smart and resourceful. He will take care of himself, and do what is right."

"Yes," Mary agreed. "He will know what is the best thing to do."

"Which is to come home, I pray!" Salome exclaimed.

"Yeshua will come home when he's ready," James said. "All we can do is to be patient and let him do the Lord's work."

One week later, Dalia walked in through the door with a smile on her face. "Yeshua is back!"

"What?" Leila asked. "Did you see him?"

"Yes, *Emma*. He just arrived. He's at Mary's house."

Leila gave me a look. "Should we go see him? Or give them some time to talk first?"

"I'm going to see him now," I said, heading for the door.

"Wait for me!" she said with a laugh. "I'm just as curious as you."

It's a very short walk to our neighbor's house, and we were there in a few moments. Yeshua was talking to Mary and Salome. He greeted us with a nod, then continued.

"All the soldiers of Antipas left once they took John away. Many of his followers became afraid and returned to their villages. I stayed for a few more days to baptize people. Then people stopped coming, and there was no reason for me to stay. I thought it best to come home."

"What will happen to John now?" Mary asked.

"No one knows," Yeshua said. "I think that Antipas is afraid to set him free, but he is also afraid to kill him."

"Does he worry that John's followers will start a revolt?" I asked.

"That seems very likely. Herod is a fearful man."

Leila shook her head, smiling at the irony. "If John is free, he might start a revolt. But if Antipas kills him, his angry followers might start a revolt then."

Yeshua nodded. "Exactly so."

"What now?" Salome asked.

"Now, little sister, I need to rest and think for a few days. Then I will make plans to start my own ministry."

Leila and Salome looked surprised; Mary did not. His statement was only a mild surprise to me, and only because it came so soon.

Salome said: "Your own ministry? But, why?"

"I am past the age of thirty, the legal age for a Jewish man to start a ministry. My time has come."

"That doesn't answer my question, Yeshua. Just because you *can* start a ministry doesn't mean that you *should* start a ministry."

Yeshua looked at his sister, his gaze calm but determined. "I will start my own ministry because this is what the Lord asks of me."

Salome gave a sigh, followed by a small nod of acceptance.

"You will rest tonight," Mary said. "We'll talk as a family tomorrow. Your brothers will be here then. Mary is in Kokhaba with her family, so we'll let her know that you're home."

"You are the voice of wisdom, as always," Yeshua told her with a smile. "Yes, we'll talk as a family tomorrow."

"You must have lost your mind!" Joses said loudly, his voice a near shout. The conversation was getting heated.

A small crowd of people gathered around the tables on the bare earth patio. The siblings James, Joses, Judah, Mary, and Shimon, and their spouses, sat at the tables or stood beside them. His mother Mary and sister Salome sat near Yeshua. Clopas and his wife Mary stood nearby. Simeon, the son of Clopas, stood near them, along with his brother James.

This was Yeshua's family. Leila and I were not family, but as friends and neighbors, we were welcomed to participate in the discussion. The reaction to Yeshua's announcement of his plans was very mixed, and very emotional.

"Be calm, Joses," James told him. "There is nothing crazy about starting a ministry in the service of God."

"Is that what you told John the Baptizer when you saw him?" Joses asked him. "Will you say that to him today, as he rots in the dungeon of Antipas?"

His sister, Mary, spoke up in agreement. "That is also my fear. It's simply too dangerous. Herod Antipas and the Romans execute those who cause trouble for them."

"You are right," Yeshua said. "There is a danger. But tell me this, Sister: should I abandon my devotion to God because I fear tyrants?"

Mary shook her head. "No. But we all fulfill our devotion to God in our own way. It does not require placing our lives at risk."

"I agree with Mary," said Shimon. "Consider this, Brother. You are now talking about leaving the family for good, not just for a few months baptizing people on the banks of the Jordan River. And worse, you put your life in danger. I don't see the wisdom in that."

"It is true, I am leaving the family. Some will say that I abandon my family duties," Yeshua said. "Yet even though you are the youngest, Shimon, you are no child. It is not abandoning you when you are able to manage your life without me."

"I *am* managing my life very well," Shimon said, sounding mildly hurt. "But know this. When you leave the family, you still abandon the family. You shame us all when you do that, my respected brother."

"James is the head of the family now," Yeshua replied. "Give your respect and loyalty to him."

His sister Mary said: "This is breaking all tradition. You understand this better than anyone, Yeshua. After *Abba* died, *you* taught us the rules for how a family should live."

"I did," he agreed. "The Law of Moses has not changed, and our rules for living are no different. There comes a time, however, when higher rules apply. Serving the Lord is more important than the rules for our family life."

"Yeshua is in the right," Clopas said. "Our devotion to God comes before our devotion to family."

Mary spoke next. She talked in a quiet but very solemn voice, and everyone gave her their full attention. "Let no one question Yeshua's love for our family. When Yosef died, he became head of the family at the age of sixteen. Let no one say that he has not done his duty to us. Our family has prospered under his guidance and love for us."

She looked around at the faces of her children. All were silent, but the respectful expressions on their faces left no doubt that all agreed with her. The only person in the family who commanded more respect than Yeshua was Mary.

"But today, times have changed," Mary continued. "Yeshua must follow the will of the Lord, as we all must. Let no one here challenge his right, or challenge the wisdom of his decision. Only Yeshua knows what path the Lord wishes him to follow."

Everyone around us became quiet and reflective. We all knew that Mary was right.

Two days later was the Sabbath day. All the men in the village gathered for synagogue, along with many of the women. The major news on everyone's mind, of course, was Yeshua and his plans for a ministry. The simple idea of a ministry was not upsetting, but what troubled many people was the notion that Yeshua's mission would be similar to that of John the Baptizer. Some strongly disagreed with John's radical ideas, and some were frightened by what he represented. The news of John's arrest frightened them even more.

The sermon was given by our neighbor, Oren. He told the story of the prophet Elijah and his contest with the priests of Baal to prove who was the one true God. We all laughed at the familiar story of how Elijah mocked the priests when their god did not answer their prayers to set fire to the sacrificial altar. Was Baal asleep, or perhaps busy relieving himself? Then Elijah built his own altar and had it soaked with water. He asked God to bring fire to it, and the Lord sent fire to consume the offering and the altar.

"And when the people saw that, they said, the Lord, he is God!" Oren said with a flourish. "And Elijah told them, seize the prophets of Baal and let no one escape! Then he took them all down by the river and slaughtered each of them."

Oren finished, then paused for a moment to look out over the faces of the congregation. His eyes rested on Yeshua, who was seated near the front of the crowd.

"The Lord is God," Oren said. "He is the only God. Some say there are many ways to worship the Lord, but I say no! There is only one proper way. The holy Scriptures provide us with very clear and strict laws for how we should do so."

He paused for a heartbeat, still looking at Yeshua. "When we go to the Temple of God, the good Temple priests, servants of God, provide us with the sacred rituals to seek purification and atonement. This is the only proper way, the only right path, to worship the Lord."

Other people followed Oren's gaze, and Yeshua became the center of everyone's attention. Some stared hard at him, which is always very rude behavior and inexcusable at synagogue. Yeshua maintained his composure through all of Oren's comments directed at him. His mother Mary, seated next to him, kept her calm poise.

One man stood up and addressed him. He was Simcha, a farmer from the east side of the village and a friend of Oren. "Will you follow the right path, Yeshua, when you preach to others on how to worship the Lord?"

"Of course I will," Yeshua replied. Then he also stood up to address the congregation.

"You all know me, neighbors and friends. Many of you have known me since I was a child. When have I ever *not* been proper and right in the worship of the Lord?"

"I knew the son of Yosef and Mary," an older woman said. "But are you the same man now, *Yeshua bar Yosef*? Or will you spread strange ideas that bring shame to your family?"

"Will you bring shame to Nazareth?" a man asked accusingly.

Their anger caught me by surprise. Perhaps Yeshua had the same reaction, but he did not show it.

"You must not worry about that," he told the woman patiently, and gave her a kind smile. "I will bring no trouble or shame to my family, or to you, or to anyone else in Nazareth."

Avner, the son of Oren, rose to his feet. "That's an easy thing for you to say, Yeshua! But if you challenge the authority of the Temple, you *will* bring misfortune to yourself. Some of that misfortune, I fear, will follow you to Nazareth."

"That is true," Simcha agreed. "We have seen it before. Don't bring the soldiers of Herod Antipas here! You put us all in peril!"

James had heard enough. He jumped to his feet.

"These are shameful accusations! Yeshua preaches no dangerous ideas. He puts no one here in danger!"

"These ideas are confusing to me," said Liva, the mother of Avner. "This reign of God that is coming soon, I don't understand what that is. My son tells me that the Temple priests consider it blasphemy."

A man sitting nearby nodded vigorously in agreement. "Preaching blasphemy will surely bring disaster to us. And not only from Herod, but also from God Almighty." He turned toward Yeshua with an angry look. "You will bring destruction to Nazareth!"

Tempers were getting much too heated. I stood and tried to calm the man down. "He will do no such thing, neighbor. Yeshua is a man of peace, as was Yosef before him. He is no troublemaker."

Oren gave me a scornful look. "*You*, of all people here, should know better. Tell him, David *bar* Matthias! Tell this preacher what happened to your father!"

I gave Oren a cold, icy stare. Violence would only worsen an already bad situation, I knew, so forced myself to stay calm and swallowed my anger. "Be respectful of my father's memory, Oren, or I warn you that you will regret it."

The older man bowed his head. "I did not wish to offend. Still, it would be far better for us if Yeshua did not start this ministry."

"I will follow the path that the Lord sets for me," Yeshua said in his surprisingly still calm voice. "Nothing will prevent me from doing so."

"Then do it somewhere else!" cried another woman. She was Zemira, the wife of Simcha. "And don't come back to Nazareth!"

Salome shot up, her face red with anger. "My brother will live and preach where he wishes! He belongs here just as much as you!"

Yeshua put a calming hand on her shoulder. "We should not argue with our neighbors, Sister. Let people say what is on their minds."

"Perhaps we should leave now," Mary said. "This is not the time or place for arguments."

Mary, the wife of Clopas, gave a sigh filled with frustration. "There is no good time or place for arguments with hotheads. But I agree, we should leave before we come to blows."

Yeshua looked around him and addressed the crowd. "I will speak with anyone in peace who wishes to speak with me. There is no cause for rancor, my friends. I will not bring trouble to Nazareth."

"Then go! And stay away!" a man replied. "Let us live our lives in peace!"

We left quietly after that. The anger toward Yeshua was shocking. At first, no one quite knew how to explain it. We walked in silence down the street.

"They are afraid," Mary said after a while. "They blame Yeshua for their fear, and then it turns to anger."

"Fear is the last thing I wish to bring them," Yeshua said. "God's message is one of faith and hope, and of love for all His children. My words are the way to God."

"But they won't hear that now," Clopas grumbled. "You heard them back there. Some of them, if they could, would kill you like a priest of Baal! Throw you off a cliff!"

Yeshua laughed softly. "Lucky for me, then, there are no cliffs in Nazareth."

"This is not a laughing matter, my son," said Mary. "Their fear and anger are real."

"I understand," he said. "But I will not start my ministry in Nazareth. I have thought about it and decided on a much better location from which to begin."

We all turned our heads to him, curious.

"Where?" Salome asked.

"Capernaum."

It took Yeshua only a few days to prepare for his departure. Matters of family business needed to be settled, and plans discussed with James for the family's future needs. Although we expected that Yeshua might visit from time to time, no one believed that he would return to live in Nazareth again. His new life of ministry would take him far and wide across Galilee, Judea, and other lands within his reach.

The evening before he left, we gathered for a farewell dinner in his honor. Mary and Asher came from Kokhaba, and brought five-year-old Saul with them. The young children, including Mary's grandchildren and those of Mary of Clopas, made a lively and playful racket while the adults sat down to talk.

"Capernaum is a very good choice," Clopas said casually. "It is five times larger than Nazareth, and much more prosperous. Its location on the north shore of Lake Kinneret is within easy walking distance to Chorazin and many other villages, and not too far from Bethsaida and Magdala."

"I'm glad to hear that you agree with my choice, Uncle," Yeshua said with a smile.

Clopas poured himself more wine and continued. "Further south of Magdala is Tiberias, but you don't want to go there."

"No!" young Shimon exclaimed with mock horror. "Stay far away from Antipas and his soldiers."

"The people I wish to see are not in Tiberias, or Sepphoris, or Sidon, or Tyre, or any of the large cities," Yeshua explained. "They live in the small villages, some even smaller than Nazareth. There is no shortage of those for me to visit."

"It sounds exciting," Salome said. "I wish that I could join you."

"Maybe one day you will," Yeshua said. "There is no reason why only men should serve in a ministry."

His sister Mary walked over and gave her brother a gentle embrace. When she pulled back, tears welled up in her eyes.

"Why do you cry for me, dear sister?" Yeshua asked in a soft tone.

Her hand went up to wipe a slow teardrop running down her cheek. "I'm afraid of what might happen," she said.

"What do you fear might happen?"

"I'm afraid for your life! You saw how some of our neighbors treated you at synagogue, and in the days since." Mary paused and frowned. "And these are the people who know you! It will be even worse when you talk to strangers in other places."

Yeshua shook his head. "No. There you are wrong. People in other villages will treat me better."

She gave him a doubting look. "I don't understand. Why would strangers treat you better than the people here?"

"Because no prophet is accepted or honored in his hometown."

Clopas chuckled, but young Mary still looked puzzled.

"What do you mean?"

"Here in Nazareth, I can only be Yeshua the carpenter, the son of Yosef and Mary," he explained. "My message is rejected and scorned by my neighbors, as you saw, because all they can see is Yeshua the carpenter. In other villages, people will see me for who I am."

Their mother Mary walked over to stand beside them. Her face was serenely calm and peaceful. She put a hand on her daughter's shoulder to comfort her, then looked into Yeshua's eyes.

"They will see you for who you are," Mary said. "You are a man of God. A messenger of God."

"Do *you* believe in my mission, *Emma*?" he asked.

"With all my heart. Since you were a child, you were always guided by what you believed that God Almighty wished for you to do. That will never change. I know that now. You were born for this, my son. Now is your time. Go on your mission with all my blessings."

Yeshua took her hand, raised it to his lips, and gave it a soft kiss. There was boundless affection in that kiss, and gratitude, and great joy at her sharing of his dreams. It touched him to the core, that was plain to see. Mary knew him best and shared his dreams completely. Over time, many others would come to share his vision and his dreams, but his mother was the first.

The next morning, at first light, Yeshua left Nazareth for the last time. He carried only a small cloth satchel that contained an extra shirt and a small bit of food. All parting gifts were politely refused, because he wished to travel light. He gave all his money to James to use for the family's needs.

"But what will you do for food on the road?" his aunt Mary worried. "Take a basket of food and a wineskin, at least!"

"The Lord will provide me with what I need on the road," Yeshua told her. "This is my new life. It is a simpler life."

"Trust in the Lord, as Yeshua trusts in Him," his mother said to Mary of Clopas. "The Eternal God watches over him."

The aunt smiled at both of them. "I see that I must do so. Very well, my nephew. The Lord guide you and protect you on your journey."

Mary told him: "When you arrive in Capernaum, go see my sister. She and your uncle Zebedee will be very happy to see you."

"Aunt Salome will be the first person I visit," Yeshua reassured her. "Then my cousins, who I haven't seen in many years. They are grown men now. I wonder if they will even recognize me?"

We kept our farewells very brief. Then Yeshua turned and began the long walk on the north road to Sepphoris. From Sepphoris, he would take a good road that went northeast to Capernaum.

Watching Yeshua walk the familiar road, in his relaxed but strident gait, brought back a flood of memories of the many hundreds of times we made that journey together. First with Yosef and Yeshua, and then with Yeshua and his brothers. The memories of Yosef and his many lessons were bittersweet. They were good memories, however, of a good man and a simpler time. They were memories worth keeping, of a man worth remembering.

Chapter 14

Capernaum

Nazareth, Galilee, Autumn 28 C.E.

Two weeks went by quickly, then three. Life in Nazareth settled into the familiar routines of the fall season. Olives and pomegranates reached their ripening seasons. We owned no olive groves, so the olive harvests required only a few days of labor here and there to help a neighbor in need. Our wheat fields would need little care until springtime. The same was true for Clopas and his vineyards.

One mild evening, the two Marys stopped by for a visit. Mary, the mother of Yeshua, and Mary, the wife of Clopas, were both in a happy mood. We exchanged pleasantries casually, but it was clear that they had news to share.

"Any news from Yeshua?" I asked, curious.

Mary, his mother, shook her head. "Not a word."

Leila raised an eyebrow. "Then why, may I ask, are you both looking so pleased?"

Mary of Clopas said cheerfully: "We're going to Capernaum to visit Yeshua. We want to see for ourselves what is happening there."

"That is good news," I said. "Did you come by just to tell us that?"

"We come to invite you to go with us," said Mary. "Do you want to go to Capernaum?"

Her offer was appealing. This was not a decision to be made hastily, however, because there were many things to consider. "How long do you plan to visit?" I asked.

"That depends on what we find when we get there," Mary said. "It may be a short visit, a week or two, or perhaps longer. Yeshua might need our help, or maybe not."

Mary of Clopas said: "But you can stay for as little or as long as you wish, of course."

"Who else is making the trip?" Leila wondered.

"My husband is coming, and our son James," said Mary of Clopas. "We'll make this like a holiday trip!"

"And Salome," Mary said. "She says she wants to keep me company and look after me, but I know she is very eager to see her brother on his ministry."

Leila caught my eye. We both knew what the other was thinking. She spoke first.

"Well, we can't take the children, and I can't leave them here for two or three weeks," she said. "Your work in the fields is done for a while. I know that you're very curious about Yeshua's ministry —"

"Oh, good!" exclaimed Mary of Clopas. "David will join us, then. It's too bad that you both can't make the trip."

Leila smiled at her enthusiasm. "David can go, not me."

"I won't be gone longer than three weeks," I promised. "But I am very eager to see what Yeshua is doing in Capernaum."

Capernaum, Galilee, Autumn 28 C.E.

From Sepphoris, we took the road that headed northeast to Magdala. That large village is located on the western bank of Lake Kinneret, which the Romans call the Sea of Galilee. From there, we travelled north along the lakeshore to Capernaum, located on the northwestern side of the lake.

We avoided Tiberias, to the south of Magdala, because we had no wish to go near the home city of Herod Antipas. That was the home of the Jewish ruling class of Galilee, the very wealthy nobles and political and military leaders who worked in partnership with the Romans.

The walk from Nazareth was very long, but pleasant. The heat of summer gave way to the more temperate days of September. It was not yet the rainy season, so the roads were dry. All along our travel route, the land was green, beautiful, and scenic. There was plenty of fresh food to purchase in the villages. Mary of Clopas packed enough food to last us for three days, which Clopas carried on his pack donkey, but even that food supply was not necessary.

Lake Kinneret is a freshwater lake about thirteen miles long and eight miles wide. The land on the western side is rich and fertile, and crops and orchards are plentiful: wheat, barley, olive groves, fruit trees, and vineyards. The lake is well stocked with fish, and particularly abundant in the northern areas around Capernaum and Bethsaida.

As we approached Capernaum, it was plain to see that we were coming to a small city, not a village. The road was busy with carts pulled by horses, mules, and oxen, and with streams of travelers on foot, like us. In the distance, we could see small fishing boats going out on the lake, or returning to shore with their catch. The best fishing was done at night, but many preferred the convenience of daytime work.

The houses of Capernaum were built small and sturdy. They appeared crowded with people, some looking out on the street from windows or doorways. Most were one-story houses, the same as in Nazareth, but here and there one could see a few two-story houses.

"Do you remember where the house is?" Mary of Clopas asked. "My memory is foggy, and all these streets look the same to me."

"Of course I remember where my sister lives," Mary said with a laugh. "You're just not used to city streets."

Unlike our hometown, the streets were bustling with people. While Nazareth was a village of three hundred people, Capernaum was home to over fifteen hundred. That is what brought Yeshua there.

The house of Zebedee was a two-story house built of stone, which came as a mild surprise. Twenty years earlier, he moved his family to Capernaum with very little money in search of a better job. He turned his fishing boats into a prosperous business, it seemed.

The man of the house was not at home, but Salome greeted us at the door with unrestrained joy. She exchanged hugs with the two Marys, then gave an even fiercer hug to her niece Salome. The three men were welcomed with a smile: Clopas, his son James, and me. We were ushered into the comfortable first floor room of the house and offered refreshments to quench our thirst.

Even more than the refreshing cups of cool lemon water, we most welcomed the comfortable chairs and a soft couch. After several days of walking on hard and dusty roads in our leather sandals, legs and feet were sore and simple rest was a blessing.

"James and John are on the fishing boats, along with their father," Salome told us. "They'll stop their work later in the afternoon, because they want to attend Yeshua's sermon today."

Clopas looked at her in surprise. "Zebedee is still working on the fishing boats, you say? The man is pushing fifty years old!"

"Yes, he took up the work again in the last few weeks," Salome said. She caught Mary's eye. "He's not very happy with our sons right now, and I'm afraid that Yeshua is to blame for that."

Mary seemed startled by this news. "What do you mean? How is Yeshua at fault?"

"Yeshua is very active in his ministry. He's doing very well," Salome continued. "However, he convinced his cousins to join him. Now they would rather be with him than go out on the lake to fish."

"Oh, Sister," Mary said. "I don't know what to say. But James and John are both grown men. They make their own decisions."

"Of course! And I don't complain about that," Salome explained. "I'm happy to see them working alongside Yeshua in the service of God. But do you see the problem? This leaves Zebedee short of help. This morning he had to beg his own sons to help him on the boat!"

Clopas gave a grunt. "Sounds like he needs to hire more help, then? That would solve the problem."

"He's trying his best to hire and train new helpers," Salome said with a frustrated sigh. She eyed James and smiled. "Young men who are good workers, like you, James!"

The young James held up both hands defensively and laughed. "Not me! I'm not made to be a fishing boat worker, as you can see. But I would be interested in working with Yeshua, perhaps?"

We all smiled or laughed at his comment. James was just past twenty years of age, but still quite thin. He was not strong enough for the arduous physical labor required on a fishing boat. His character was mild and thoughtful, which was better suited for ministry work.

Young Salome grew impatient. "Ah, Uncle Zebedee will find new workers. I want to know more about what my brother is doing."

"You can see for yourself in a few hours," her aunt Salome replied. "Yeshua is giving a sermon at the house where we meet for synagogue. Fifty or more people come to listen to him every time he speaks."

"Then Yeshua is doing very well," I said, pleased to hear that news. "In Sepphoris, only the good speakers draw that kind of crowd unless the sermon is on the Sabbath."

Mary smiled at that. "It will take some time for his name to grow. These are the first small steps in building a ministry."

"Very true," said Mary of Clopas. "But tell me, Salome, how are James and John helping him?"

"They also talk to people about the ministry," said Salome. "They are Yeshua's disciples, along with two men from Bethsaida."

"From Bethsaida?" young Salome asked. She shot me a questioning glance. "Those two men we met at the Jordan River, the disciples of John the Baptizer. Weren't they from Bethsaida?"

"Yes, I think so. Philip and Matthias."

Salome of Zebedee shook her head. "No, these two men are called Peter and Andrew. They are brothers. They will be at the sermon also, along with my James and John. You will meet them then."

Mary gave her a sublime smile. "This is why we came, Sister. Your kind hospitality is a blessing, as always. Now let's rest for a bit, then we'll go to hear Yeshua give a sermon."

We were greeted outside the synagogue house by James and John, along with their father, Zebedee. They were still dressed in their fishing clothes and carrying the strong pungent smell of freshly caught fish. Nobody cared about that, least of all these young men.

"Yeshua is doing God's work, truly," James told Mary in a reverent tone. "Capernaum has never seen a minister like him."

"We're blessed to work by his side," John added. "His life is entirely devoted in service to God Almighty. And now, I'm happy to say, my life is as well."

I had not seen them in many years, and barely recognized them now as fully grown men in their middle twenties. Both were built wide across the chest and shoulders, with legs and arms strengthened by years of demanding physical labor. They had black hair, cut short, and hazel eyes sparkling with energy. They were both born with passionate temperaments, and that part of their characters would never change. They were quick in temper and given to quarreling.

"I'm very pleased to hear that," Mary replied. "The Lord will bless you both beyond measure for the work you are doing."

Zebedee walked up to stand beside Salome. "Our sons have our blessings, as well. A wonderful thing is happening here since Yeshua arrived in Capernaum, Mary."

"That's what we came to see," Mary said. "But where is Yeshua?"

"He's inside the house, greeting people," John said. "Come, I will take you to him. All of you, come inside!"

The one-room house was longer and wider than most houses, built to hold a large number of people for synagogue. It was half full when we arrived, with perhaps forty people in attendance. More people gradually drifted in behind us.

We saw Yeshua standing at the far end of the room, which would be the speaker's place once people were seated. He greeted people cheerfully as they walked up to greet him. Each one received his kind attention in equal measure: young and old, firm and infirm, dressed well or poorly dressed. This was the Yeshua we knew well, who treated everyone with the same acceptance, respect, and affection. The very kind boy had grown into a very kind man.

Standing close to Yeshua, and also greeting people, were two men who bore enough resemblance to be brothers. The older of the two was about the same age as Yeshua. He was of medium stature, with a sinewy build. His dark brown hair flowed down to his shoulders. Even from that far distance, his piercing iron-gray eyes gave him an intense look, almost fierce.

James of Zebedee noticed my gaze. "That's Simon, but Yeshua calls him Peter, his rock," he explained with a grin. "The man beside him is Andrew, his brother. We are all Yeshua's disciples."

I acknowledged him with a nod. Andrew was perhaps two or three years younger, with the same sinewy build. His light brown hair also fell down to his shoulders. His facial features and dark brown eyes looked softer and less fierce than his brother's. He looked, at first glance, to have a gentler disposition.

Yeshua saw us and promptly walked over to meet us. He greeted his mother and sister with joy, then each of the others with heartfelt smiles. He looked to be in very good spirits, but there was something more. Something about him felt different. His presence felt different.

It took a moment of observation, and then it hit me. Yeshua was the focus of everyone in the room. He had a commanding presence about him that filled the room, felt but unspoken. What made it more impressive was that this did not happen through any effort of his own to make it so. It was spontaneous, natural, unaffected.

This could never happen in Nazareth, his hometown, I knew. It was a new day for him and for us all. Yeshua's life was no longer bound to Nazareth.

"These men are my disciples, Peter and Andrew," he introduced the two men who joined us. "They were fishermen, like my cousins, but now they devote themselves to a much greater mission."

"We are now fishermen of men, not fish," said Andrew with a smile. "We follow the true path to God."

Peter took Mary's hand and gently kissed it. "Blessed are you among all mothers, for you brought Yeshua to us."

Mary looked pleased but also very surprised by this attention. It was something new and unexpected for her.

"We are all blessed, Peter," she replied. "And we must do all that we can to lead our people on the path to God."

"We're doing much already," Yeshua said. "Now, wait for me here until I finish the sermon. The congregation is ready for me to start."

"My words are the way to God," Yeshua began. "I tell you truly, the reign of God is near! Rejoice! Father God is a loving God. He is not an angry and vengeful God. He will wash away the evil in this world and relieve the suffering of His children."

"The first commandment from God is this: you shall love the Lord your God with all your heart, and with all your soul, and with all your strength. And the second is this: love your neighbor as yourself. There is no other commandment greater than these!"

"The Law of Moses teaches us how to be pure, and we must obey God's commandments. But the word of God equally teaches us to be loving," he said with a tone of patient and gentle assurance. "Both are demanded of us if we are to be worthy of salvation in the eyes of God. This is how we prepare the path to God's reign."

Yeshua spoke in a clear and calm voice that filled the room. When John the Baptizer preached to a crowd, he was loud and strident, even harsh and angry at times. Yeshua, in contrast, was calm, reassuring, and comforting. His voice was soothing, and the effect was plain to see in the faces of the people listening to him.

"Prepare for God's reign by purifying your body through baptism, and by your good behavior in how you worship the Lord and how you treat others." He paused for a moment, and his eyes scanned over the crowd to make sure he had their full attention for what came next.

"Baptism is the first step, but it is *not* enough. Repentance for your sins does not come from baptism alone, but comes only through your good behavior. I tell you, be the tree that bears good fruit if you wish to be worthy in the eyes of God!"

This was different from what people were used to hearing about repentance from the Temple priests. The priests demanded offerings and sacrifices for atonement that must be performed at the Temple. Still, many of the people listening nodded in silent agreement. What Yeshua said next was even more surprising and, to some, shocking.

"Purification and repentance do not require blood sacrifices. We are not meant to make blood sacrifices to please the Lord."

A few people looked skeptical, but all continued to listen. No one challenged Yeshua on these new ideas. He was not preaching to them as a religious scholar would, quoting passages from Scripture, but was speaking straight from the heart.

"Rejoice in the coming kingdom of God! Blessed are you who are poor, because yours is God's reign! Blessed are you who are hungry, because you'll be full! Blessed are you who mourn, because you'll be comforted!"

"Love your enemies and pray for those who persecute you. You'll become children of your Father, who makes the sun rise on those who are evil *and* those who are good, and sends rain on those who are just *and* those who are unjust."

These were more teachings that did not come from the familiar priestly sermons, but from Yeshua himself. He was not quoting some other religious authority. Yeshua was his own authority. He continued.

"When someone slaps you on the cheek, offer the other one too. When someone asks you for your shirt, give them your coat too. When someone makes you go one mile, go an extra mile. Give to everyone who asks you. And when someone borrows your things, don't ask for them back."

The room was very quiet except for the sound of Yeshua's voice. People listened carefully, some struggling perhaps to understand the deeper meanings of his message.

"Treat people how you want them to treat you. If you love only those who love you, why should you be rewarded? Don't even the tax collectors do that? Be merciful, just like your Father."

"If your brother offends you, correct him. If he changes, forgive him. Even if he offends you seven times a day, then forgive him seven times!"

"Don't judge, and you won't be judged, because you'll be judged the way that you judge. And you'll be measured the way that you measure."

"These are the things that God Almighty asks of us. Rejoice and be glad, because your heavenly reward is great!"

Yeshua finished speaking, and for a short while the room remained silent. Many people looked deep in thought. Some were enchanted, gazing at him with adoration. Yeshua remained standing and looked over the assembly with a serene and loving expression. He was doing exactly what he wished and looked very pleased with the results.

Over the following months, this became a familiar scene of people listening and reacting to Yeshua's sermons. He spoke with honesty and passion that no Temple priest could match. He spoke well with words, but also with his hands, his facial expressions, and with his eyes.

The common people of Galilee listened to him as one of them, because he *was* one of them. His lessons did not come from a book, but from his own life. They listened, and contemplated, and believed.

After the sermon, Salome of Zebedee and the other women prepared the evening meal at her house. The men gathered around tables on a patio paved with stone. Signs of Zebedee's more than modest wealth showed in his choice of furniture, finely crafted wooden tables and chairs instead of the familiar roughhewn benches we used at home.

Yeshua was in a happy mood as the wine cups were filled, drained, and filled again. He greatly enjoyed a gathering with family and friends, with ample good food and plenty of good wine.

Clopas raised his wine cup in a toast to Yeshua, who was seated flanked by his disciples James, John, Peter, and Andrew.

"Now there is a sermon I never heard at synagogue in Nazareth. It is a new kind of sermon."

"What do you mean, Uncle?" Yeshua asked.

The older man paused for a moment to reflect. "You don't talk like the old prophets. They frightened people with stories about the wrath of God. Your message is quite different. This is a new kind of teaching."

Zebedee said: "I agree. I see this at every sermon now, Yeshua. You don't frighten people, but instead you" — he searched for the right word — "you *enchant* them with stories of a loving God."

"I don't wish to frighten people," Yeshua said. "God's word is the love that He shows for all His children. The Lord's commandment is that we love God, and that we love one another."

I said: "When we listened to John the Baptizer on the banks of the Jordan, he sounded very much like an old-time prophet. But that is not your message."

"Yeshua is a different kind of prophet," Peter said firmly. "He brings a different message to guide us to God's kingdom."

"Oh, is Yeshua a prophet now?" Clopas asked good-naturedly.

"I am what I am," Yeshua replied. "I am God's messenger."

Zebedee frowned. "Be cautious about what you call yourself, Nephew. Some people will attack you for the things you say."

James, the son of Zebedee, gave his father a defiant look. "Should we hide the truth because people might feel offended? I say no!"

John and Andrew nodded in agreement. Peter smiled at James' fierce declaration of faith and loyalty. The younger James, the son of Clopas, also smiled to show that he agreed.

Yeshua raised his hand for calmness. "Brothers, let's not argue with one another. Soon we will go out and preach the word of God to God's children, and each one of them will receive us in their own way."

The women brought the food to the tables, and we settled in for our meal. Mary sat next to her son, still full of joy at seeing him again. Salome of Zebedee and Mary of Clopas joined their husbands. Young Salome found a seat beside me, eager to join the discussion.

"I heard what you said before, about John the Baptizer," she said to me. "He sounded like Elijah from Scripture. Yeshua is not the same."

"No, he's not," I said. "Yeshua sounds like Yeshua, not like anybody else. No different from the Yeshua I've known since he was a child."

Mary looked up with a pleasant smile. "You're right. Now the time is here for other people to know him."

"Truly, Yeshua, the people listening to you today were very eager to hear you," Mary of Clopas said. "You touched their heats."

"Should that surprise us?" Yeshua asked. "I only described to them what is already in their hearts. The Lord is already in their hearts. I teach people how to repent and prepare themselves for God's reign. Are these not things we have all been praying for?"

Salome of Zebedee gave him a solemn look. "Yes, these are things that we know as true in our hearts. But they don't come from books, or from priests. They come from you."

"*This* is why we join Yeshua in his ministry," Peter said.

"Exactly so, Brother," Andrew said. "We do what the Pharisees and Sadducees cannot do. Let them go on taking money from poor people for rites of purification and repentance, while *we* do the Lord's work freely with people who suffer and need God's mercy the most."

"Amen," said Yeshua in a serious tone.

James, the son of Clopas, turned to him with a look of affection close to reverence. "When will you go out to other villages and towns to spread your mission?"

"Very soon," Yeshua replied. "But first, we must gather many more followers to help us spread the word."

James looked eager to say something, but Salome interrupted.

"Oh, look! We have visitors! And I know one of them."

Two men approached the table, looking tired and road weary. One was a familiar, stocky, middle-aged man with curly reddish-brown hair. The other one looked to be a few years younger, but with the same stocky build. Yeshua stood up from the table to greet them.

"Philip! I am glad to see you."

"I am happy to see you again, Yeshua," Philip said. "This is my good friend, Nathanael Bartholomew."

"Welcome, Bartholomew," Yeshua said pleasantly. "I am thankful that you could join us."

"Peace to you, Yeshua," Bartholomew said. "I'm very grateful that you would accept me to help in doing the work of the Lord."

Philip said: "We've just arrived, thankfully before night fell. Could we bother you for a cup of wine? It's a long walk from Bethsaida."

"Come! Sit! Dine with us," Yeshua invited them.

"I remember you, and your friend Matthias," Salome said to Philip after the men were seated. "Did he not come with you?"

"Mathias will join us in a few weeks," Philip explained. "Until then, he will be very busy with his family's olive harvest."

"Then he will join us when he's ready," Yeshua said. "More people are coming to join us every day."

The young James shot a quick glance at his parents, Clopas and Mary, then addressed himself to Yeshua in a serious tone.

"I wish to join your ministry, if you will accept me. I believe with all my heart that your teachings are the true path to God. I wish to serve the Lord at your side."

"Then I welcome you, James," Yeshua told him in a voice just as serious. "You are my cousin, but now you are also my brother."

James beamed with pride. Clopas and Mary, although surprised by this unexpected announcement, gave their approval with their eyes.

John, the son of Zebedee, enthusiastically slapped James on the back. "Now you're one of us!"

"We are asking men in town to join us," Peter said. "You can help us with that, James."

"Are you asking women to join you and become disciples, as well?" the young Salome wondered.

Peter looked uncertain, but Yeshua answered instead.

"Yes, Sister. We welcome everyone who wishes to do God's work. Will you also join us?"

"I will," Salome replied without hesitation.

Mary of Clopas turned to Mary with a smile. "My goodness, it might be a lonely walk back to Nazareth!"

"God's will be done," Mary replied. "I think I will stay in Capernaum for a while longer, myself."

"Then I will stay, as well," said Mary of Clopas.

"Ah, that brings me joy!" Yeshua said.

"And you, David?" Clopas asked. "What are your plans? Am I to walk back to Nazareth by myself?"

Yeshua gave me a questioning look. I gave him an honest answer.

"In time, I hope to join your ministry, but not today. Family duties wait for me in Nazareth, and I must leave soon."

He gave a nod. "I understand. In time, perhaps that will change."

Chapter 15

Miracles

Capernaum, Autumn 28 C.E.

Y eshua spent most of his days talking to people in the city, or walking in the surrounding areas around Lake Kinneret with some of his disciples. On most days, his mother Mary and his sister Salome, along with his aunt Mary of Clopas, accompanied him on his walks. It was much easier for the women to approach other women to talk with them, as it was more acceptable for the men to approach other men. Yeshua had a gift for talking to men, women, and children with equal ease.

The group of disciples devoted to Yeshua's ministry soon grew to over forty. Most were men, but also a good number were women. His closest disciples were Peter and Andrew, the sons of Jonas, James and John, the sons of Zebedee, Philip and Bartholomew from Bethsaida, and James, the son of Clopas. All travelled with the group and attended Yeshua's talks and sermons, then afterwards talked with people who wished to join the ministry.

On the Sabbath day, a large group of one hundred people crowded into the synagogue house to hear Yeshua's sermon. Each was greeted warmly as they arrived, by Yeshua or one of the disciples. I was glad to see that the young people, Salome and her cousin James, the son of Clopas, were eagerly greeting people along with the older disciples.

I sat with the older relatives: Mary, Clopas and his wife Mary, and Zebedee and his wife Salome. We sat near the back of the room for this service, so that new arrivals who wished to hear Yeshua could sit closer and be able to see and hear him better.

As always, the service opened with a prayer. Yeshua then faced the congregation that was eagerly waiting to hear him. Some had attended services before, but many in the crowd were new faces.

A young woman sitting in the front was nervously fretting with her hands. Yeshua noticed her anxious face and walked up to her.

"What troubles you so fiercely, sister?" he asked in his gentle voice.

"I worry every day, Rabbi," she replied. "Some days I worry about not having enough food. Today I worry because I don't have money to buy cloth to make a new robe for my husband." She lowered her head and blushed. "I don't know how to stop worrying."

"Put your trust in the reign of God," Yeshua told her. He turned to face the full congregation again. "I am telling you, ask and you shall receive. Look and you will find. Knock and it will be opened for you, because everyone who asks receives."

He paused and turned to the young woman again. Her hands were folded in her lap, and she gave him her full attention.

"So, I'm telling you not to worry about your life, sister. Don't worry about what you'll eat. Don't worry about your body, or what you'll wear. Isn't life more than food, and the body more than clothes?"

"Think about how the ravens don't sow, reap, or gather grain into barns, yet God feeds them. Aren't you more valuable than the birds?"

"And why worry about clothes? Look at how the lilies grow. They don't work or spin, yet I'm telling you that even Solomon, in all his glory, wasn't dressed like one of these!"

"But if God clothes the grass of the field, which is here today and is thrown into the oven tomorrow, won't God clothe you even more? So don't worry. Don't ask, 'What are we going to eat?' or 'What are we going to drink?' or 'What are we going to wear?' Look for God's reign, and all these things will be given to you too."

A man stood up and asked: "But, I wonder, how does God know what we need?"

"Father God is a loving God," Yeshua said. "Which of you would give your child a stone if they ask for bread? Or who among you would give them a snake if they ask for a fish? So, if you know how to give good gifts to your children, and give them what they need, how much more will the heavenly Father give good things to those who ask!"

The service continued in this manner. Once again, Yeshua was not retelling familiar stories from the Scriptures, but instead talked about God and the things that people cared about in their daily lives. He talked about the loving Father God who would care for and provide for them, not judge and punish them.

And again, Yeshua talked about the coming kingdom of God. His was a message of hope, not despair. He spoke of God's gifts and the heavenly rewards to come. He talked about preparing the way for the reign of God, and about the responsibility of each man and woman to prepare themselves for God's reign.

An older man stood up to ask a question.

"Rabbi, tell us, how may we understand the coming of the kingdom of God? How do we prepare ourselves?"

Yeshua's eyes flowed over the assembly and saw that many people had the same question and were eager to hear his answer. He still showed no signs of tiredness and spoke in a clear and loud voice.

"What is God's reign like, and to what should I compare it? It can be compared to a mustard seed which someone sowed in their garden. It grew and became a tree, and the birds of the sky nested in its branches. And again: to what should I compare God's reign? It can be compared to yeast, which a woman hid in fifty pounds of flour until it was all fermented. She made many large loaves of bread from it."

"God's reign will grow as it is nourished by the good deeds of His children. Remember this, because each of you will be measured by the fruit you bear before the Lord!"

"I tell you again, no good tree bears rotten fruit, nor does a rotten tree bear good fruit. Every tree is known by its own fruit. Are figs gathered from thorns, or grapes from thistles? The person who's good brings good things out of their good treasure, and the person who's evil brings evil things out of evil treasure."

In this sermon, as in many others, Yeshua taught us again how to take responsibility for our lives and our behavior. He told us as well what actions to take to please the Lord and to prepare for the reign of God. People listened attentively, and the lessons were well received.

As the service drew to a close, a young man asked: "Rabbi, how should we pray to Father God?"

"When you pray, say: Father, we honor your holy name. Let your reign come. Give us our daily bread today. Forgive us our debts because we, too, forgive everyone who's indebted to us. Don't put us in harm's way."

The young man bowed his head in humble gratitude. It was a good way to end the sermon.

The peace of the service was suddenly and shockingly interrupted by a loud and crazed scream from a man sitting in the back, not far from us. He was dressed in dirty and tattered clothes. His face was drenched in sweat and his hair disheveled. The man jumped into the center aisle and took a few unsteady steps forward, wild eyes full of hate staring directly at Yeshua.

I started to rise, alarmed for Yeshua's safety, but Clopas put a hand on my shoulder to restrain me. Mary stared at the scene in disbelief. At the front of the room, the brothers James and John bolted from their seats, but Yeshua calmly raised a hand to signal them to stop. The congregation sat in stunned silence to see what he would do.

The crazed man shuffled forward on wobbly legs. His hands shook and trembled in agitation, closing into fists and then opening again.

"We know who you are, Yeshua of Nazareth!" the man screamed at the top of his voice. "We know why you're here!"

Yeshua raised his arm, the open palm facing outward toward the approaching madman. He looked directly at the man, but somehow seemed to be looking through him.

"Shut up, and leave him!" Yeshua shouted in a booming voice that filled the room.

The man stopped in his tracks. His whole body shook with a violent convulsion, his arms flailing and head lolling from side to side on his spastic neck. Then he shrieked hideously, an anguished cry of defeat, and collapsed on the floor.

Yeshua walked over to him. The man was breathing with rapid and shallow breaths, like a frightened animal, but otherwise unmoving.

"He will be well now," Yeshua said.

It took a few moments for people to recover from their shock. Mary started walking briskly toward Yeshua, with her daughter Salome right behind her.

A man sitting nearby spoke loudly, his voice filled with wonder: "He commands demons, and they obey him!"

All around us, people were talking, and a surge of excitement filled the room. We were all astonished.

"What did we just witness?" I asked, just thinking out loud.

"An exorcism," Clopas replied. "Yeshua drove out unclean spirits from that poor man."

The young woman who spoke earlier with Yeshua now faced him. She raised her chin proudly, and her eyes shined with adoration.

"You are a prophet, truly," she told him.

"Yes!" cried a man standing beside her. "We are all witnesses to Yeshua, who performed a miracle here!"

Yeshua shook his head. "No. God performed a miracle here today."

Peter looked at him in wonderment. "God Almighty performed a miracle here, but you were His agent."

The man who nearly attacked Yeshua was helped to his feet by two people in the congregation. He looked around, somewhat dazed and confused, but quickly understood from other people's reactions that Yeshua was his savior. He bowed his head in a gesture of gratitude.

"You are blessed by the Lord, Rabbi," he said in a soft voice. "I was unclean, but now I am well."

Yeshua put a hand on his shoulder. "Praise God Almighty and thank Him that the unclean spirits are banished. Go now, and do good deeds to honor the Lord so that the unclean spirits do not return to you. Go in peace. Enjoy life."

The man bowed his head again. "Be you blessed too, Rabbi."

People came up to Yeshua to say a few words, and to see him face to face. Some touched him on the arm or shoulder, or shyly touched his robe, their faces filled with awe and affection. Yeshua's family and disciples patiently stood and waited until each man and woman paid their respects and said farewell.

Every person there left the sermon knowing that they witnessed something wonderful, so astonishing that it could only have been an act of God. After they left, they shared their stories with other people they met, and with family, neighbors, and friends. Word of Yeshua's exorcism spread like wildfire. It seemed that, by the time evening fell, all of Capernaum knew about it.

"Will you join us at my house for a meal?" Peter asked us after the service concluded and all the people drifted away. "You are all invited! Yemina and Tiva prepared a large meal."

When he stayed in Capernaum, in the early days of his ministry, Yeshua lived as a guest of Peter, his wife, Yemina, and his mother-in-law, Tiva. Later, in the coming weeks, Yeshua would attract wealthy supporters to his ministry who helped to provide housing for him, the twelve apostles, and many of his other disciples.

It was a generous offer that we happily accepted. Peter and Andrew led the way down the busy street, followed by Mary and Yeshua, then all the other relatives and disciples. As we walked through the streets, people began to point us out. Or rather, they pointed out Yeshua, who was drawing more and more attention from the people along the way. Some joined us, trailing along behind the disciples. It was a peaceful and friendly crowd in a mood for celebration. They all wished, perhaps, to be in the presence of the miracle worker.

The house of Peter's mother-in-law was a modest house on the lakeside, built around a common patio with two other houses. At the back was a small dock where the fishing boat was tied. The boat was small, just big enough to accommodate three men and the fishing nets.

We were welcomed by Yemina, the wife of Peter, a woman with a very sensitive and kind face. She showed us to tables that were already prepared with pitchers of water and wine, and wooden drinking cups.

"Word reached us even before you arrived," Yemina said to Yeshua, looking at him wide-eyed. "Our neighbor witnessed the miracle you performed, and now everyone is talking about it."

"As well they *should* be talking about it!" Peter exclaimed. "We all witnessed an act of God. This day will be long remembered."

Andrew came up to them. "Brother, there is a crowd of people gathered in the street. They clamor to see Yeshua."

Mary of Clopas laughed. "I don't wish to sound impertinent, but can they wait until after he eats his meal?"

"There is no hurry," Yeshua said. "I will talk to everyone after our meal. They will be patient and wait."

Peter looked around, his eyes searching. He asked Yemina: "Where is your mother? She should be here to greet our guests."

"*Emma* is unwell," Yemina answered gloomily. "She has a very bad fever, since yesterday."

Mary touched her arm in sympathy. "I am sorry to hear that. Is she feeling any better since yesterday?"

"No. She couldn't get up from her bed," Yemina said. "She's very disappointed that she can't help me. I'm terribly worried about her."

Mary and Yeshua exchanged glances. No words were spoken, but the message was understood.

"Will you take me to see her?" Yeshua asked.

When Yemina looked surprised, Peter gave her a reassuring smile. "Yeshua is a healer," he said. "Let us go and see Tiva."

"Of course," Yemina said. "I would be so grateful if you could help her. Nothing that I gave her has helped."

Yeshua followed Yemina and Peter into the house. Some of us went with them, including Mary and the young Salome. There was concern for the poor woman lying sick in bed, but also a curious interest to see what Yeshua could do for her.

Tiva was a stout woman in her middle years. She was stretched out on her bed, covered by a blanket. Her face looked drawn and tired and shiny with perspiration. She struggled to lift herself up when she saw us approaching, but Yeshua raised his hand and motioned for her to remain as she was. We waited near the door at a respectful distance.

"Rest, blessed child of God," Yeshua told her. "God is with you. You will be well."

He bent down at the waist and took her hand in his hand. They spoke to each other in very soft voices that the rest of us could not hear. An old memory flashed through my mind then, from twenty years earlier, of Yeshua comforting my sister Eva as she lay sick on her bed. Holding her hand. Talking to her softly.

Yemina whispered: "God be praised, she is looking better already."

"We have seen this before," Mary told her. "Yeshua has the healing touch."

"God provides the healing touch," Peter said. "Praise the Lord."

"Yes," Mary agreed. "It is a gift from God."

Tiva stirred, then slowly sat up in bed. Still holding Yeshua's hand, she put her feet on the floor and stood up. She looked unsteady for a moment, then gained her balance. Yeshua led her to us, walking slowly but steadily on her feet.

"*Emma*, do you feel well?" Yemina asked.

"Yes, I'm well now," she replied. "The fever is gone."

"God be praised!" Yemina said with a sigh of relief.

Tiva looked around impatiently. "Why are we all standing here? We have guests, and there is work to be done."

Peter laughed. "That's our Tiva! Always the gracious hostess."

"Oh, shush," the woman scolded him. "I am only being sensible."

We went back out on the patio, where Tiva was greeted with looks of delighted surprise. She greeted people politely, then set about with Yemina and some of the other women to bring the food out on the tables. Our simple meal quickly became a celebration.

Some of the men standing among the crowd on the street called out to Peter. He walked over to them.

"What has happened?" a man asked. "What made everyone so happy after you came out of the house?"

"My mother-in-law was very ill with a fever," Peter explained to them. "Yeshua held her hand and talked to her, and now her fever is gone. She is healed! Praise to God!"

This news spread quickly from one person to another. The crowd grew more excited as people discussed the events of the day. First the exorcism in the morning, and now this healing before them. Peter stayed with them a while longer to answer questions about Yeshua and his ministry.

"Yeshua is a prophet!" a man declared with strong conviction. "God Almighty is showing us signs!"

A woman turned to Peter, her expression very earnest. "Is he truly a prophet? Tell us honestly. You are his disciple and know him well."

Many others were also staring at Peter with the same questioning looks on their faces. He answered them in a serious tone.

"I tell you truly, Yeshua is a messenger of God. Today, God Almighty sent us two signs to show us who Yeshua is."

A man cried out: "It is so! I know it!"

Others in the group murmured agreement. More people passing by noticed the excitement and stopped to hear the discussion, which swelled the size of the crowd.

"What has happened?" a newcomer asked.

Peter said: "I witnessed Yeshua of Nazareth perform two miracles today. He banished unclean spirits from a man possessed by demons. And just now, in this house, he healed my mother-in-law of her fever by holding her hand. These are miracles brought by the hand of God."

"Hosanna! God blesses us with His prophet!" a man cried with joy. Others picked up the call, which became a shout that filled the street.

Yeshua looked up from his plate to pay closer attention to all the commotion. So did we all, because the passion of the crowd took us by surprise. Although Yeshua had been well received by many people in Capernaum, this was something entirely new.

"Listen to them! They call me a prophet," Yeshua said. "Is it because of the exorcism at the synagogue?"

"No, Yeshua," replied John, the son of Zebedee. "They call you a prophet because that is what you are."

"Amen," said his brother James.

The person at our tables most surprised by their statements was Yeshua himself. He did not call himself a prophet, and never expressed a desire that others should think of him that way.

"Listen to them, Yeshua," Clopas said. "This is what you have done, and in a very short time."

"They wish to hear from you," Mary told him.

"Then I won't keep them waiting any longer," Yeshua said, rising from the table. "They are thirsty to hear the word of God, and I am our Father's messenger."

As he walked toward the enthusiastic crowd, the joyful cheers grew louder and filled the street. The clamor did not stop until Yeshua began to speak to them.

Chapter 16

Magdalena

Capernaum, Galilee, Autumn 28 C.E.

S he walked for ten miles, in her bare feet, over cold and muddy roads from her home in Magdala to Capernaum. Her sandals had fallen apart from overuse some time ago, or perhaps were stolen from her. The robe she wore was made from good quality cloth, but threadbare after long use and being patched and mended.

Although poorly dressed and near the point of physical exhaustion, the young woman held her head high as she approached the house of Zebedee and Salome. She walked with a proud gait, her determined look telling everyone to not get in her way. Her face, finely featured with almond-shaped hazel eyes and high cheekbones, was framed by long brown hair that cascaded down over her shoulders.

Conversations stopped, and we all turned our heads to watch as she came nearer. There was something tragic and sublime in the look of this forlorn figure. For reasons that at the time I could not put into words, she commanded attention.

The woman stopped and looked around, searching, at the people seated around the tables. Suddenly her shoulders sagged, and she looked unsure and perhaps a little afraid. A pained and haunted look came into her eyes.

The first one to rise and go to her was young Salome, the sister of Yeshua. The two women looked to be close in age, which perhaps made Salome feel the most sympathetic toward her.

"Sister, are you looking for someone?" Salome asked when they stood face to face.

The woman gazed at her with an intense look for a moment. "Yes. I need to speak with Yeshua the Nazarene. Do you know him?"

"He is my brother," Salome said. She turned to look for Yeshua, but he was already up and striding toward them.

"I am Yeshua of Nazareth," he told the stranger in a gentle tone. "What is your name, sister?"

"I am Mary of Magdala." Her voice was mildly hoarse, but strong and determined. "I come to you because you are a great healer."

"What is your affliction, Mary?" he asked compassionately.

Mary suddenly became tense, her shoulders rigid. Her lower lip trembled, and a muscle twitched high on her cheek. The pained and haunted look in her eyes returned.

"I am possessed by demons," Mary whispered.

"Come with me," Yeshua said. He nodded to a walnut tree growing on the side of the patio. "We can talk more privately over there."

He guided her slowly and gently to stand underneath the tree. We tried to be respectful and not stare, but it was impossible to turn away from them completely. There was a feeling of anticipation in the air.

Yeshua spoke to Mary in a soft voice. She answered him in a voice just as quiet. Her body suddenly began to tremble from head to toe, but she was able to maintain her balance. Yeshua reached out with both hands and placed them on each side of her head, holding her tightly. He looked into her eyes and shouted loud, sharp commands. Mary trembled more violently, her whole body shaking. Her mouth opened wide and let out a terrible scream, and then she went limp. Her knees buckled and she would have fallen, but Yeshua caught her and gently lowered her down on the grass.

Salome grew alarmed and rushed to them. Yeshua looked up at her, his face completely calm.

"She will be all right now. Would you be kind, Sister, and fetch her a cup of water?"

Mary Magdalena was taken to rest inside the house. Young Salome became her companion and nurse. The older Salome, the woman of the house, went to her closet and provided a clean robe and sandals for her to wear. Mary, the mother of Yeshua, and her sister-in-law, Mary, the wife of Clopas, applied ointments and medicinal herbs to soothe the cuts and bruises on her feet.

Outside, we continued our discussion about finding housing for new arrivals who wished to become Yeshua's disciples. More people were arriving every day.

"We have more than fifty people who wish to join our ministry," Peter told Yeshua. "Half are from Capernaum, but the other half are from villages as far away as Cana and Naim. They need a place to live here in town, but most are poor, as we are."

James, the son of Zebedee, shook his head. "We have no money to rent or buy houses."

"Well, neither can we leave them out in the streets," said Philip of Bethsaida. "They come here to do God's work."

John, the son of Zebedee, grew impatient and irritable. "Then sell your house in Bethsaida and buy one here!"

Yeshua raised a hand to calm them down. "For now, the disciples who live in Capernaum should be the hosts for the disciples from other towns. God will provide us with money to rent more houses soon."

"Amen," said James, the son of Clopas. "God will provide."

Young Salome came out of the house. Her face looked tense and strained with concern. She took a seat beside her brother.

"Is Mary Magdalena resting well?" Yeshua asked.

"She's resting, but she is still very weak," Salome replied. "She is very grateful to you for making her well. Also, she tells me that she wishes to join your ministry and become your disciple."

Peter chuckled. "Another bed to provide! And does her husband approve of this idea?"

Salome frowned at him. "She has no husband, and her condition is nothing for you to laugh about." She looked at Yeshua. "Mary told me her story. I will tell you if you wish to hear it. She is not ashamed for people to know."

"Yes, I wish to hear her story," Yeshua said. "Please continue."

"Her husband divorced her last year because she is barren," Salome said bitterly. "He married another woman, who can give him children."

"That is his moral and legal right," Philip said. "But forgive me for interrupting."

Yeshua eyed him dubiously. "*Legal* right, yes, that part is true. What is morally right in the eyes of God, that's a different matter."

"Allow me to continue," Salome said, a tone of irritation rising in her own voice. "Mary's husband's legally correct but morally repulsive divorce left her alone and destitute, with no property and no money of her own. She has no relatives in Galilee, so she was all alone. No man wants a woman who is divorced and barren. She slept in a barn and worked odd jobs for her meals."

Yeshua listened, grim-faced. "And that's when the demons found her, because they prey on the weakest. Is that not so?"

"Yes, that is so," Salome replied. "Mary has suffered from being possessed for almost a year now. She heard of your miracles, Yeshua, because people talk about you even in Magdala. That is why she placed her trust in the Lord and walked alone to Capernaum."

Salome finished her story, and the table became very quiet. We were all touched by this young woman's plight.

"We will make a home for her in our ministry," Yeshua said. He gave Peter a patient look. "And we will provide a bed for her."

"Of course," Peter replied in a serious tone. "God sent her to join our flock, and we will provide for her."

Andrew looked around at the faces at the table. "Should we ask the wealthier supporters to donate to the ministry?"

"Yes," Yeshua replied without hesitation. "Not to enrich ourselves, but to provide for the poor and needy among our disciples. People like Magdalena."

Chorazin, Galilee, Autumn 28 C.E.

Three days later, Yeshua and a group of fifteen disciples made the trip to Chorazin, a small farming village three miles north of Capernaum. The time was drawing near for me to return to Nazareth, but I decided to make this trip with them. I wished to extend my stay a while longer.

As became his habit, Yeshua walked at the very front of the group. His long energetic strides set a fast pace and forced the rest of us to keep up. Time was precious and there were many places to go, things to do, and people to see.

Walking by his side that day were Mary, his mother; Mary of Clopas, his aunt; and the newest member of his ministry, Mary Magdalena. Throughout the course of his ministry, these women became known as the Three Marys. They were Yeshua's closest companions other than the Twelve.

In time, Magdalena would become the closest companion of them all. Yeshua embraced her in all areas of his life. On that day, however, she was an avid listener as Yeshua discussed his faith and his plans for the ministry. Mary was a fast learner. Soon she was able to share her own views, which closely matched Yeshua's. She put her past life in Magdala behind her, and never mentioned it again.

The small houses and narrow streets of Chorazin reminded me of Nazareth. We walked to the center of town and found that a crowd was already gathering there to greet Yeshua. Word of his arrival spread quickly through the village, and people were eager to hear him speak.

"Rabbi, give us a blessing!" a man asked.

Yeshua looked out over the crowd and spread his arms. "Blessings on you, Chorazin! The time is fulfilled, and the reign of God is near! Repent and make yourselves ready for the kingdom of God!"

People listened to Yeshua's message of a loving God, but it was a new message they were still not used to hearing. All their lives, the common people of Galilee had been told of the terrible wrath of God, who would bring down harsh judgements on them.

Yeshua did not speak of this angry and vengeful God, but instead talked of God as a compassionate and caring Father to all. God saw their suffering. He cared about them and would soon bring salvation and justice to this sinful world.

"How can you say, do not be afraid of the wrath of God?" a man asked. "Don't even the Temple writings tell us: He will rise up from His throne with indignation and anger?"

Yeshua's voice remained calm. "I am telling you, Father God does not come as a terrible and angry judge. He does not come to judge and punish you. He comes with compassion, overflowing with love."

Many people in the crowd looked joyful listening to what Yeshua said, yet many other faces remained grim and clouded with doubt. They seemed reluctant to believe his lessons about the coming kingdom of God. Looking at some of the faces, it was clear that their spirits were crushed, and despair came easier than hope.

One man said: "Tell us who you are so that we may trust you!"

Yeshua shook his head, growing impatient. "You know how to read the face of the sky and the earth. When it's evening, you say, 'There'll be good weather, because the sky is red.' In the morning, 'There'll be wintry weather today, because the sky is red and threatening.' You know how to interpret the appearance of the sky, but why don't you know the one right in front of you?"

The man continued stubbornly: "Scripture tells us that the true kingdom is God's kingdom. As every child knows, it will only come with the Messiah. So tell us, are you the anointed one sent by God Almighty to free us from our oppressors?"

"I am what I am," Yeshua replied. "My words are the path to the kingdom of God. Why do you doubt the Lord's message that I bring to you?"

The man frowned. Some of the people standing beside him, his friends and neighbors, grumbled unhappily.

Finally, Yeshua lost his patience. His voice erupted.

"Oh, you people of little faith! Are the demons not cast out? Are the sick not healed? Do the blind not see? Do the deaf not hear? Yet you still doubt that through God's power I am able to do these things!"

For a few moments, the crowd looked stunned at his show of anger. Many of the doubters lowered their heads and stared at the ground.

"Yes, I believe!" a woman cried. "You are blessed by God, Yeshua of Nazareth!"

"Is the woman from Magdala here with you?" another man asked. "The one they say was possessed by demons?"

"Yes, she is here." Yeshua turned toward Mary, standing nearby with the other women. She bowed her head gracefully to the crowd, a gesture of humility.

Yeshua told them: "She is Mary Magdalena. Four days ago, she was possessed by unclean spirits. Today she stands here clean and healthy, by God's mercy and compassion. The power of God Almighty cast her demons away!"

"God be praised!" people in the crowd shouted.

"God be praised!" Mary Magdalena echoed their cries, her strong voice rising above the crowd.

Mary took a step forward to stand beside Yeshua. She looked over the assembly in a calm and serene manner, as he had done. People stood silently and waited for her to speak.

"The kingdom of God is near," Magdalena told them. "The Lord has shown me the way. God's love and compassion made me whole again.

Chorazin, embrace God's love and goodness! Rejoice with all your heart, as I do!"

The mood of the crowd changed, as if the sun had emerged from behind a dark cloud. People looked at her with kindness and affection. She continued in a clear voice filled with passion.

"Chorazin, I tell you: Yeshua the Nazarene is a messenger of God. I have seen his work, which is the blessed work of the Lord."

A woman in the front shouted: "*You* are the blessed work of the Lord! You are a sign! I see God's light shining on you!"

Magdalena continued: "Yeshua teaches us that those who seek will find. And that anyone with two ears should listen. I know in my heart that he guides us on the true path to the kingdom of God. Rejoice, Chorazin! The reign of God is near!"

Shouts of praise and acclamation from the people standing before her told Mary that her words were well received. They knew that she was one of them, and that her message was heartfelt and pure. She was living testimony to Yeshua's message to them.

Mary allowed herself a small smile of satisfaction. Yeshua gazed at her approvingly, and his smile was not restrained.

Yeshua finished his sermon to an amicable crowd. In the months to come, he would pass through Chorazin often, as did the apostles and other disciples, because it was located on the road to Capernaum. The village provided many supporters who wished to join the ministry. Mary Magdalena as well always found a very warm welcome there.

Capernaum, Galilee, Autumn 28 C.E.

We left for Capernaum in the late afternoon. The walk back was a more leisurely stroll and took the better part of an hour. Magdalena walked with young Salome, and it was gratifying to see the friendship growing between them. The older women walked behind them, pleased with how we were received in the village.

Yeshua walked with the disciples Peter and Andrew, and James and John the sons of Zebedee. They were discussing the twelve tribes of Israel. Curious, I joined them.

"The prophet Jeremiah predicted it," Peter said. "The twelve tribes of Israel will be reborn, and God Almighty will break the yoke from off the neck of His people."

"That is so," Yeshua agreed in a serious tone. "And the Lord of Hosts said, I shall restore the fortunes of my people, Israel and Judah. I shall bring them back to the land that I gave their ancestors, and they shall take possession of it."

"On that day," said Peter, "the kingdom of God will be with us."

We were all familiar with the prophesies of the restoration of the twelve tribes, who would form the true nation of Israel. Our people had been praying for it for generations on end. I, sadly, had little hope of seeing it happen in my lifetime.

"How will this restoration of the tribes happen?" I asked. "It would take a miracle."

"Ah, David, be of strong faith," Yeshua said. "Yes, it's true that it will take God's miracle. But isn't that what we're working for? With the blessings of God Almighty, we are here to create that miracle."

"Amen!" said John of Zebedee in a passionate tone.

Although I was pleased to see their enthusiasm, it did not dispel my doubts. The long history of failed Jewish rebels was on my mind.

"As you know well, Yeshua, many have tried before to restore the twelve tribes. How will you succeed where others failed?"

"With God, everything is possible," Yeshua said. "We will take the first steps. The Lord will do the rest."

"What first steps do you mean?"

"I am appointing twelve apostles to lead the ministry," Yeshua said. He paused very briefly and lifted his eyes to the heavens. "With the blessings of God Almighty, they will sit on twelve thrones and rule over the twelve tribes when the reign of God is with us."

I heard then, for the first time, the echoes of true rebellion in his voice. Yeshua certainly wanted to do God's work, to ease the suffering of our people and guide them to salvation. But clearly, he also wanted much more than that.

This new idea of twelve apostles ruling over the twelve tribes was a vision of radical change. I prayed then that Yeshua was right, that the reign of God was indeed near. Only the reign of God, coming soon and fully implemented here on earth, could sweep away the oppression and overcome the military might of our Jewish and Roman rulers. If that did not happen, the alternative was a frightful thing to consider.

At the house of Zebedee, Salome and other female disciples had the evening meal prepared for us when we arrived. The setting sun lit the skies with glorious bands of red and orange. We were happy to sit and dine with them at the tables that filled the stone patio.

Salome of Zebedee poured Yeshua a cup of wine, then told him: "A traveler has arrived to see you. She is resting inside the house."

"Who might that be?" he asked.

"Her name is Susanna. She rode here in a horse-drawn carriage, from Sepphoris."

An image came to mind of a kindly woman who hired us to build an addition to her house. She gave me a small bundle of lemon candies for my children. It's funny how such small things stick in your memory, even thirteen years later.

"Oh, yes! I remember her," Yeshua said. "Please ask her to join us when she is rested enough."

Salome laughed. "I don't have to ask her. Here she comes now."

Susanna was as I remembered her, a slender woman of medium height. She was now a woman of fifty years, and her long black hair was streaked with white. Her styled and perfumed hair, along with her robe made of fine cloth, made it clear that she was a woman of wealth.

Yeshua stood up to meet her and took her hand in greeting. "I am happy to see you, sister. Welcome to Capernaum."

She bowed her head modestly in greeting. "Yeshua of Nazareth, I rejoice to see you again. I heard about your healings and exorcisms and knew that I must come to see you."

"Are you in need of healing, sister?" he asked in a compassionate tone.

She smiled at his concern, then shook her head. "No. I come to help you do the work of the Lord."

"Then you arrived just in time," Yeshua said with an easy laugh. "Come, join me at my table."

We made room for Susanna next to Mary, his mother, and Mary Magdalena. She acquainted herself with the two women while they ate. After the meal, the discussion turned to matters of the ministry with Yeshua and some of the disciples. Peter spoke first.

"What we need most urgently are funds to rent or buy houses for our brothers and sisters to live in, those who are from out of town," Peter explained. "Four or five houses should be enough, for now."

"I can help you with that," Susanna said. "My brother and I live in Sepphoris, but we also own a large house in Capernaum." She turned to Yeshua. "It is yours to use as you wish, to house your followers. It is also large enough to hold a gathering of one hundred people for a meeting or synagogue, if you wish."

"You are truly a blessing from God," Yeshua told her gratefully. "The Lord sent you when we most needed you."

"No," she said humbly. "I am truly blessed by God. As are you, and all those who follow your path."

"More people join our ministry every day," Yeshua told her. "I planted a seed in Capernaum, and it grows into a tree!"

Mary, his mother, smiled. "May its branches grow and spread."

"Amen," Susanna said. "But tell me, will you need money for food and housing when you travel to other villages?"

"Not a penny!" Yeshua replied. This surprised most of the people around the table, including the disciples. "The people we talk to will give us food, because a worker should be paid for his labor. They will give us a place to sleep, even if only a spot on their patio."

"That would suit me just fine," proclaimed John, son of Zebedee.

His brother James gave him a friendly slap on the back. "You've slept in worse places than a patio!"

"Yes, I have," John replied. "And so have you!"

"Hardships are easy to bear in service to the Lord," Yeshua said. He turned toward Mary Magdalena. "Mary walked here from Magdala, through the cold and mud, in bare feet and wearing a threadbare robe. Cold did not stop her, nor hunger or thirst, and not even demons. And see how strong she looks now!"

Everyone turned to Mary with looks of pride and affection. She did not shy away, but held her head high and met their glances.

"Everything is possible with God," Mary said.

"I am discovering that more and more, each day that I spend here in Capernaum," said young Salome. She gently touched Magdalena on the shoulder. "You are also teaching me that lesson, sister."

"All things are possible with God," said Yeshua. "This is a lesson we must teach to everyone we meet. Teach it with all your heart, and with all the strength of your love for God Almighty."

"It is a lesson that saved my life," Magdalena said.

Yeshua smiled. "It is a lesson that will change the world."

As the evening grew late, people retired to their homes or to their beds in the house of Zebedee. Yeshua, Clopas, and I were among the last to sit around the table, lit dimly by an oil lamp, and share a last cup of wine. Early the next morning, Clopas and I would be leaving to return to Nazareth. The others who came with us—his mother Mary, sister Salome, and Clopas' wife Mary and their son James—were staying with Yeshua in Capernaum.

"I'm very glad that I came to visit, Yeshua, to see your work," I said. "I wish that I could stay longer, but my family needs me at home."

He nodded. "You are always welcome to come back, David. But tell me, did you find what you expected to see here?"

"Truthfully, you have already surpassed my highest hopes of what I expected to see. What you are doing here is astonishing."

"Oh, I agree with that," Clopas said. "You are gathering your flock very quickly. Why, just look at us! Six of us came to Capernaum for a short visit, but only two are going home to Nazareth."

Yeshua laughed. He drained the last of his wine cup, then refilled his cup and ours as well.

"The Lord welcomes all people in His service. How could I do less? Everyone is welcome to follow the path to God."

"Even sinners?" asked a new but strangely familiar voice from the darkness. There was a pleading, haunted tone to that voice.

We all turned to the sound. "*Especially* sinners!" Yeshua answered. "Who are you? Show yourself!"

The figure who approached us, reluctantly at first, was a man of average height and build. He looked to be about my age and was dressed in a fine robe. Within a few more steps, he came close enough so that we could see his face in the flickering light of the oil lamp. I stared at him in surprise.

"You!" Clopas hissed. "You, of all people?"

Yeshua stood up to face him. "Levi. Yes, you are welcome here. All sinners are welcomed."

"Even a tax collector for Herod?" Levi asked. "You all despise me, I know that. You have hated me for many years."

Yeshua put a hand on his shoulder and looked him in the eye. "We are all God's children. Come, join our table."

Levi sat across from me, and I poured him a cup of wine. He took it gratefully, then drained half the cup in one big gulp. I had known Levi since we were boys, and as adults we had unpleasant discussions twice a year during tax season. Yet, somehow, he seemed different now. Perhaps it was the soft look in his eyes—it lacked the cold and haughty arrogance of old.

I asked: "Are you still a tax collector for Herod Antipas?"

"No," he replied. "I resigned my position as tax collector."

"For what reason?" asked Yeshua. "Your job as a publican made you a wealthy man."

Levi shook his head. "I no longer wish to be that man. I'm ashamed of the things I've done as Levi, the tax collector."

"That shame is well earned," Clopas said evenly.

"You are right to say so, Clopas. But I have sinned enough."

Levi turned to Yeshua with a pleading look in his eyes. "I wish to repent and begin a new life. I see what you are doing here, Yeshua. Now I want to join you in your work for the Lord."

"Then you are no longer Levi, the tax collector," Yeshua told him. "Repent through good behavior and love for the Lord, and join me in God's work. I welcome you as a brother."

The tension drained from Levi's face. He took a breath and let it out quickly, a sound of deep relief. He struggled to hold back tears, but these were not tears of sadness — they were tears of gratitude.

We were all glad for him, even Clopas. Yeshua looked at him with patience and kindness, and a stronger sense of forgiveness than I was capable of.

"Well, if I am no longer Levi," the former tax collector said, "then who am I?"

Yeshua reached out and placed both hands on the shoulders of his new disciple.

"From this day on, you are Matthew, servant of God."

Chapter 17

The Twelve

Nazareth, Galilee, Autumn 28 C.E.

Word of Yeshua's wondrous feats reached us in Nazareth over the following weeks. In many villages throughout Galilee, other than Nazareth, people repeated amazing stories about the many miracles that Yeshua performed. He cured a leper just by touching him. A man who was born deaf could now hear. Demons were exorcised and cast out from those who were possessed. Most astonishing, a young girl who died was raised up from the dead, and she lives again.

News about these things came to us mostly from travelers. They heard the many stories about Yeshua of Nazareth, and many who were passing by were curious to talk to people in his hometown. Who was this worker of miracles, the man some people were calling a prophet?

Far too often, the visitors who asked those questions in Nazareth left feeling more confused than when they arrived. We know of no prophet from Nazareth, the local people said. Yeshua is the son of Yosef, who was a carpenter, and Mary.

Those of us who knew Yeshua best thought more highly of him, of course. Still, it would do no good to argue with people who only wished to stubbornly hang on to their old beliefs. As the wise saying goes, there are none so blind as those who will not see.

"I am going to Capernaum to join my brother," James announced one morning. I was working on replacing the old straw in our children's mattresses with new material, while Leila was mending some of their clothes. We both put our work aside to consider this news.

"He'll be very pleased to see you, indeed," I said. "The ministry is growing fast, and there is no one Yeshua trusts more than you."

"Is Kitra joining you?" Leila wondered.

"No, not this year at least," James said. "Our youngest is too young to live away from home."

Leila gave me a look. "Well, that won't be a problem for us."

James raised his eyebrows. "What do you mean?"

"We also talked about going to help the ministry," I said. "Yeshua's work is important. I don't want to just sit and watch from afar."

"It would be wonderful to have you join us," James said. "Dalia is old enough to watch the younger children while you are gone, no?"

"She's sixteen, old enough to manage the household for a few months," Leila said. "And if she needs any help, she can turn to Kitra, who is just next door, or her Aunt Eva and Uncle Uziel."

"This is very good news," James said. "Yeshua appointed twelve apostles, but many more disciples are needed for the work ahead."

Leila raised an eyebrow. "Twelve apostles?"

"Yes. Twelve men who are his most trusted disciples. Trained to go out on their own, without Yeshua's supervision. They are the leaders of the other disciples," James explained.

"Ah, the twelve tribes of Israel reborn," I said lightly.

James frowned. "We should *not* call them by that name, David. I think you understand the reasons why."

I nodded. "A foolish jest. It will not be repeated."

Leila gave a sigh. "Herod will not think it's funny, and neither would the Romans who rule over him. John the Baptizer sits in prison today because Herod fears a revolt. We don't want him to fear Yeshua in the way that he fears John."

"On that we can all agree," James said. "The twelve are religious apostles, not rebel leaders, but who knows what Herod Antipas might think of them?"

Capernaum, Galilee, Autumn 28 C.E.

In Capernaum, we were welcomed once again by Salome, the wife of Zebedee. She took delight in greeting her nephew, James, and Leila, after not seeing them for many years. I noticed right away that her house, which was brimming with people and bustling with activity the last time I was there, was now empty and quiet.

"Where are all the people?" I asked. "Are they on the road, visiting other towns?"

"They are at the meeting house. Yeshua has seventy disciples now, and he rents several large houses for them."

James chuckled. "Then money is no longer a problem, I see?"

"No, funds to support the ministry are no longer a problem. Some *quite* wealthy supporters have come to us." With an amused smile, Salome nodded toward the back of the house. "Come outside with me to the patio. You can meet one of them now."

We followed her, growing more and more curious. Two women were seated at the nearest table on the stone patio. The one facing us was Mary, the mother of Yeshua. She paused in her conversation and stood up to greet us. The second woman followed suit and stood up with her, then turned to face us.

I recognized her immediately, and it came as a mild shock. I had only seen her once, on a street in Sepphoris, some eight years ago. One did not forget the face, however, of a Jewish noblewoman as regal as Joanna, the wife of Chuza.

As Salome made the introductions, Mary came around to greet us and gave her son and Leila warm embraces.

"James is my second oldest son. David and Leila are our neighbors in Nazareth," Mary explained. "I have known David since he was born. He taught Yeshua how to herd sheep when Yeshua was a young boy."

"Peace be with you," Joanna said in a casual and friendly tone.

We all sat around the table and exchanged pleasantries. I tried not to look too much at Joanna, but she looked different now and that made me curious. Her long brown hair was still styled in curls, but she wore no cosmetics. She was dressed in a simple white robe and wore no jewelry. At nearly forty years of age, she still carried her famed beauty well. She looked poised and confident still, as I remembered her from that one brief encounter, but carried no air of privilege or arrogance. Her manner of treating those around her was no different from Mary, Salome, or Leila.

"How did you come to join Yeshua's ministry?" Leila asked, curious. "Capernaum is a very different world from the royal court of Herod!"

That made Joanna smile. "It is different indeed. But to answer your question, I came to see Yeshua because I needed urgent healing." Her expression turned very serious for a moment, then relaxed. "He cured my illness. And even knowing of my wealth, he did not ask me for even a penny."

"That sounds like my brother," James said. "And then you decided to stay here?"

"Yes. After that I decided to stay in Capernaum, because I knew then that Yeshua is much more than a healer. He is a messenger from God." She looked around to gage our expressions. "Some people say that he is a prophet."

Mary shook her head politely. "Some may say that, but Yeshua does not call himself a prophet. He has no wish to glorify himself, but only to give glory to God."

"I too believe that is the right path, sister," Joanna said. "Yeshua tells us that whoever exalts themselves will be humbled, and whoever humbles themselves will be exalted. I *know* in my heart that is true."

"But, if you stay here, won't you lose favor in Tiberias with those who are loyal to Herod?" Leila asked. "Your husband is the minister of finance for Antipas, is he not?"

"My husband agrees that I should do this," Joanna said. She saw the looks of surprise on our faces. "Chuza is grateful to Yeshua for his healing of me. He is a loving and generous husband. And, truthfully, I don't care about any of the fools at Herod's court, or what they might think of me."

"We are humbled to have you with us," James said with a small bow of his head. "You are truly a blessing from God."

Joanna gave him a patient smile. "We are all humbled in the eyes of the Lord, James. Here I am one of many in a family of equals, but I tell you truthfully, I feel more exalted now than when I was living in Herod's palace."

It was a remarkable thing to hear from this noble woman. She said it with such humility that it left no doubt she meant what she said.

"We should go to see Yeshua," Mary said. "He's going to give a talk to the twelve and the other disciples."

"That's what I came to see," James said eagerly. "So many good things are happening with Yeshua in Capernaum."

Yeshua spoke to his followers on the ground floor of a large two-story house. Perhaps eighty people crowded into the room, some sitting on the floor and some standing along the walls. Yeshua stood in the front of the room and was already addressing the crowd. He was flanked by the twelve apostles, six on each side of him. Mary Magdalena was also standing close by.

"The path to the reign of God has been shown to you," Yeshua told the group of disciples. "Blessed are the eyes that see what you see. I'm telling you that many prophets and rulers wanted to see what you see, but didn't see it; and to hear what you hear, but didn't hear it."

Young Salome, his sister, noticed us entering the room and made her way through the crowd to greet us. She was particularly cheerful in greeting her brother, James.

"The Lord God has seen the suffering of the poor and heard their cries of anguish. The time for salvation is here! Purify your bodies through baptism, and renew yourselves in devotion to God Almighty, and so prepare the way for the kingdom of God. But I tell you, those things are not enough!"

Yeshua paused, then said with firm conviction: "The time has come for us to go out and deliver God's word to all His children. Follow me, leave your homes and your families behind, and go from town to town, village to village, to teach others the path to salvation."

I paid close attention to the apostles, standing in rows of six. I knew eight of them. James and John, sons of Zebedee. The brothers Peter and Andrew. Philip and his friend Bartholomew. Young James, the son of Clopas. And Matthew, who I once knew as Levi the tax collector.

Yeshua continued: "It's not possible for anyone to mount two horses or stretch two bows, and it's not possible for a servant to follow two leaders. No one can follow two masters, because they'll either hate one and love the other, or they'll be devoted to one and despise the other. You can't serve both God and Mammon!"

Of the four apostles I did not recognize, three were younger men in their middle twenties. One was tall and thin, with a nervous and gloomy expression on his face. Another was short, with a husky build. His manner seemed placid, a follower perhaps rather than a leader. The third was a tall, broad-shouldered man who might once have been a soldier. His piercing black eyes moved across the room impatiently, as if he disliked standing for long and doing nothing.

"Everyone who hears my words and acts on them can be compared to someone building a house on bedrock," Yeshua said. "When the rain poured, and the floods came, and the winds blew and pounded that house, it didn't collapse, because it was founded on bedrock."

"But everyone who hears my words and doesn't act on them is like someone who built a house on sand. When the rain poured, and the floods came, and the winds blew and pounded that house, it collapsed immediately. How great was its fall!"

The fourth apostle I did not know was a few years older, in his early thirties, about the same age as Yeshua. He was tall and thin, his black hair and beard trimmed short. His eyes drifted casually around the room, from one face to another, in a calm and calculating manner. His name, I would later learn, was Judas Iscariot.

Yeshua's tone of voice grew softer, and it appeared that he was near the end of his sermon. The eyes of every disciple in the room were still focused on him intently.

"Nothing is concealed that won't be revealed, nor hidden that won't be made known. Whatever I tell you in the dark, say in the light; and whatever you hear whispered in your ear, announce from the housetops!"

His address to them concluded, Yeshua relaxed his posture and looked over the crowd. People began to talk with one another, turning to their neighbors to discuss Yeshua's lessons.

We made our way to Yeshua. He also greeted his brother James with an enthusiastic embrace, then welcomed the rest of us.

"So, your disciples will visit other towns on their own?" James said. "This will spread the word of God quickly across all of Galilee."

"The time has arrived," Yeshua replied. "I won't wait to have people come to me, as John did. I will go to meet people where they live and talk to them in their homes. My apostles will do the same."

Leila said: "That's a wonderful idea. Will the women disciples also travel with the men?"

"Yes. It is best to have the men and women travel together."

Mary Magdalena gave Leila a friendly smile. "That way, women like us can approach the women in the villages, who will not wish to talk to a strange man from outside their village. And the men there will listen to the men disciples."

"A very good idea," I said. "We are also here to serve the ministry in any way we can. If that means travelling on the road as a couple, then we shall go together to where we are needed."

"God's blessings be upon you, my good neighbors," Yeshua said. "You will walk with me, or with one of the apostles."

"I want to meet all your apostles," James said.

Yeshua nodded. "There will be time for that, Brother. Soon we shall leave in groups and go in different directions. But until then, everyone will be here in Capernaum."

James and I sat in the afternoon sun, enjoying a cup of wine, when Andrew, the brother of Peter, approached our table. Walking beside him were two men who I now recognized as two of the new apostles.

"Peace be with you, James and David," Andrew greeted us. "These men are apostles. They asked to meet James, the brother of Yeshua."

James stood up to greet them. "I am James. Will you join us?"

"I am Thomas Didymus," the taller one said. "Didymus is my Greek name, but please call me Thomas."

"I am Thaddeus, the son of James and Lebbaeus," said the shorter man. He turned to me and spoke in a very polite voice: "And you must be David the Nazarene, Yeshua's neighbor?"

"That's right," I said. "Please, join us for a cup of wine."

"How did you meet Yeshua and come to join the ministry?" James asked them once the men were settled in.

"On the fishing docks," Thomas replied. "Most of us are fishermen, and that's where Yeshua found us. Come with me, and be fishers of men, he tells us!"

Thaddeus smiled. "And it works! But in my case, Andrew here spoke to me first. After Yeshua, he is the best recruiter of disciples."

"You joined the ministry after just one talk with Yeshua," Andrew said humbly. "The credit belongs to him."

"One talk was all I needed to know that this is the path the Lord wants me to follow," said Thaddeus.

James asked: "I know Matthew, the tax collector, but are the rest of you all fishermen?"

"Matthew *was* a tax collector," Thomas corrected him. "He is a changed man now and no longer a sinner. But yes, most of us were fishermen."

"Other than Judas Iscariot and Simon the Zealot," Thaddeus added. "Judas handles money, and Simon wished to be a soldier until Yeshua showed him the true path to God."

"In what way does Judas handle money?" I asked.

"Yeshua appointed him treasurer, so he handles our money," Thomas said. He shrugged. "That job is not for me. He can have it."

Andrew gave him a small, good-natured grin. "You would worry yourself to death over our finances."

Thomas frowned. "As I said, that's a job he can have! Judas is good with numbers, they say, so he's good with money."

"It must be true. Yeshua trusts him for a reason," Andrew said.

"Different men are good at different things," James said. "Your brother Peter is a leader, but you are better at talking to people and bringing them into the ministry. The sons of Zebedee are better at making sure nobody starts trouble for Yeshua, or putting down trouble quickly if it starts. We all serve the Lord in our own way."

Thaddeus bowed his head in a gesture of humility. "That is so. God asks for both leaders and followers. Some men must be shepherds, and some must be sheep."

"In this ministry," said Andrew, "we all have but one shepherd."

"Amen," said Thomas. "We are blessed by God to be in his flock."

"Amen," I repeated after him.

How far you have come, Yeshua, I thought to myself, since your childhood days tending sheep in Nazareth. How far you have come.

Later in the afternoon, I was approached by the tall and burly man whose name, I learned, was Simon the Canaanite. Sometimes he was called Simon the Zealot. He greeted me in a friendly manner.

"Peace to you, David of Nazareth."

"And also to you."

"You have known Yeshua since he was a boy, they tell me?"

"Yes," I said. "Our families are neighbors."

Simon motioned toward the nearby lakeside. "Will you walk with me? I wish to speak with you."

This was an unexpected, but reasonable enough request. "Yes, of course," I replied. In truth, I wished to speak with him as well.

We walked in silence for a while. This was a quieter section of the lakeside, away from the busy boat docks. In places on the lake, the afternoon sun reflected brilliantly off the turquoise blue water.

"What kind of man is Yeshua?" Simon asked in a casual tone. "You surely know him well."

I took a moment to ponder his question. He dedicated himself to serve in Yeshua's ministry and deserved to hear an honest answer.

"A very good man," I said. "He's very smart. And most of all, he is devoted completely to serving the Lord."

Simon gave a small nod. We walked on.

"Tell me, Simon, why do you ask me that question?"

"I know Yeshua is all those things," he replied evenly. "I still wonder sometimes if he will be the kind of leader that we'll need."

"What do you mean? What kind of leader?"

"A leader who will free God's chosen people from the tyranny of Rome," he said bitterly. The anger in his voice made it clear why some people called him the Zealot.

"That is what Yeshua wants as well," I told him. "As do I. As do you. The coming reign of God will sweep away the injustice of this sinful world. That includes the tyranny of Rome and the Jewish rulers who betray our people and work with Rome."

"I believe that," Simon said. "But you see, I also believe that God's reign can only be ushered in by those with the zeal to fight for it."

I paused in my walk. He stopped also and turned to face me.

"Yeshua will not lead a violent revolt," I told him. "He is not a man of violence."

"I know this. He is a man of peace."

I said: "They call you Simon the Zealot. Tell me, do you wish for a military rebellion?"

Simon's face grew taut, a muscle in his jaw twitching. "And then King David said to God Almighty, 'Zeal for your house has consumed me.' Should we expect any less from ourselves?"

"No, we should not expect less," I told him. "Yeshua is not lacking in zeal to serve God, but he will *not* lead a violent revolt. If you are seeking that kind of leader, then look elsewhere."

Simon looked out over the lake, his thoughts turned inward while his eyes gazed into the distance. Then he quickly grew calmer, as if his inner fury abated.

"Yeshua is a prophet," he said. He turned to look me in the eye. "I don't know if he is the right kind of prophet. That is what troubles me, when my thoughts grow dark and I grow restless and impatient."

"I understand what you mean," I told him. "When a man's anger turns to helpless rage, he is tempted to turn to violence. Many years ago, my father Matthias took that path and joined the revolt of Judas the Galilean. He was crucified by the roadside, along with Judas and two thousand others."

Simon paused for a moment to reflect. "I know the story of Judas the Galilean. And I understand you as well, David. Yeshua won't take us down the path of violence. I still believe, however, that the tyranny of Rome can only be ended by force."

"It will surely be ended by force!" I said. "But it will be done by the force of God, not the force of men. As God Almighty struck down the armies of Pharaoh, so He will smite the armies of Rome."

He said: "Your faith is very strong. My faith sometimes wavers."

"Then be stronger in your faith," I told him. "Yeshua is Yeshua, and he will only do what he believes the Lord asks him to do. I have learned over the years not to question that. He is truly a messenger from God."

"You are right," Simon said in a solemn tone. "I must be patient, and stay hopeful, and not question my faith."

"Sometimes faith will be questioned, most of all in our moments of weakness," I said. "The most important thing is that we don't turn away from it. Question Yeshua if you have doubts, and he will answer your questions, but don't turn away from him."

"I won't turn away," Simon declared. It was a calm assurance that told me he truly believed it. We walked back to the meeting house in silence, because all that mattered was already said.

Two groups of apostles gathered at tables in the courtyard. Yeshua was very engaged in a spirited discussion with Peter and the brothers James and John. Peter raised a finger to make a point, but was cut off by James, who argued his point in a loud and energetic tone. John raised his voice to disagree. James dismissed his brother with a wave of his hand and turned his attention back to Peter, who was losing his patience with being interrupted. John voiced his objections.

I nodded a greeting to them in passing. They ignored me, except for Yeshua, who threw up his hands.

"Do you see why I call them *Boanerges*?" he said loudly, to be heard over the Zebedee brothers. "The Sons of Thunder!"

At the next table, Philip raised himself up and shouted to Yeshua: "Thunder is intermittent! Don't these two ever stop?"

Everyone laughed except the sons of Zebedee. It's possible that they never even heard Philip's question while arguing with each other.

James, the son of Clopas, waved to invite me to join him. He was seated at the table with Philip, Bartholomew, and Matthew. I was happy to accept his invitation.

I had not spoken with Matthew since that late evening when he first approached Yeshua and asked to join his ministry. There was a different look to him now, and not only because he abandoned his fine clothes for a plain robe of brown cloth. He looked calmer, more at peace with himself.

"Are my father and brother well?" James asked. "When you last saw them in Nazareth, I mean."

"Both are well," I replied. "Your father is his usual industrious self, and Simeon is helping with the vineyard."

James smiled. "That is good. But I wish they were here with us."

"Perhaps they will join us in time," said Matthew. "Along with more people from Nazareth, I pray."

"Perhaps not so many will come from Nazareth," said Bartholomew wryly. "Yeshua's ideas for a ministry were not received kindly there."

Philip shook his head. "Indeed not. His sister Salome is still upset about how Yeshua was treated."

"I can't blame her for being upset," I said. "But that's the nature of people everywhere. As Yeshua said, no prophet is accepted in his own hometown. The people there can only see him as one of them."

"Ah, but people sometimes change," Matthew said.

"Indeed. Look at you!" James said with a grin. "My father used to hate you. I don't think he would hate you now."

Matthew gave a small shrug. "Many people hate me still. They only see me as the man I was. Levi, the tax collector. Levi the sinner."

"I don't hate you," I said. "I forgive you for your past injustices. You are not the same man now."

"Thank you for that kindness, David," he said in a humble tone. "But what is most important is that God Almighty forgives me. I am reborn, and I dedicate my life to serving the Lord."

I found Yeshua in a room on the second floor of the large house, which was called the treasury room. This was where the ministry's money was kept, in a locked box in a locked room to discourage thieves. The keys were kept by the man appointed as treasurer, Judas Iscariot.

Judas was there with Yeshua, along with Joanna of Chuza, and the three Marys: Yeshua's mother, Mary of Clopas, and Mary Magdalena. Magdalena was a woman of bright mind and good judgment. She had quickly become a close companion of Yeshua, and an advisor along with his mother and his aunt.

Joanna addressed herself to both Yeshua and Judas. "We have enough funds here to pay the rents for the next six months, and to buy food for those staying in Capernaum. As Yeshua has instructed, the disciples travelling on the road will not need money to take with them. They will make their own way for food and other needs on the road."

Judas said: "People are kind and generous. They will provide."

"God will provide," Yeshua said. "And yes, people who love the Lord are kind and generous, as we are."

Joanna gave them a patient smile. "The people who collect rents are no kinder or more generous than the tax collectors. Judas, mind that funds are always on hand for at least three months of rent payments, otherwise we must raise more money."

"Of course," Judas said evenly, but his dark eyes narrowed slightly. He disliked being given instructions by a woman, as would any Jewish man. This woman, however, was the wife of the finance minister of all Galilee, and the biggest donor of money to Yeshua's ministry. Judas listened politely.

"Your instructions will be followed," Yeshua assured Joanna. "And when Judas is travelling, the treasury will be minded by you or one of these three good women named Mary."

"As you wish," Judas said. "Magdalena, have you ever managed a household yourself? Managed the household finances, I mean."

"Yes, I managed my husband's household," she replied politely but firmly. "I know how to pay bills."

Mary of Clopas laughed. "Judas, when it comes to stretching a penny, women are much more practical than men. We learn from hard experience."

"Well, that settles the matter of money," Yeshua said. "Now let's go for a walk through the town and minister to people there."

"Ah, that's what I came to tell you about," I said. "There are already a dozen people waiting outside who wish to talk with you."

"Let us minister to them first, my son," said Mary. "Devotion and patience should be rewarded."

As Yeshua spoke to the small crowd of people gathered in front of the house, the four women stood a short distance away and talked among themselves. At times Mary, the mother of Yeshua, was shown a higher level of respect and even deference, but in most things, the women treated each other as equals. They shared a common vision in their complete devotion to Yeshua and his work.

Judas Iscariot came to stand beside me. His eyes drifted to the four women talking.

"Yeshua values the female disciplines just as much as the men," he said in a casual tone. "He is unorthodox, in that way."

"He is," I agreed. "Do you think that is wrong?"

"It is very unusual," he said. "A woman's place is in the home. They bear and raise children, cook, sew, and manage the household. From birth, women are ruled by their father, then their husband. The Law tells us that women must be obedient to men."

"Yeshua does not treat women that way," I said. "And if he did, they would make poor servants to the Lord! You see for yourself how much the women do to help the ministry. Mary, his mother, Mary of Clopas, Salome of Zebedee, Susanna, Joanna, and now Magdalena. Should he treat them like servants and insist they be subservient to him?"

"In the holy Scriptures, women are subservient to men. The same applies in our synagogue meetings, and of course in the Temple."

"In Nazareth, in our synagogue meetings, women are free to speak just as freely as the men," I told him. "We don't consider that unusual. That is the tradition Yeshua grew up with."

"But it goes so much further than women at synagogue meetings," Judas said. "Yeshua treats *everyone* the same. Man, woman, rich, poor, clean, unclean. He breaks a multitude of our Jewish traditions."

"A new day is coming," I said. "The reign of God is coming soon. Yeshua is the shepherd to lead us to it."

Judas stood in silence for a moment, then continued in a soft voice that was meant only for me to hear. "Simon tells me that you and he talked. That you are certain Yeshua is the right kind of shepherd to lead us to the kingdom of God."

"Yes. I believe that completely, with my heart and soul." I turned to look at him directly. "Do you have the same questions as Simon?"

"At times," he replied. "Simon and I came here as the most zealous of the apostles. I travelled here from Judea when I heard about Yeshua the Nazarene, praying to God along my journey that he is the one to deliver us. Like Simon, I sometimes wish for a more aggressive path."

I shook my head. "*Zealous* does not mean aggressive or violent. No disciples are more zealous in their faith than the sons of Zebedee, or Peter, Andrew, or young James."

"You are right," Judas said. "No one questions their love for God."

I motioned to the crowd. "Look. The most zealous of us all stands there before you. No man or woman is more passionate and zealous in service to the Lord than Yeshua. And none preach more strongly that we live in peace and love one another."

"Yes, I see that," Judas Iscariot said. "Man, woman, rich, poor, clean, unclean. He even loves the sinners. Sometimes I wonder, why does Yeshua do this?"

I told him why.

"Because this is what God Almighty asks of him."

> Chapter 18

Why Do You Dine With Sinners

Capernaum, Galilee, Autumn 28 C.E.

A large group of people gathered to hear Yeshua's sermon on the Sabbath day. That became a common occurrence in Capernaum. When news spread that he would speak at a synagogue meeting, the meeting house was always filled to overflowing. On many days, if the weather was not rainy or too cold, we moved the service outdoors to accommodate the crowd.

So it was that Leila and I stood along with more than two hundred others in a grassy clearing near the shore of Lake Kinneret. There was a gently sloping rise from the water's edge to the first row of houses, and Yeshua's stood at the top of the rise so that people could see and hear him better.

"Rejoice! The reign of God is near," Yeshua said, repeating what for many was becoming a familiar message. "The Lord God, who is Father of us all, has heard the cries of suffering from His children. Blessed are you who suffer, because God is coming to take away your misery."

Although Yeshua knew many passages from the scriptures because he heard them quoted in the past, he almost never quoted from the scriptures. He did not speak the language of the priests and scholars, but the language of the common people. Most of all, he spoke from his heart. He talked of hope, not fear. Forgiveness and compassion, not punishment. Love, not anger and hate.

Leila discreetly nudged me with an elbow. "Look, over there," she whispered in an amused tone. "We have spies among us."

I followed her gaze and looked to the side of the crowd. Not too far away, two men wearing fine white robes were standing by themselves and watching Yeshua. To my surprise, I recognized the younger one as Avner from Nazareth, the newly trained Pharisee priest who had brought us the news of the arrest of John the Baptizer. The older man, based on his clothing and his demeanor, was also a priest.

"Maybe they're not here to spy," I said in a low voice, but already knew that was a false hope.

"Don't be so blind!" she whispered back. "Just look at their faces. They're not here to enjoy the sermon, like everyone else."

"You're right. They do look rather taciturn."

Avner saw me looking and gave a small nod of his head in greeting. I returned the nod to be polite. He was very obviously not in favor of Yeshua's ministry, and now I was curious about his purpose here.

The young man said something to his companion, then both started walking in our direction. We were near the back of the congregation, where the crowd was thinner.

"We have company," I told Leila.

"Oh, joy," she whispered dubiously, keeping her attention to the front.

"Peace to you, David," Avner said. "This is Ezra, my teacher."

"And also to you," I replied. "Have you come from Jerusalem to hear Yeshua give a sermon?"

"We hear stories in Jerusalem," Ezra said curtly. "But of course it's better for us to hear him talk directly."

He was a short and stout man, with streaks of gray in his hair and beard. Avner was deferential toward him, which was proper in their roles as teacher and student.

"Of course," I said evenly. "Yeshua has much to teach us. Some of his ideas are unique, as you have surely already heard."

Ezra made an unpleasant face, but said nothing. We turned to the front again to watch Yeshua continue his sermon.

"Blessed are the hungry children, and the beggars who are despised in the streets. Blessed are the sick and the demon possessed, the tax collectors and other sinners, because Father God loves you all as His children and offers you salvation," Yeshua said with a ringing voice that carried to the water's edge.

"The reign of God is most of all for you! Repent through your good behavior, love the Lord with all your heart, and you will be embraced and welcomed into the kingdom of God!"

"That is sacrilege," Ezra muttered with indignation. "There is no path to repentance and salvation except through the sacred rites of purification and sacrifice to God Almighty."

"That is correct," said Avner in a proud tone.

Ezra continued: "Only *we*, the priests of God, can offer those rites, as the Law demands. Who is this uneducated preacher from Nazareth to tell people otherwise?"

"Look around you," I told Ezra politely. "Many people here believe that Yeshua is right."

"Nonsense!" the priest said dismissively.

"Mind that you speak more respectfully, Priest," a man standing nearby growled. "You offer us rites of repentance and purification, but only if we pay for them. Yeshua the Nazarene is different. I believe him, and so should you, because he is a messenger from God."

Ezra looked too stunned to reply. He stood stone-faced, as did Avner, and turned to the front again to listen. They were Pharisee priests, and not used to being challenged this way in public.

A man near the front asked Yeshua: "For generations we have been told to look toward Jerusalem when we pray. Yet when you pray, you look up toward the heavens. Why is this?"

Yeshua paused to look over the congregation. He surely knew that, once again, he was breaking with old tradition and telling people something that many would find very surprising, confusing, or even disturbing. When he spoke again his voice was very solemn.

"We all have one Father, who is our Father in heaven. When we pray, we should pray to our Father and not to Jerusalem. The Eternal God is not tied to one place. He is everywhere."

Many people reacted with surprise, as did I. For my entire life I had been taught there was one proper way to pray. At least three times in a day, we were to face toward God's Temple in Jerusalem and pray. Now Yeshua was telling us something very different indeed.

Ezra again scoffed angrily. "Come, Avner, we should leave. This is a congregation of sinners. It's not fit for holy men of God."

They turned and walked away without any words of farewell. I was not sorry to see them go.

"Are Pharisee priests always so impolite?" Leila wondered casually. "I can understand why they might not wish to talk to me, since in their eyes I am a mere woman unworthy of their attention, but *you* are one of the Jewish male tribe."

Her comments made me smile. "They do carry a certain arrogance about them, no doubt. However, as my uncle Abram likes to remind us, the Sadducee priests he works with at the Temple are even worse. They treat themselves as the nobility of the priestly classes."

Leila's face turned serious. "Before Yeshua's work is done, he will make a great many priests unhappy, I think."

"I think so too," I said. "What Yeshua is telling us, and also telling the priests, is that when it comes to renewing our covenant with God, the priests and their rituals are no longer necessary. Which means, of course, that the priests are no longer necessary."

Yeshua and the disciples were invited after the service to the house of Matthew for a meal. We walked there as a group, with Yeshua in the lead. Many people still remembered Matthew as Levi the tax collector, and harbored ill will toward him. Those of us in the ministry knew him better, as a changed man and an apostle for Yeshua.

Many people greeted Yeshua with affection as we walked by, or stopped briefly to speak with him. He was well known by then to the people of Capernaum and many of the nearby villages. He never turned down a soul who sought his attention, even as we moved along at a brisk pace.

A middle-aged woman, who was leading a man of similar age by the arm, called out to him from the side of the street.

"Yeshua from Nazareth, you who are blessed by God Almighty, will you help my husband?"

He stopped for them. "What help do you seek from me, sister?"

She bowed her head in modesty. "I will let him tell you himself."

"I was once a shoemaker," the man said in Yeshua's direction. His eyes were blank, looking into the distance. "But now I am blind, and I am helpless to do my work. Will you call on God's mercy and heal my blindness, blessed one?"

"Everything is possible with God," Yeshua said. "Do you have faith in the Eternal God?"

"Yes, I do," the man replied, his voice trembling. "I love the Lord our God with all my heart, and with all my strength."

"Then your faith shall heal you," Yeshua said. "Close your eyes and listen to me."

Yeshua spoke to the man in a soft voice. Next, he touched the man's eyes with his fingers and slowly rubbed them over the closed eyelids as he continued to talk to him. After several seconds, he pulled his hands away and took a step back.

"Open your eyes now and tell me what you see."

The man opened his eyes, hesitantly at first, and blinked twice to clear his vision. "I see you," he said to Yeshua. He turned to his wife and said with a sob: "I see you."

"God be praised!" the woman cried, then buried her head in her husband's chest as her tears flowed.

"God be praised!" many people around them exclaimed.

Yeshua told the man: "Go in peace. Enjoy life."

We moved on and left the happy couple and their friends behind. Every person in our party felt the power of God as we watched Yeshua perform the healing. Our spirits were lifted higher and our faith in the Lord grew even stronger.

Two men did not share in the happiness. Ezra and Avner watched from a distance. They did not look pleased.

Matthew's house was large and well built, a reflection of the wealth he earned from his work as a publican for Herod Antipas. The side of the house facing the patio was decorated with an elegant fresco made of colored stones, which pictured a forest scene with animals. He gave up his privacy to host many of his fellow disciples, so that now the house was brimming with people.

Several tables were set up outside to accommodate all the guests. In addition to Yeshua, his family, and his disciples, the guests included Matthew's neighbors and even some of his friends who still worked as tax collectors.

In the spirit of Yeshua's ministry, which was now also embraced by Matthew, we all sat, ate, and drank together without regard for social status. Matthew invited beggars from the street to join the feast. Women and men sat together, which, after a short period of confusion and discomfort, was accepted by Matthew's friends.

Yeshua sat at Matthew's table, along with his brother James, his sister Salome, and the three Marys. Young James, the son of Clopas and Mary, joined his mother and was attentive to her needs. Yeshua's closest apostles, the brothers Peter and Andrew, and James and John, were never too far from him.

Leila and I joined some of Matthew's neighbors. They were friendly and polite, but traditional in their views and not quite familiar with this new religious ministry. Not surprisingly, the conversation soon turned to the guest of honor.

"Yeshua has four brothers and two sisters, we hear?" asked the man sitting across from us. "What are their names?"

"James, who is sitting next to Yeshua, is the second oldest brother," I told him. "Salome is the youngest sister. She is sitting there, next to their mother. The other siblings are Joses, Judah, Mary, and Shimon."

"Are they all living in Nazareth?" one of the women asked.

Leila said: "The brothers are, yes. Mary lives in Kokhaba with her husband and their son."

"And their father? He was a carpenter?"

"Yosef was a builder," I told them. "He worked as a carpenter and stonemason. He trained Yeshua and me to work in those crafts. We took many day trips to Sepphoris to find work."

One of the women smiled. "Such humble beginnings for such a wise prophet."

I nodded agreement. "Yeshua is unique in many ways."

Leila gave a low groan. "Oh, no. Here they come again."

Ezra and Avner, the two Pharisee priests, approached at a brisk pace. They did not greet any of the people there, but made a beeline straight for the table where Yeshua and Matthew were sitting. The looks on their faces told us they were not in a social and friendly mood.

Matthew, being the host, greeted them. "Welcome, friends. Will you join us at our meal?"

The older priest, Ezra, spoke first. "We are only here to speak with Yeshua the Nazarene."

"Peace to you, Avner," Yeshua said politely to the younger man. "You are a Nazarene, but who is your companion in priestly robes?"

"This is Ezra, my teacher," Avner said. "We are Pharisee priests, as you can see."

"And what do you wish to speak to me about?"

"Why do you dine with these tax collectors, beggars, and sinners?" Ezra asked brusquely. "They are unclean, as you well know."

Yeshua gave him a patient smile. "Since when do the healthy need a doctor? It is only the sick who do. Sinners need to hear the word of God even more than those who are just."

Matthew said: "I bear witness to that truth. Praise the Lord!"

Many people around him laughed good-naturedly, but not the priests. They stood grimly, facing Yeshua like accusers at a trial.

"The Torah is God's teaching to us," Ezra said. "It instructs us on how to live our daily lives, and how to live with each other. Do you tell your followers to observe the Torah?"

"Yes, the Law must be strictly obeyed," Yeshua said. "It is easier for heaven and earth to disappear than for one smallest letter or one tiny pen stroke to drop out of the Torah."

Ezra raised his eyebrows. "My heart is glad to hear you say so. But I ask again: why do you eat and drink with sinners, who are unclean? You flout the Law of purity brazenly, for everyone to see."

"Because the Lord also tells us to love one other, and to treat each other with compassion," Yeshua replied. "While doing God's work we must serve all His children equally, including sinners."

"Are you telling me, then, that *compassion* is more important than following the Law of purity?" Avner's tone was incredulous.

"Yes," Yeshua replied calmly.

The priest looked shocked for an instant, then became outraged. "That is blasphemy!"

"Let God Almighty be my judge," Yeshua said.

Avner could no longer hold his tongue. "Tell us, why do you heal people on the Sabbath day, as you did with that blind man? The Law of Moses teaches us that this is a day of rest for the whole family. Men put aside their work. Women do not bake bread."

"Yes!" Avner cried. "The pig people don't practice a weekly rest, but for God's chosen people it is a sacred tradition. When you profane the Sabbath, you dishonor our covenant with God!"

Yeshua said: "And suppose your son, or your sheep, falls down a well on the day of the Sabbath. Would you hesitate for a second to pull them out? Or would you let them drown?"

Ezra frowned. "Of course I would not let them drown."

"Ah, you would not hesitate to save a life or to save your property," Yeshua said. "And indeed, your acts would be praised. But don't you see? We do the work of the Lord in preparing His children for salvation and the coming reign of God. Is that work not *more* important?"

"But you are not doing God's work properly!" Ezra accused. "The disciples of John the Baptizer are always fasting and offering prayers, and so are those of the Pharisees, but yours just eat and drink. And here you are, in the company of sinners, eating and drinking as if you were at a wedding!"

We expected Yeshua to take offense at this insult to us and him. To our surprise and delight, however, he leaned back in his chair and laughed heartily.

"You hypocrites! John didn't come eating or drinking, and you say, 'He's demonized!' I come eating and drinking, and you say, 'Look, a glutton and a drunk, a friend of toll collectors and outsiders!'"

Avner's face turned red. Ezra maintained his defiant posture.

Yeshua continued: "Everything you Pharisees and Sadducees do is for show. You expect the best seats at a banquet, or at a synagogue. You demand money from the poor to perform sacrifices of atonement. Woe to you, Pharisees! You tithe your mint, dill, and cumin, but you ignore justice, mercy, and trust!"

Ezra puffed out his chest and protested: "That is not so!"

"Woe to you, Pharisees!" Yeshua continued. "You clean the outside of the cup and dish, but inside they're full of greed and decadence. Clean the inside of the cup, and its outside will be clean too."

"God Almighty will punish you for these unjust words!" Ezra said hotly. He turned on his heels and walked away. Avner gave Yeshua one last unhappy glare, then also turned and followed his teacher.

James turned to his brother. "You spoke well, Yeshua. Traditions should be tempered with compassion and justice."

"I agree," said his sister Salome. "But I also fear that now these men will become your enemies."

"Don't be afraid, little sister," Yeshua reassured her. "Those who become my enemies also become the enemies of the Lord. Woe to them on that terrible day!"

Mary said: "God's will be done. We are all in His hands, and we can only follow His wishes."

"Amen," said Peter the apostle. "You are a bedrock of God's faith, Mary. You are blessed by God above all mothers."

Matthew said: "I think so, too. But come! You are my guests, so let us enjoy this dinner."

Everyone was in happy agreement. We resumed dining as before the priests' interruption, but for me some troubling feelings lingered. Perhaps Salome was right. Yeshua's message to the two priests, by his actions and with his words, was that the Temple system was corrupt and ineffective. The rites of purification, atonement, and sacrifices were useless, and a new way was needed for us to commune with God.

Although I agreed with Yeshua, this was a very harsh message for the priests and the rulers in Jerusalem. It would not be taken lightly.

Yeshua and the Twelve met indoors, at the house provided by Susanna of Sepphoris, to take shelter from the windy and rainy weather. I joined them, along with Salome and Mary Magdalena. The discussion was about practical matters that the apostles would encounter during their visits to villages beyond Capernaum.

"We share their lives, as poor and humble as they be," Yeshua said. "We live as they live. Do they carry gold when they walk? No. Neither do we. Do they wear fancy clothes? No, and neither do we."

Thaddeus asked: "What foods should we eat, and what should we tell them?"

"Eat what is given to you," Yeshua said. "Show gratefulness for what they can provide you, but don't lie, and don't do what you hate, because everything is revealed in the sight of heaven."

The door swung open suddenly, and a cold gust of wind and rain chilled those of us standing near the entrance. Yeshua's brother James walked in, trailed by a young man whose robe was drenched from the rain and clinging to his short and thin body.

"Oh!" Salome exclaimed. "It's Matthias!"

We had not seen him since our visit to the Jordan River, and his appearance caught us both by surprise. He looked downcast, with the gloomy expression of someone who bears bad news. Yeshua stopped talking and waited for the two men to approach.

James said: "Here is Matthias. He came looking for you."

"Peace to you, Matthias," Yeshua said. "What news do you bring that made you walk here through a pouring rain?"

"That madman, Herod Antipas, finally did it," Matthias said bitterly. "He had John executed."

Although this news was not completely unexpected, in the moment it still felt like a terrible shock. To expect it as likely is one thing, but to hear the actual truth of it is another. The room grew silent.

"How was John executed?" Yeshua asked. His voice remained calm, but there was pain in his eyes. He admired John the Baptizer as much as any of us, and perhaps more.

"He was beheaded," Matthias told him. "At Herod's fortress of Machaerus, where John was imprisoned since his arrest."

Philip's cry of anguish filled the room. He had been a disciple of John, along with Matthias, and had followed him faithfully.

"Herod has killed a prophet and a messenger from God," Philip said. "God Almighty will punish him for this sin."

Simon the Zealot became angry. "We should strike back! John was loved by many thousands of people, and now they mourn his death."

This was exactly the hotheaded response that would only make things worse. The rest of the apostles appeared to agree, because no one joined Simon in his angry outburst.

"We will not turn to violence," Yeshua told them, looking from one face to another. "Our path to serving the Lord is clear, and we shall not stray from it."

Peter spoke for the other apostles: "We honor John by loving and honoring God, and doing all that we can to bring forth God's reign and sweep away the evil of men like Herod Antipas."

"Yes," Yeshua said. "Our path to God is the true path. John was a prophet, and much more than a prophet, because it's written about him: Look, I'm sending my messenger ahead of you, who'll prepare your path for you."

He paused for a moment to look at each apostle again. "I'm telling you that John was the greatest among those born of women. But I'm telling you, whoever among you will become a little child and follow the path will know God's kingdom and become greater than John."

We all stopped to reflect on Yeshua's passionate message. From the beginning, he shared some ideas with John the Baptizer, but he chose a very different path to serving God. He wished to accomplish things that went far beyond what John had accomplished.

Philip spoke next: "I followed John as his disciple, as did Matthias. I know that he was a great prophet. And I believe, like Yeshua, that John was preparing us for the coming of a prophet greater than he."

"I agree with you," Matthias said. "John talked about these things, as well."

Philip continued in a solemn tone. "And I know, too, in my heart, that I have seen a greater prophet."

Young Salome and Mary Magdalena exchanged a look. Salome asked with a soft voice: "What prophet do you mean?"

"Yeshua. He is the greater prophet."

No one was surprised by Philip's declaration, and no one disagreed. We were all believers.

Chapter 19

From Village to Village

Capernaum, Galilee, Autumn 28 C.E.

Mary Magdalena worked with Yeshua every day to instruct the newest disciples on what was expected of them in the ministry in the days to come. She also worked tirelessly to provide them with their basic needs, such as housing and clothing. Yeshua's mother Mary, and Mary the wife of Clopas, assisted greatly in managing those practical matters.

Yeshua was discussing these things with the three Marys, and with Joanna of Chuza, on the day before groups of disciples were to go out on the road. Young Salome and I joined them at their table.

Salome addressed herself to Magdalena: "There are a few things I wish to discuss with you, whenever you are free, sister."

Magdalena looked up. "Yes, of course," she replied, but her voice was faint and strangely distant.

Salome gave her a look of concern, along with other people at the table. Magdalena's face suddenly turned very pale. There was a mild tremor in her hand that was resting on the tabletop.

"Are you feeling unwell?" Salome asked, looking more worried.

Suddenly Magdalena looked physically exhausted, as if all energy drained out of her. The haunted look reappeared in her eyes, and the tremors in her hands became more pronounced. Everyone around the table became fearful for her then, except for Yeshua. He understood what was happening.

He took Magdalena's hand to comfort her and said: "The unclean spirits are trying to come back."

She returned his gaze and nodded weakly.

Salome frowned and shook her head, puzzled. "But how can that be? The demon was exorcised, the day when Magdalena first arrived."

"When the impure spirit leaves someone," Yeshua explained, "it journeys through arid places looking for rest, but doesn't find it. Then it says, 'I'll return to the home I left'; and when it comes back, it finds it swept and organized."

"The demon returns?"

Yeshua said: "Yes. Then it goes out and brings seven other spirits that are even more evil, and they move in and live there. That person ends up even worse off than before."

"How terrible!" Salome said, looking at Magdalena with sympathy and concern. "Then what is to be done?"

"We must perform another exorcism," Yeshua calmly replied. He stood up and put his hand on Magdalena's arm. "Come with me, Mary. Let's go inside the house where I can do the exorcism in privacy."

She nodded again with a grateful expression, then stood up to go with him. They walked slowly to the house, Magdalena holding on to his arm for support.

"The poor woman," Mary of Clopas said. "What torment she must be going through."

"Sometimes exorcisms need to be repeated many times," said Mary, the mother of Yeshua. "Let's be thankful that she has Yeshua to take care of her."

"Magdalena is very thankful, as am I," Joanna said. "The Lord has blessed us with a wonderful healer."

Salome turned to her mother, her face solemn and determined. "This is why I commit myself to serving the Lord with Yeshua. I will not return to Nazareth."

"Neither will I," said Mary. "Our lives are joined with Yeshua now."

Later that day, Yeshua gathered the twelve apostles and all the other disciples in a group. We met again at Susanna's large house. These would be his final instructions before we left in small separate groups, each heading for different destinations.

He began with a parable.

"Someone was making a bountiful dinner and planning on having many guests. When dinner was ready, they sent their servant to call the visitors."

"The servant went to the first and said, 'My master invites you.' They said, 'Some merchants owe me money. They're coming tonight. I need to go and give them instructions. Excuse me from the dinner.'"

"The servant went to another one and said, 'My master invites you.' They said, 'I've just bought a house and am needed for the day. I won't have time.'"

"The servant went to another one and said, 'My master invites you.' They said, 'My friend is getting married and I'm going to make dinner. I can't come. Excuse me from the dinner.'"

"The servant went to another one and said, 'My master invites you.' They said, 'I've just bought a farm and am going to collect the rent. I can't come. Excuse me.'"

"The servant went back and told the master, 'The ones you invited to the dinner have excused themselves.'"

"The master said to their servant, 'Go out to the roads and bring whomever you find so that they can have dinner. Wealthy buyers and merchants won't enter the places of my Father.'"

Yeshua paused for a few moments to let people reflect on the story. He continued: "We are the servants sent to gather the guests for our Father's great dinner. We won't find them in palaces, wearing fancy clothes, but in the small villages, towns, and streets of Galilee."

"The harvest is plentiful, but the workers are few. So, the Lord of the harvest commands that we send workers into the fields. Go!"

"Look, I send you out like lambs among wolves. Don't carry a purse, bag, sandals, or staff. Don't greet anyone on the road to stop and talk, but look to make your way to your next destination."

"Whenever you enter a house, first say, 'Peace to this house.' If a peaceful person is there, let your blessing rest on them; but if not, then take back your blessing."

"Stay in the same house, eating and drinking whatever they give you, because the worker is worthy of their wages. Don't move around from house to house. If they welcome you in whatever town you enter, eat whatever is set before you. Sleep wherever they provide a place for you to sleep, even if that is a spot on a patio or in a barn."

"Do not approach women who go out to get water or wood, be they single or in a group, because a righteous woman will not speak to a strange man who is not her relative or neighbor. If a woman disciple is with you, then that disciple may approach the other woman and ask to speak with her. Travel in a group of both men and women, so that we may talk to everyone we meet."

"Heal those who are sick there and tell them, 'God's reign is at hand!' Do not accept money for your healings, because God Almighty gives us the power to heal for free. We use God's power to heal for free, because we are not like the priests who take money from the poor to pay for God's blessings."

"But if the people don't welcome you in whatever town you enter, when you're leaving that town, shake the dust from your feet. I am telling you that on that day, it'll be better for Sodom than for that town!"

Yeshua's voice had a powerful tone of determination and passion. It was mesmerizing and held everyone's full attention. He was nearing the end of his talk and continued by telling us another parable.

"A certain sower went out, took a handful of seeds, and scattered them. Some fell on the roadside; the birds came and gathered them. Others fell on the rock; they didn't take root in the soil and ears of grain didn't rise toward heaven. Yet others fell on thorns; they choked the seeds and worms ate them. Finally, others fell on good soil; they produced fruit up toward heaven."

We listened intently, because each of us saw ourselves as that sower. God Almighty, speaking through Yeshua, was giving each of us our own handfuls of seeds.

"The time is here when we travel to other towns and spread the word of the Lord. We are the sowers of God's word. Find the fertile soil and spread the seeds there!"

"Don't despair if you are not welcomed, but continue on your way. I am telling you: whoever welcomes you welcomes me, and whoever welcomes me welcomes the one who sent me."

Yeshua's instructions were very clear. We would live like the poorest people in the villages and towns of Galilee. Walk as they walk, dress as they dress, eat as they eat. And if need be, suffer as they suffer.

We would gather the lost sheep among God's children, most of all the very poor and forsaken who suffered the most, and guide them on the true path to the kingdom of God. No money would be asked for or accepted from people. We would ask only for repentance, through their good behavior and devotion to the reign of God.

We are all God's children, Yeshua taught over and over again. Rich or poor, sinner or just, healthy or unhealthy – in the eyes of the Lord, we are all the same. In sharing the sufferings of His people, in showing God's love and compassion in everything we do, we show others the path to God's kingdom in which God will reign as Father of us all.

Yeshua's ministry was very well prepared for the work to come. He and the twelve apostles would lead the way, but more than seventy other disciples would also serve and lend a helping hand. The seed had found fertile soil, and the tree was reaching up to heaven. The time to branch out had arrived.

At first light, we all gathered at Susanna's house, where Yeshua and the Twelve were staying. The twelve apostles would travel two by two, each pair accompanied by a group of other disciples that included both men and women. We had our instructions and knew our destinations. The groups would travel on a month-long mission through Galilee, then re-unite in Capernaum to make new plans for the next mission.

That early morning get together was a time for final arrangements and brief farewells. Yeshua bade farewell to each group in turn as they left and gave them his blessing.

Peter travelled with Andrew and, not surprisingly, one of the larger groups of other disciples. Andrew had recruited many of them to join the ministry, and many of the lesser disciples already admired Peter as one of Yeshua's most trusted apostles.

"We wish to be the first on the road," Peter told Yeshua.

"Yes, the point of God's spear," Andrew added happily.

Yeshua smiled. "Lead the way, my brothers. You will inspire many others with your zeal for service to the Lord."

"You inspire us daily with your faith," Peter said. "We cannot expect less of ourselves."

The other disciples came after them, each giving Yeshua a brief nod or a small bow, and some shyly reaching out to touch his robe. He greeted each and gave his blessing with a loving smile.

Salome, the wife of Zebedee, travelled with her sons, James and John, whom she favored above all others. She embraced her sister, Mary, then gave her nephew Yeshua a farewell embrace as well.

"Show God's love and compassion to everyone you meet," Yeshua reminded his cousins.

"Don't worry about us," John replied. "We know what our mission is, and it is *not* to argue with people who disagree with us."

"The trust and faith you place in us will not be dishonored," said James. "We will follow your path in serving the Lord."

"I know you will, my brothers," Yeshua told them. "You will follow my instructions, but most important, always honor the Lord and obey His wishes for us."

"It will be so," Salome assured him in a calm tone. "We shall see you back here in a month, Nephew. And farewell for now, Sister."

Mary squeezed Salome's hand. "Be strong and blessed, Sister."

Thomas and Thaddeus, one tall and thin and the other shorter and husky, looked like an odd pair when standing next to each other. Both men were kindly and mild-mannered, however, and would travel well together with their small group of disciples.

"The Lord bless everyone as we embark on this mission," Thomas said. "I am grateful and humbled to be one of your apostles, Yeshua."

Yeshua placed a hand on his shoulder. "We are all humbled before the Lord, Thomas. We are all equally blessed to serve our Father."

"This is a happy moment for me, and for all of us," Thaddeus said. He glanced at Thomas and smiled. "Why, look here! Even Thomas doesn't look so gloomy today."

Thomas chuckled, and Yeshua laughed with him. There was no hint of worry on Thomas' face that morning.

"The Lord bless you on your travels," Yeshua said. "Be strong and of good courage."

Philip and Bartholomew, who at times seemed inseparable, also travelled together. Matthias from Bethsaida joined them, along with several other disciples from their hometown. Matthias was not yet an apostle, although at a much later time that would change. He was just as dedicated to Yeshua as any of the current apostles, however.

Philip stood before Yeshua and gave him a small, respectful bow. "When we first met on the bank of the Jordan River, I knew then that you were a man of God. An uncommon man, who one day would do great things in service to the Lord. Everything you have done since that day shows that I was right in my judgment."

"I see that as well," Matthias said. "We were disciples of John, but the journey that we begin now shows that you are a greater prophet."

Bartholomew agreed with a nod. "I believe the same, Yeshua. You are a messenger of God, and the Lord works through you."

"We're all servants of the Lord," Yeshua said. "As was John."

"Where you lead us, we follow," Philip said. "Today is the beginning of something wonderful."

"Be strong and blessed in your journey," Yeshua told them. "Many good and wonderful things will come from your service to the Lord."

James and Salome, the brother and sister of Yeshua, travelled with the apostle James, the son of Clopas, and with Matthew, the former publican once known as Levi. They would be there in support of their young cousin. The much older Matthew was the more worldly of those two apostles, and he would take the younger James under his wing.

Yeshua gazed at them, and at the other disciples accompanying them, with pride and affection. Mary, his mother, and Mary of Clopas, did the same in watching the happy faces of their children.

"My heart overflows with joy to see you start your mission," Yeshua said. "Father God smiles down on you at this moment, as well."

"That is the greatest of blessings," James of Clopas said. He turned to his mother. "A brief farewell, *Emma*, then we must go."

Mary of Clopas embraced him tightly, then took a step back to look him in the eye. "God bless you and protect you, my son."

Young Salome became sentimental, as was her nature. First, she embraced Yeshua, then her mother, then her aunt Mary. Finally, she turned to Mary Magdalena and also gave her a warm embrace.

"You look well, Sister," Salome told her. "Be healthy and strong."

"I am well. God be praised," Magdalena replied. "Good health to you as well, Sister."

Matthew bid farewell to Yeshua with a few words of kindness and gratitude, then, surprisingly, turned to me with a small smile. "Have you forgiven me yet for all my past sins toward you, David? Can we be friends now?"

I couldn't help but return his smile. "Seek forgiveness from the Lord, Matthew, and from yourself. But, yes, we can be friends now. You are no longer the sinner that you once were."

He acknowledged with a small nod. He was indeed a changed man, and he was at peace.

Yeshua bid farewell to his brother, James, as did their mother.

"Salome will be under my protection," James told them. He looked at his cousin and added: "And so will James."

"Ha!" James exclaimed with a grin. "I thank you, cousin, but we are all under the protection of God Almighty."

"Amen," Yeshua said. "Trust in God, and He will protect you."

Their group turned and left, heading for the north road to Chorazin. They would travel among the villages in the northern part of Galilee, venturing as far north as Caesarea Phillippi, perhaps.

The final group was that of Judas Iscariot and Simon the Zealot. Not surprisingly, they decided to travel together. I did not know whether to be concerned about that or not. They appeared to have tempered their zealotry, or at least the aggressive notions of it. Whether that would last, or what it might lead to, was still to be seen.

Simon's piercing black eyes scanned our group quickly, then settled on Yeshua. He gave him a small bow of respect, almost reverence. "God Almighty blesses us in this mission. The Lord delivered you here to lead us and be our shepherd, Yeshua. Now our work begins."

"Indeed, Simon," Yeshua said. "We are brought here by the Lord for a great purpose. Now our work begins."

"That is so," Judas agreed. "You prepared us well, Yeshua, as any good shepherd would. Now we go out and teach others what you have taught us so well these past few weeks."

"Ah, but there is only one shepherd, Judas," Yeshua replied. "He is Father God, and we follow His guidance. The lessons I teach you come from the Lord alone."

"Of course," Judas replied. "The lessons come from God Almighty, and you are His messenger."

"You made all necessary arrangements with Joanna to manage the treasury, I am told?" Yeshua asked him. It was perhaps a question asked out of politeness, since Joanna of Chuza was sitting on a chair nearby and no doubt had already discussed the matter with Yeshua.

"Yes, I have. While I am travelling, the treasury is in the hands of Joanna," Judas said. He glanced at Joanna with a mildly haughty look and added: "I know that she will manage the money well."

Joanna fought to keep from laughing. "How kind of you to say so, Judas," she said, giving him a mirthless smile.

Leila, standing next to me, giggled softly. She knew that Joanna's understanding of financial matters would put Judas to shame.

Yeshua gave Judas, Simon, and their group of disciples a warm and loving farewell. They turned and briskly walked away, happy to be on their way.

Yeshua trusted Judas and Simon, and I trusted that he had good reasons for doing so. Judas would continue as treasurer, which was a position of high responsibility. The ministry was not designed to make money, but certain regular expenses, such as rents, needed to be paid.

As the rest of us stirred and prepared to leave, Joanna approached Yeshua. It was time to say farewell, and she also had a question.

"I was wondering," Joanna said, "what made you decide to appoint Judas as treasurer for the ministry?"

Yeshua looked mildly surprised. No one had ever brought up the matter before.

"Judas is good with numbers," Yeshua told her. "Also, he showed strong interest in being treasurer, a job that others preferred to shun."

Joanna gave him a cold sober look. "Be careful about the ones who show strong interest in controlling your money."

He looked mildly surprised again, but only calmly acknowledged her advice with a nod.

Interestingly, Joanna, the Galilean noblewoman and wife of Chuza, was the only one to express doubts to him about Judas. Yeshua was nobody's fool, but he was a trusting soul, and I don't know whether he took Joanna's words of caution very seriously. As we learned much later, there were times when Judas took money from the treasury for his own personal use.

Finally, it was our turn to leave. Yeshua turned to face us with a joyful smile. I had seldom seen him happier.

"The time has arrived. The road before us is long, and there is much work to be done. We do it with hearts full of joy, and faith, and love for our heavenly Father," Yeshua said. "Today the Lord beckons us to start our journey. Blessed ones, let us begin."

At Mary's invitation, Leila and I joined this group, along with Mary of Clopas and Mary Magdalena, that would travel with Yeshua. She enjoyed Leila's company based on many years of living as neighbors, and also believed that I was someone from home Yeshua could talk with honestly. Or, at least, I like to think the second part was true.

Our group headed west, toward Cana. We would visit many of the villages of central Galilee, then head south toward Samaria. We would bypass Sepphoris because the soldiers of Herod Antipas would not be pleased with our presence there. Sadly, we would bypass Nazareth as well, except for brief family visits.

Yeshua led the way at the front, along with Mary Magdalena. She looked fully healthy and fit again. Leila and I walked in the second line with the two other Marys, Yeshua's mother and aunt. A string of other disciples followed behind us, half of them men and half women.

"Was Yeshua always this devoted to serving the Lord?" Leila asked Mary, his mother. "I always knew he was very devout, but I only saw him now and then, as a neighbor. I did not know him well."

"Yes, always," Mary replied. "We saw that in him even as a boy."

Mary of Clopas agreed. "Almost from the time he learned how to talk. Few children like talking in synagogue, but Yeshua did."

I said: "He was curious and inquisitive from a young age, as very bright children often are."

"You told me the story of how he shocked you when he was eight years old," Leila said with a chuckle. "And how you knew then that he was no ordinary little boy."

Mary of Clopas raised an eyebrow. "Shocked you, David?"

"No, I would not say that I was shocked," I said. "He impressed me very much with his maturity and knowledge of religion. And his strong devotion to God, which I thought was unusual for such a young child."

"That is simply how Yeshua is," said Mary. "He is blessed with many gifts from God."

"Very true," Mary of Clopas said. "And now, Yeshua is using those gifts to serve the Eternal God."

"Ah, *this* is his purpose," Leila said with a tone of wonder in her voice. "Now I understand."

Mary shot a questioning glance. "What do you mean?"

"There were times, over the years, when I wondered what Yeshua meant when he spoke about the reign of God," Leila said. "He sounded like someone who knew things that the rest of us did not know. Like someone with a vision that the rest of us could not see."

"Ha! I know what you mean," Mary of Clopas said with a soft laugh. "I often have the same feeling."

"It was always about this," Leila said. She spread out her arms to include Yeshua, us, and the road ahead. "This journey. This mission. This was always Yeshua's vision."

"I agree, Leila dear, but there is more," Mary said. "I think that you are half right."

"Only half right? In what way?"

Mary looked at us with her gentle eyes. "This is Yeshua's vision and his mission for the Lord. And this is the Lord's mission for Yeshua."

Appendix: Names of People and Places

Author's Note:
- Names of cities and locations are historically accurate.
- With the exception of Yeshua's neighbors in Nazareth (of whom no historical records exist), the major characters portrayed in this book are historical figures.
- For the purpose of this list, fictional characters in the book are identified as "fictional" in the character descriptions.

<u>NAMES OF VILLAGES, CITIES , AND PLACES</u>

Bethany – a small village east of Jerusalem, on the far side of the Mount of Olives. Home to Martha, Mary, and Lazarus.

Bethsaida – prosperous fishing village, on the northern side of the Sea of Galilee

Caesarea by the sea – luxurious coastal city where Pontius Pilate lived and kept his Roman army (as did all Roman governors of Judea). The prefect made the three-day march to Jerusalem during the High Holidays to keep the peace while a vast number of pilgrims gathered there.

Caesarea Philippi - a Roman city north of the Sea of Galilee that served as the seat of the tetrarchy of Herod the Great's other son, Philip

Cana – farming village, north of Sepphoris and west of Capernaum

Capernaum – large and prosperous fishing and farming village, on the northwestern side of the Sea of Galilee

Chorazin – small farming village, three miles north of Capernaum

Gadara – village in the Decapolis, southeast of the Sea of Galilee

Gerasa – village in the Decapolis, southeast of the Sea of Galilee

Gergesa – fishing village, east of the Sea of Galilee

Hippos – village in the Decapolis, southeast of the Sea of Galilee

Japha - village south of Jerusalem

Jericho – a major city east of Jerusalem, on the west side of the Jordan River. An oasis area surrounded by a dry desert area.

Jerusalem – the largest city in Judea and spiritual center of Jewish people around the world. One week's walk south of Nazareth.

Kokhaba – farming village near Nazareth. Some of Yeshua's relatives lived there.

Lake Kinneret – very large freshwater lake in Galilee. The Romans called it the "Sea of Galilee" or "Sea of Tiberias."

Magdala – prosperous fishing village, south of Capernaum

Naim – farming village, south of Nazareth

Nazareth – a small village in Galilee, an hour's walk south of the capital city of Sepphoris. Described as "no place found on any map." Home to Yosef, Mary, Yeshua, and their family.

Pella – village in the Decapolis, southeast of the Sea of Galilee. Members of the early Christian church in Jerusalem fled there before Jerusalem was destroyed and its people massacred in 70 C.E.

Sea of Galilee – the very large freshwater lake in Galilee. The locals called it Lake Kinneret.

Sepphoris – the first capital city of Galilee. Built by Herod Antipas. Located in central Galilee, an hour's walk north of Nazareth.

Sidon – a very large coastal city

Tiberias – the second capital city of Galilee. Built by Herod Antipas in 20 C.E. On the west side of the Sea of Galilee.

Tyre – a very large coastal city

YESHUA'S FAMILY

Yosef – husband of Mary. Father of Yeshua.

Mary – wife of Yosef. Mother of Yeshua.

(Siblings of Yeshua listed in order of birth)

James – became leader of the early Christian church in Jerusalem after the crucifixion of Yeshua. Was executed by stoning in 62 C.E. on orders of the High Priest. Well-known and highly respected in his time as "James the Just."

Joses – third son of Mary and Yosef

Judah (Jude) – fourth son of Mary and Yosef

Mary – first daughter of Mary and Yosef

Salome – second daughter of Mary and Yosef

Shimon (Simon) – fifth son of Mary and Yosef

YESHUA'S RELATIVES

Clopas family:

Clopas – the older brother of Yosef. Yeshua's uncle. Clopas was his Aramaic name; Alphaeus was his Greek name.

Mary the wife of Clopas – Yeshua's aunt. Married to Clopas, the older brother of Yosef. Became a key supporter in Yeshua's ministry.

James the son of Clopas – son of Clopas and Mary. Yeshua's cousin. Became one of the twelve apostles; sometimes called James the Younger to avoid confusion with James the son of Zebedee. Clopas was the Aramaic name; Alphaeus was the Greek name.

Simeon – son of Clopas and Mary. Yeshua's cousin. Took over as the leader of the Jerusalem branch of the Christian church after James the Just was executed by stoning in 62 C.E. Led the Jerusalem branch of the church to safety out of Jerusalem before the Romans destroyed the city in 70 C.E.

Nimura – daughter of Clopas and Mary (fictional)

Zebedee family:

Zebedee – husband of Salome, Mary's younger sister. Father of James and John, who became two of the twelve apostles.

Salome the wife of Zebedee – younger sister of Mary. Yeshua's aunt. Mother of James and John, two of the twelve apostles.

James the son of Zebedee – son of Zebedee and Salome. Yeshua's cousin. One of the twelve apostles. One of the two *Boanerges*, or "Sons of Thunder."

John the son of Zebedee – son of Zebedee and Salome. Yeshua's cousin. One of the twelve apostles. One of the two *Boanerges*, or "Sons of Thunder."

Rina – daughter of Zebedee and Salome (fictional)

THE TWELVE APOSTLES

Peter – also called Simon Peter. Older brother of Andrew. Along with James and John, the sons of Zebedee, became part of Yeshua's inner circle of apostles. Later became leader of the Christian church in Rome. Executed by Emperor Nero in 67 C.E.

Andrew – younger brother of Peter

James the son of Zebedee – older brother of John. Along with Peter and John, became part of Yeshua's inner circle of apostles. Called by Yeshua one of his "Sons of Thunder."

John the son of Zebedee – younger brother of James. Along with Peter and James, became part of Yeshua's inner circle of apostles. Called by Yeshua one of his "Sons of Thunder."

Philip – from Bethsaida. Originally a disciple of John the Baptizer.

Bartholomew – friend of Philip

Thomas – later became known as "Doubting Thomas"

Matthew – former tax collector (*publican*) known as Levi

James the son of Clopas – also known as the son of Alphaeus. Clopas was the Aramaic name; Alphaeus was the Greek name.

Thaddeus – sometimes called the son of James and Lebbaeus

Simon the Zealot – sometimes called Simon the Canaanite

Judas Iscariot – also called Judas the Betrayer. Served as treasurer for the apostles. Came from Judea, near Jericho, not from Galilee.

NEIGHBORS AND FRIENDS IN THE BOOK

Abana – neighbor of Yosef and Mary in Nazareth (fictional)

Abram – uncle of David of Nazareth. A Levite, helper who assisted the Sadducees priests with Temple care and functions. (fictional)

David of Nazareth – narrator of the story. Husband of Leila. Father of Dalia, Matthias, Gila, and Eitan. (fictional)

Eva – sister of David of Nazareth. Neighbor and childhood friend of Yeshua. (fictional)

Iacob – husband of Abana. Neighbor of Yosef and Mary. (fictional)

Leila – wife of David of Nazareth. Mother of Dalia, Matthias, Gila, and Eitan. (fictional)

Sarah – mother of David of Nazareth and Eva. Neighbor of Yosef and Mary. (fictional)

Uziel – husband of Eva (fictional)

DISCIPLES, SUPPORTERS, OTHERS

Joanna the wife of Chuza – Galilean princess and famed beauty; married to Chuza the Nabatean, who was finance minister for Herod Antipas. Healed by Yeshua, then became a key supporter, financially and in other ways.

John the Baptizer – evangelist and zealot, possibly from an Essene family. Critical of Temple priests and Herod Antipas. Baptized people along the Jordan River, including Yeshua. Executed by Herod Antipas.

Lazarus of Bethany – supporter; brother of Martha and Mary

Martha of Bethany – supporter; sister of Mary and Lazarus

Mary of Bethany – supporter; sister of Martha and Lazarus

Mary Magdalene – key disciple and close companion of Yeshua during his ministry. Cured of demons and tremors. One of the "Three Marys" in Yeshua's inner circle, along with Mary the mother of Yeshua and Mary the wife of Clopas. Became a leader in the early church after the crucifixion of Yeshua. Became a victim of false and malicious character assassination centuries later by the later church (portrayed as "harlot," prostitute, etc.)

Matthias – early disciple of Yeshua. Originally a follower of John the Baptizer. Was elected the "13th apostle" after death of Judas Iscariot.

Susanna – key supporter for Yeshua's ministry, financially and in other ways

Historical Note

Chicago, July 2024

Jesus of Nazareth, in this book called by his more historically accurate name of Yeshua of Nazareth, is both a historical figure and theological and religious figure. Very little is known about his history that was not shaped by later theology, however it is possible to gain a sense of the person who predates the theology.

The Roman-Jewish historian Flavius Josephus, writing toward the end of the first century, some seven decades after Jesus was crucified, described him as "a wise man," who "worked surprising deeds," and "was a teacher of such people as accepted the truth gladly." Sadly, few details are provided about this teacher of wisdom and miracle worker who clashed with the Jewish priestly order in Galilee and Judea and was executed by the Roman occupiers who ruled those regions.

It is nonetheless possible to paint a picture of the historical figure (the person) who came before the theological figure (the Christ) by giving careful and respectful attention to the history, theology, and culture of those ancient times.

History, theology, and cultural studies are rich sources of valuable information and insights. This author chooses to consider the insights and contributions of all three of these perspectives. The picture that emerges then of the historical Jesus of Nazareth is a fascinating picture indeed. This is the unique advantage of historical fiction — to make people and events from the past come to life in a way that history books and theology cannot.

The people who shared the life of Jesus — family, followers, friends, enemies — were real people with lives of their own. One limitation of the canonical gospels is that they omit many basic details. We are told that Jesus had sisters, for example, but not how many, and no names or other details are provided. His four brothers are named, but only by digging through some of the "lost" gospels do we discover that he had two sisters whose names were Mary and Salome.

This kind of information enriches our understanding of who Jesus of Nazareth was. It certainly does not diminish it in any way. We no longer live in a world where women are considered so unimportant that history only records the names of their brothers, but treats them as irrelevant and not worth mentioning.

Based on our best historical information, the writings of the early Christian church that became known as the "Q" source materials were written between 50 C.E. and 70 C.E. Many of the quotes attributed to Yeshua in the later chapters in this book are quoted verbatim, or nearly verbatim, from the "Q" source materials in the public domain. These include many quotes in the early sermons, the heated discussion with the Pharisees priests at Matthew's house, Yeshua's instructions to his apostles and other disciples, and parables such as the story of the man who invited guests to dinner.

These stories and quotes from the early church, which eventually became the "Q" written materials, were passed along for many years from person to person as oral history before being recorded in writing. This was not unusual for that time in Galilee and Judea, when illiteracy was very high (over 97%) and only the wealthy and educated political, economic, and religious elites could read or write.

All the gospels that followed, canonical and "lost," were written in Greek, many decades after the crucifixion of Jesus. The oldest of the canonical gospels, the Gospel of Mark, was written in Rome around 73 C.E., three years after the destruction of Jerusalem. It incorporates a great deal of material from the "Q" source materials, including familiar stories and quotes that are repeated in the later gospels.

The Gospel of Matthew was written in Damascus around 80 C.E. The Gospel of Luke was written in Antioch around 90 C.E. The writer or writers of the gospels of both Matthew and Luke clearly copied a good deal of their material from the earlier Gospel of Mark.

The Gospel of John was written in Ephesus around 100 C.E. John includes material from the earlier gospels, of course, but also wanders much further into theology than the other gospels. For that reason, religious scholars consider the earlier gospels of Mark, Matthew, and Luke to be in a category of their own, called the Synoptic Gospels, in terms of their style and following the historical narrative.

Modern scholars, including historians and archaeologists, continue working to discover information relating to the historical figure. It is an effort well worth pursuing, because the monumental historical figure who lived in ancient Galilee, whether we call him by his Aramaic name Yeshua or the modern name Jesus of Nazareth, was someone well worth knowing.

Yeshua: The Young Jesus of Nazareth is the first novel in a series of three planned historical fiction novels. The second novel in the series is titled *Yeshua's Mission: The Ministry of Jesus of Nazareth,* and covers the period of the ministry years from 28 to 30 C.E. The third novel is titled *Yeshua's Disciples: The Early Christian Church*, and covers the history of the formative years of the Christian church from 30 to 70 C.E., with special focus on the lives of James the Just in Jerusalem, Peter and Paul in Rome, and the lives of other apostles and some important disciples.

Readers are encouraged to read the novels in sequence, or as individual stand-alone books, depending on their interests. These books are not meant to dispute or challenge any religious beliefs, but rather to enrich our understanding of a remarkable individual, the culture and history of the world he lived in, and the tremendous impact he made in many people's lives that continues to this day.

Peter Jaksa

Thank you for reading *Yeshua: The Young Jesus of Nazareth*. I hope you enjoyed this novel. If you have a moment, please review *Yeshua* on the Amazon book page or other location where you obtained the book. Help other readers with an interest in the historical Jesus of Nazareth, and the history of ancient Galilee and Judea, and tell them why you enjoyed this book. Thank you!

ABOUT THE AUTHOR

Peter Jaksa, Ph.D. is a psychologist and author
living in Chicago, Illinois

Books by Peter Jaksa

Yeshua: The Young Jesus of Nazareth (3 – 28 C.E.)
In production:
Yeshua's Mission: The Ministry of Jesus of Nazareth (28 – 30 C.E.)
Yeshua's Disciples: The Early Christian Church (30 – 70 C.E.)

The Rome – Dacia Series (e-book, print, and audiobooks):
Decebal Triumphant (85 – 99 C.E.)
Decebal and Trajan (100 – 102 C.E.)
Decebal Defiant: Siege at Sarmizegetusa (103 – 107 C.E.)
Dacia In Rebellion (117 – 118 C.E.)